MW00327354

MINE TO PROMISE

When two worlds crossover. From the This Is Series and The Southern Series. From *Wall Street Journal & USA Today* bestselling author Natasha Madison *comes a small town, one night stand, secret baby, second chance romance.*

Addison

I never thought I would see him again.
Especially while I was planning someone else's wedding—yet there he was holding hands with his girlfriend.
Our one night was wild and passionate; I could never forget him because it changed my life.
Now he's here—and the result of our one night is twirling in a princess dress at our feet.

Stefano

I didn't make mistakes.
I was the one you called in when you needed answers.
I was cutthroat but they didn't pay me to be nice.
I was in control every single second.
The only time I let my guard down was five years ago.
If I thought seeing the woman I could never forget again would throw me off—it's nothing like seeing our daughter for the first time.

BOOKS BY NATASHA MADISON

Southern Wedding Series
Mine To Kiss
Mine To Have
Mine To Cherish
Mine to Love
Mine To Take
Mine To Promise
Mine to Honor
Mine to Keep

The Only One Series
Only One Kiss
Only One Chance
Only One Night
Only One Touch
Only One Regret
Only One Mistake
Only One Love
Only One Forever

Southern Series
Southern Chance
Southern Comfort
Southern Storm
Southern Sunrise
Southern Heart
Southern Heat
Southern Secrets
Southern Sunshine

This Is
This is Crazy
This Is Wild
This Is Love
This Is Forever

This Is
This is Crazy
This Is Wild
This Is Love
This Is Forever

Hollywood Royalty
Hollywood Playboy
Hollywood Princess
Hollywood Prince

Something So Series
Something Series
Something So Right
Something So Perfect
Something So Irresistible
Something So Unscripted
Something So BOX SET

Tempt Series
Tempt The Boss
Tempt The Playboy
Tempt The Ex
Tempt The Hookup
Heaven & Hell Series
Hell And Back
Pieces Of Heaven

Love Series
Perfect Love Story
Unexpected Love Story
Broken Love Story

Faux Pas
Mixed Up Love
Until Brandon

SOUTHERN WEDDING SERIES TREE

Mine To Have
Harlow Barnes & Travis Baker

Mine To Hold
Shelby Barker & Ace

Mine To Cherish
Clarabella & Luke

Mine To Love
Presley & Bennett

Southern Family tree
Billy and Charlotte
(Mother and father to Kallie and Casey)

Southern Chance
Kallie & Jacob McIntyre
Ethan McIntyre (Savannah Son)
Amelia
Travis

Southern Comfort
Olivia & Casey Barnes
Quinn (Southern Heat)
Reed (Southern Sunshine)
Harlow (Mine to Have)

Southern Storm
Savannah & Beau Huntington
Ethan McIntyre (Jacob's son)
Chelsea (Southern Heart)
Toby
Keith

Southern Sunrise
Emily & Ethan McIntyre
Gabriel
Aubrey

Southern Heart
Chelsea Huntington & Mayson Carey
Tucker

Southern Heat
Willow & Quinn Barnes

Southern Secrets
Amelia McIntyre & Asher

Southern Sunshine
Hazel & Reed Barnes
Sofia

Cover Design: Jay Aheer
Editing done by Jenny Sims Editing4Indies
Editing done by Karen Hrdicka Barren Acres Editing
Proofing Julie Deaton by Deaton Author Services
Proofing by Judy's proofreading www.judysproofreading.com
Cover picture by: Britt & Bean Photography
Formatting by Christina Parker Smith

Southern Wedding Series

NATASHA MADISON

Prologue

Dearest Love,
   Well, well, well, what can I say.
   Two universes are about to meet again.
   Five years later.
   Just this time there is more than the two of them.
   How will Stefano react when he sees Avery?
   How will Addison react to them co-parenting?
   How will the family react?
   Only time will tell.
   XOXO
   Love NM

One

Addison

"What do you mean she fell?" I ask with my teeth clenched, one step away from a total panic attack.

"I mean, she drank a little bit too much sweet tea and she fell," Zara says from the other end, trying not to laugh but laughing still the same. "It will be fine. We'll take care of it." Zara, the future groom Mathew's aunt, was supposed to be taking care of things.

"Where is Ingrid?" I look over my shoulder to make sure no one sees me panic. "Can I talk to her?" Ingrid was in charge of serving drinks and food in the bridal suite, something we should have not been doing from the sounds coming through the phone. The bridal suite where they were supposed to be resting and waiting until the bride was ready. I can confirm they were not in fact resting and waiting.

I hear yelling from the other end of the phone, some giggles, well, lots of giggling, and then Ingrid comes on the line. "Hello." She sounds like she's one step away from losing it.

"There will be no more drinking," I order. "It's coffee and water and get them some food."

"On it," she replies and then quickly hangs up.

"She's coming," someone says, and then I turn to watch. I can hear myself breathing heavily but try to do it as silently as I can, which is proving to be harder than I thought. My heart is beating a million times a second, if that is even possible. I have never in my life been this nervous. Well, that isn't exactly true. There have been other moments. Monumental moments, actually.

I can count on one hand when my life undertook a major change. One was the time I had my first ever one-night stand. The second was when I found out I was pregnant from said one-night stand. The third was being cut off from my whole family and giving birth alone. The fourth was getting this job, and now the fifth is them giving me the reins for this wedding.

I swear to God, I can feel the drops of sweat pouring off me as my hands shake. I look over at Clarabella, Presley, and Shelby—the four of us are hidden in the middle of a forest, waiting for the surprise proposal to happen. We all know Sofia is going to say yes; she's been in love with Matty since they went to college together. Sure, they had a break between and he did get engaged to someone else, but that led them to be together again. I mean, it's not every day your wedding planner is the ex-love of your life. It's also not every day, you leave your fiancée for your wedding planner once you realize you've been in love with her and only her your whole life.

"The wait is killing me," I whisper to Clarabella, who stands beside me. Shelby stands on the other side of Clarabella next to Presley. The three of them have the biggest and most prestigious event-planning business. They originally started out just doing weddings and then slowly started adding in corporate events. That took off so much, they have recently decided Clarabella, Shelby, and Presley would take care of the corporate side of the company, leaving Sofia to handle the wedding side. The first thing she did was officially place me as a junior event planner. I have been working under her to make sure I would be ready. News flash, I was not ready. I mean maybe I was, but I was definitely not ready for today.

When Matty came into the office last month to let us know he was proposing, we went wild. He then told us he not only wanted to propose to her but also get married at the same time. If I thought that was nuts, imagine my surprise when he left and the three of them looked at me and said, "Congratulations, you just landed your first client." I was shocked to say the very least. I told them I couldn't do it. I wasn't ready, but push came to shove, and they said they were going to be there in case I needed them. From that day, the next two weeks were the most stressful of my life. Not only was I planning this wedding but I was doing it in secret, which made it even more stressful. Let's just say, tonight I'm going to have the biggest drink of my life, then properly collapse.

"It's happening?" someone whispers from beside me, and I see Sofia and Matty walk into the open space we spent the morning decorating. I wanted it to be magical, so the trees have tea lights wrapped around them. I made the men wrap every single tree you could see in the distance with lights. I got a lot of huffing and puffing, but for Sofia and Matty, they did it.

Sofia looks around confused, and then she gasps when Matty gets down on one knee. My hand goes to my heart. I don't know about everyone else, but I stop breathing as we listen to him.

"Sofia." You can hear the smile and love in the way he says

her name. She doesn't say a word. Instead, she steps back and shakes her head.

I don't hear what she says, but I see Matty smile at her. It's a look I see often. It's a look I secretly wish for myself one day.

"From the moment I laid eyes on you, I knew two seconds later I had to know who you were." She laughs at his joke. He calmly says the two words that will change them from dating to engaged. "Marry me?" he asks her, and I can't stop the lone tear from running down my face. "After all the ways I practiced asking you this, the only two words I can remember are those two. When I was getting ready to propose to you, I went to my father and told him. He came with me to ask your father for your hand in marriage." Sofia mumbles something, and then her laughter fills the forest. I look at the other side of the clearing to see her family there waiting for her to answer. "Yeah, well, he said no. Luckily for him, I was going to do it no matter what he said." He takes the black box out of his pocket, and all I can do is hold my hands up and cross my fingers. My eyes are closed as I wait for the words. "So, what do you say, Sofia? Will you marry me and make me the happiest man in the world?"

I wait for her to say yes, but instead, all I hear is gasps from all around me. I open my eyes in time to see the ring box flying out of his hand. My eyes follow the ring box to make sure I know where it lands. "Oh my God!" Sofia shrieks. "The ring!" she yells, and I hear voices.

"He had one job," her father, Reed, says from the other side of the forest. I look at the sisters, who all shake their heads.

"She charged him," Viktor, Matthew's father, says coming out of their hiding place. "Was he supposed to let her fall?" Matty quickly reaches out and grabs the box. "He found it, you see," Viktor proclaims loudly.

"This was supposed to be just the two of us," Matty tells Sofia, and she just grabs his face and kisses his lips, saying something else to him.

"I really wish she would speak up," Clarabella says from beside me.

"We should have snuck mics into their clothes," Shelby hisses.

"Can you imagine if we did that, and they had sex before?" Presley looks over at us.

"Can you imagine if we did that and gave everyone headsets to listen to it? Or better yet, broadcasted it to everyone waiting at the barn?" Shelby shakes her head.

"Why would your mind even go there?" Clarabella chides. "It's always the worst-case scenario."

"No, it's not true. Remember when Travis was going to get married, and our event space almost burned down, and then the 'bride'"—Shelby uses her hands to do quotations—"ended up in the emergency room? I never once said we shouldn't do this."

"Yes, you did." Presley laughs. "You said if Mom wasn't going to kill me, I'd tell him to perhaps rethink things."

I can't help but roll my lips when I see Shelby tilt her head to the side as she remembers it. "I mean, if that wasn't worst case, I don't know what is."

"I'm not saying no!" Sofia yells over her shoulder, making all of us look at her again. "I will never, ever say no."

"Is that a fact?" Matty asks her, and I just smirk. "So, if I said, let's get married today?"

"He did not," Reed groans. "Did he just—"

"Here we go," Shelby states, "do or die."

"Why is it die?" I hiss. "Never die. Always live."

"Matthew," she says, and I hold up my hand.

"What if I said I took care of everything, and all you have to do is choose the dress?" She isn't the only one who hisses at that. All the men do as well. You see, to pull this off, we had to sneak around and pretend it was going to be just an engagement celebration. But what they didn't see was all the details we snuck in. They were so busy worrying about the proposal space, no one picked up on the fact we had wedding dresses delivered. We had to bring in Zara, who owns Zara's Closet and is the most sought-after personal stylist in the world, to ensure all dresses were available. We swore her to secrecy, and it was hard since Matty's mom is her twin. Do I think she kept her word? No. Do I think Zoe hid it well? Yes.

"How—how did you do all this?" Sofia asks, and I hear laughing.

"It's go time," I say, and the three sisters nod at me as we walk out of our hiding space.

"How do you think he did?" Shelby asks, and Sofia's head whips around to stare at us. The sisters all look at her with a smile, and I wave awkwardly beside them.

"So, what do you say," Matty asks her again, "want to get married?"

"You didn't think we would miss this, did you?" Clarabella asks, shaking her head.

"We would have killed him if he did this without us," Presley declares, smiling.

"So." Shelby smirks at Sofia. "Are we doing this? Are we getting married?" She tilts her head to the side. "Today?"

All I can do is wait with bated breath. This is it. To tell you the truth, there was only one answer we were going with. No one ever thought about what we would do if she said no, not even me. "Yes."

I can't help but let out the biggest cheer, along with the girls. "Okay, people." Shelby claps her hands. "We have things to do."

"I thought we did everything we had to do?" Casey, Sofia's

grandfather, looks over at me, putting his hands on his hips.

I stare back at him, and if this was any other time, I think I would apologize to him, but I feel like I'm going to throw up, so instead, I just shake my head. "You thought wrong."

"You." Clarabella goes to Sofia. "Congratulations, but this is no time to celebrate." She puts her hand around her arm. "It's time to get you dressed and drunk."

"Um," Matthew asks, "does she need the ring?" He holds up the ring he crawled around for right after Sofia tackled him.

"She does." I finally snap out of it and smile at him. "Go put it on her." I clap my hands happily when he finally does.

"Sofia," Matthew says, picking up her hand, "will you marry me?"

"We don't have time for this," Presley states. "She already said yes, so just slip it on her. The girls are waiting."

"Well, we're trying to sober them up, but most of them are really excited," Clarabella explains. "Your grandmother is losing her mind with all the dresses Zara was able to get. She even bowed down to her and then fell." Casey takes a step forward. "She's fine." Then she mumbles, "Nothing a little makeup can't hide.

"We have her," Clarabella assures, looking at me, and all I can do is nod my head. "You two." She points at Shelby and Presley. "Gather the men."

"Gather the men," Matty's uncle Matthew says. "What the fuck does that mean?"

"I think it means if you try to run, she's going to…" Matthew's uncle Max tries to say without laughing but can't stop, "lasso you."

"Dibs," Casey calls, folding his hands over his chest as Uncle Matthew glares at him.

Clarabella grabs Sofia's hand and pulls her toward a golf cart.

"Get in."

"Where are we going?" she asks us, and all I can do is smirk at her. After all, the one thing I'm happy about is I didn't blow the surprise.

I get into the back of the cart as Clarabella starts to drive through the path on the way to Sofia's great-grandfather's barn.

The sight of her pink tractor outside makes her gasp. I grab the clipboard from the seat beside me and look down at it.

"We have a lot to get ready for," I say, getting out of the golf cart and looking toward the barn that is being transformed as we speak.

"Fun fact," Sofia shares, "I was conceived in this barn."

"Well, it's full circle now," Clarabella says. "Do you want to see the reception space or do you want to go and do the dresses?"

"Please, I trust you guys with my life," she declares. "Take me to the dresses."

"Yay." I clap again. "I'm so excited, we all have bets," I finally say as we usher her toward the side of the barn. As soon as we get close enough, I can hear the laughter and the giggles.

The door opens, and the squealing becomes even louder, and all I can do is watch in shock as the women try to blink away the drunkenness.

"It's going to be fine." Clarabella must see the frantic look I have on my face. "The only ones who need to be sober for this are Presley and Shelby."

"What?" I blurt, thinking that there has to be more people sober for this.

"They have the men who are going to be putting the finishing touches on the ceremony space," Clarabella informs me. "All we have to do is make sure no one's boobs are falling out and all private areas aren't showing."

"Can we pick a dress?" Zara says, sticking her head out of

the office.

I follow Sofia into the room and see that all my hard work from before has paid off. What was once an office is now filled with twenty mirrors all around the four walls, with tables of makeup in front of them and antique chairs. In the middle of the room are small round tables with benches so people can sit. "This is…" She looks up at the elegant chandelier hanging there.

"This is nothing," I state, pointing at the door that leads to the reception space. "You should see in there." I glance at Clarabella. "Now, if you don't need me, I have to make sure everything is in place for the ceremony and the reception." I look at Sofia. "You are my first client."

"Well then, I guess I'm in the best hands," Sofia replies, smiling at me. We have gotten very close in the past nine months, and I consider her my best friend. She has even helped me out babysitting Avery when I was stuck.

"I'll see you soon," I tell her as I turn and walk away from her and straight into the barn.

I barely make it out of the door when I hear shouting on the side. I walk over and see Casey and Matthew looking down at the shotgun in Casey's hand. "I think as soon as they say I do, we do the gun salute."

"What the hell are you two doing?" I storm up to them.

"We are going to shoot off the guns at the end," Casey informs me. "We have enough guys." I hold up my hand while he talks.

"Immediately no! There is no way you are doing that. I am drawing the line." I look at Casey. "And you don't even know how to hold a gun," I hiss at Matthew, who just rolls his eyes.

"Yes, I do. Look," he says, running over to the far end of the field.

"Oh my God, is he actually going to shoot a gun?" I ask Casey, looking around to see if there is anyone I can reason with.

"Don't worry, I gave him a gun that fires blanks," Casey reassures me, laughing, but all the laughing stops when we hear the shot being fired. "Dumbass," Casey says, shaking his head.

Matthew runs back to us. "You see, it's fine."

"I see nothing of the sort!" I shout at him. "You." I point at Casey. "No guns. You." I point at Matthew. "No nothing. I want you to go help set up the ceremony space." I point to the side where the rest of the guys are working. "If I even see a gun, I'm telling Billy and Cooper." I mention their dads to them.

"Buzzkill," Matthew grumbles, handing the gun back to Casey as he storms away, with Casey following him.

I close my eyes and look up at the sky. "This better be perfect."

Two

Stefano

"You have reached your destination." The woman's voice fills the car. "Your destination is on the right." I look out of the window at the huge house on the side. Cars line the whole street in both directions. People look like they are running around in a panic. I spot my cousins and I can't help the smile that fills my face. It's been way too long since I've seen them last.

"Finally," Jenna huffs from beside me, "I feel like we've been in this car for five days."

I look over at her. "It's been two hours." I shake my head.

"Two hours since we got into this car, you are forgetting driving nine hours before this." She opens the car door and steps out, stretching as she looks around.

"I wasn't going to miss this wedding." I open my own car door and step out, the humidity hitting me right away. "They grounded all planes in San Francisco because of the fog, what did you think was going to happen?"

"I didn't expect you to say, let's drive to Vegas and take a plane from there," she huffs again, and I close my eyes, wondering if bringing her was a mistake. We've only been dating for over a month.

"You could have stayed back." I open the trunk, grabbing my luggage. "I told you I was only going to be here for three days."

"How would that look to your family if your girlfriend decided to skip the wedding?" She pushes her blond hair behind her ear before folding her arms over her chest. "It would look like I don't want to see them."

"I don't think my family would give it that much thought, they have other things to worry about besides why you wouldn't have been here," I tell her as I hear the sound of gunshots.

Jenna jumps up and then ducks down. "What the fuck was that?"

"Sounds like gunshots," I say, trying to hide my laugh. "Do you want me to grab your bag or are you okay?"

"A gentleman never asks." She glares at me.

I chuckle at her. "If I would grab one of my sisters' or my cousins' bags, they would kick me in the balls and then wait for me to bend over and then kick me straight in the ass," I inform her. "I've seen it happen to many others."

"Well, I'm not your sister or your cousin, I'm your girlfriend," she declares, opening the back door of the car, "and I'm okay with you carrying my bag."

I walk over to the back of the car, grabbing her bag before I see a golf cart zoom across the grass going toward the barn with a pink tractor in front of it. The woman's long blond hair flies in the wind.

"Look who the cat dragged in." I turn my head toward the

voice of my cousin Stone. I dump my bag and Jenna's bag on the ground, going over to him and hugging him. "Dad said you might not make it."

"I would have called in every single favor I have to get here," I tell him when we let each other go, my hand slapping his shoulder and I squeeze. "You look skinny."

"Fuck you," he retorts. "You look like you've been skipping the gym." He taps me on the stomach but there is nothing there but muscle.

"Think again." I give him the chin up. "Stone, this is Jenna," I introduce her to Stone. "Jenna, this is one of my many cousins, Stone."

"He forgot best cousin," Stone says, going over to her and kissing her cheek. "Nice to meet you."

"Do you know where we have to go?" I ask him, looking around and spotting my uncles Matthew and Max trying to talk to another guy. I stare a little more and see that they are holding shotguns, and I'm about to ask questions when Stone starts talking.

"The women are in there." Stone points over to the barn. "And then the men are in there." He points at a house that isn't far away from the barn.

"There is also a changing whatever you call it, over there." He points at the small house in the back of the big house.

"I'll go over there and change," Jenna says, "I'll meet you later." She comes to me and kisses me.

"I'll be around," I tell her as she grabs her bag and walks away from us.

"Bringing a girl to a wedding," Stone grumbles as soon as she is far enough away. "What the hell are you even thinking?"

"What was I supposed to say to her, you can't come?" I throw back, grabbing my bag.

"Um. Yeah," he states and I laugh. "It's been a week."

"It's a month," I point out, which doesn't make it any better. We met a month ago when I was working for the company she is employed with.

He slaps my shoulder. "Did you tell your parents you were bringing her?" he asks me.

"Did you tell Romeo you are hooking up with his sister?" I counter and he stops.

"I'm not hooking up with his sister." He stops walking. "I'm trying to hook up with her, there is a difference."

"The difference is, you aren't used to people telling you no," I point out to him as I walk up the steps to the house, and I can already hear the guys' voices.

"Here we go," Stone says, opening the door. "Look at what I found." He walks in and all the heads turn toward the door.

"Stefano!" everyone shouts my name. I can't help but smile when I look around the room at all my cousins. I mean, technically we aren't blood related, but my mother, Vivienne, has been with the family from before I was even born. They are her second family and we have grown up together.

"Look who it is," I say, seeing Matty, who is standing with a beer in his hand. I drop my bag and walk over to him.

"How you doing?" I ask him, giving him a hug. He slaps me on the back before letting me go.

"I feel so fucking great right now!" he exclaims, his chest puffing out. "What about you?"

"I'm good. Driving in was fun," I say, chuckling. "I felt like I was going through security checks every five minutes." He just looks at me. "There are cameras everywhere taking pictures. Did you guys not see?" I ask the room, and all of the guys just shake their heads.

"What did you expect?" I hear a voice say from the front

door. "That we are going to let just anyone drive in?"

I look him up and down, but he needs no introduction. I mean, he doesn't to me because I've already checked him out a while ago. Casey Barnes. Owner of CBS Corporation. The biggest security firm in the world. He has major contracts with the US government and some that no one knows about. Well, except for me, that is.

"Relax," my uncle Matthew soothes, coming into the room. "Stefano." He comes over to me and gives me a hug. "I see you've already riled his feathers." He laughs. "Casey." He looks over at the man. "Meet the biggest pain in your ass you will ever meet." He squeezes my shoulder. I look over at Casey and just nod at him.

"Nice to meet you," I say, and I can see him sizing me up. When Matty started dating Sofia again, we found out who her family was. I got a call from my uncle, and when I heard the name, even my balls shriveled up. You didn't do my job and not know who Casey Barnes was.

He walks over to me and holds out his hand. "Finally get to see the man who cracked my firewall," he jokes, and all I can do is laugh.

"If it makes you feel better," I reply, shaking his hand, "it took me a whole day."

"That doesn't make me feel better at all," he returns, letting go of my hand. "What would have made me feel better is knowing someone was cracking my firewall."

"What is going on right now?" Matty asks, looking at me and then at Casey.

"Shop talk," Casey shares, putting his hands in his pockets and smirking when he knows it bothers Matthew not being in control.

"Where is Dad?" I turn around, looking for him.

"He was with Quinn, Sofia's uncle," Matty says. "They are discussing bringing some of the dogs to his rehabilitation center." My father used to play professional hockey but always had a side business of dog walkers. You would think it was a funny business but he not only opened them in big cities, but smaller ones, too; he was one of the first to start doggy daycares also. Now he has over two hundred and fifty stores all around the country. They cater to dog walking, dog daycares, dog sitting, and newly, dog training.

"Nice," I say, looking around. "I should go and get changed."

I grab my bag and walk up to Matty. "Do you need me to do anything?"

"I'm good," he replies and his eyes beam with happiness. "I'll show you where to change."

He leads me up the stairs to one of the bedrooms where there are three suits hanging. "You can change in here. One of those is yours." He points at the three suits hanging and I see one of them has SD on it, so it must be mine.

I dump my bag on the bed. "I can't believe you are getting married," I state, unbuttoning my jeans and kicking them off.

"I can't fucking wait." His face goes into a smile right away. "I would have married her as soon as we got back together." I nod at him.

"Shit," he swears, his face going white. "I forgot the gift." He rushes over to his bag on the chair in the corner. He grabs the light-blue box out of his bag with a white ribbon. "I had one job."

"I think you had more than one job," I tease, grabbing my tan linen pants and slipping them on. "It's no time to stress. I'm going to get dressed and I'll go over and give it to her."

He runs his hands through his hair. "Thank you. I would take it over myself, but I think my mother will shoot me in the foot."

"I did hear shots when I got here," I tell him, taking off my white T-shirt and grabbing the white linen shirt. "Vest or no vest?"

"Vest for the ceremony and no vest for the reception. I'm sorry I can't have all of you standing up with me at the altar." I shake my head and laugh.

"Can you imagine how many bridesmaids she would need?" I shake my head. There are a couple of things I love more than anything in this world, and my family is number one on that list. We may each have our own lives and everyone is scattered around the world, but once a year we all get together. It's chaotic and we used to always bitch about it, but now it's the one time of year I look forward to. Well, that and Christmas but that usually lasts a day or two. The vacation is always two weeks.

Matty walks over to me and hands me the box. "I can't wait for her to be my wife."

I look at him. "Do you want me to tell her that?" I grab the box. "I mean, I will but…"

"It's in the note." He glares and hisses all at the same time before turning and walking back to the bag. "I guess I'm more nervous than I thought I would be." He grabs the white card and hands it to me.

"Hey," I say to him, "you've got this."

"Yeah." He takes a huge inhale when someone calls his name from downstairs. "You good?"

"I'm good, go and do the groom things." He nods at me, smirking.

"I'm getting married," he states, his chest beaming with pride. "It feels good, you should try it."

"Let's calm down there." I hold up my hand. "My longest relationship was five months, I think. And that was only because I didn't see her for like three and a half months of that."

"Who knows? Maybe you'll meet someone you can't live without," he says right before he walks out of the room.

I grab the box and card after putting on my shoes. "Who knows?" I repeat once I get downstairs and walk out the door. "Maybe I just might."

Three

Addison

I park the golf cart right next to the barn and look around, seeing the ceremony space is as it should be. Making my way toward the wooden path that was just laid down as the aisle for Sofia, I walk down toward the trees and see the lights even from here.

Wisteria vine ratta white flowers are hanging all the way to the ground and are then pinned at the side, giving a curtain effect. The minute I saw this picture online, I knew it would look amazing here. I pick up a strand of flowers and smell it while I continue to walk down the wooden path. White rose petals are along the pathway, the tall trees closing off the sun from coming in. The soft yellow tea lights add some extra light besides the sunlight that is trying to cut through the trees. "Hey," I greet as I walk down and see Ace and Bennett putting the white and gold chairs on each side of the aisle. "How is it going?"

"It would be going a lot better if we could be in the barn drinking," Ace complains, huffing as he puts the last chair down. "Do you know how many people we had at my surprise wedding?" His wedding to Shelby was after they found out their significant others were sleeping with each other. Shelby found out the night before her wedding and then walked down the aisle and exposed him like the boss she is. Then the two of them went on her honeymoon, and from the way they act, they are still on their honeymoon. I shake my head.

"Maybe sixty people," he fills me in and then looks over at Bennett.

"Mine doesn't count; it was really a gender reveal and there were about two hundred people," Bennett says of his and Presley's wedding.

"What was the head count?" Ace asks me, putting his hands on his hips.

"I think it was something close to three hundred, if not a touch more," I reply, and Bennett whistles. "They both have huge families." The sting of tears still shocks me, even after all this time. "This looks amazing," I praise, looking toward the end of the aisle where there is a canopy of flowers and lights. "I have to check the reception space. Why don't you guys come and enjoy a cold one while you can?" I motion with my head toward the golf cart that is waiting for me.

"Don't have to tell me twice," Ace says, the both of them following me to the golf cart. I drive them to the barn and they quickly get out and walk into the building.

I look around, making sure no one is trying to shoot off any more guns before I see Shelby and Presley walking toward me, holding up a glass of champagne. "What is that for?"

"That is for this," Shelby declares, holding her hand up, and I look around at all the hard work I did the past two weeks to make this a reality. I can't help but feel proud I actually pulled it off.

"It was easy with you guys helping me," I tell her, and she just throws her head back and laughs.

"This was all you," Presley compliments, "the little touches of detail are everything." She turns and points at the empty wine barrels I found with rustic glass vases on top with candles. Instead of round tables, I put long tables so everyone can more or less be together. In the middle of the tables are little round pieces of wood that hold the flowers on them.

"That *shake it like a Polaroid picture* is amazing," Shelby declares, pointing at the big board that has string hanging, waiting for pictures to be added. There will be a photographer snapping pictures of everyone when they arrive and then hanging the pictures up. "She's going to love it."

"I hope so," I tell them. "Speaking of the bride, I need to make sure everything is going okay, and everyone is less sweet tea and more normal." I smile at them as I turn and walk out of the barn.

The sound of birds chirping off in the distance fills me with a peace, of sorts. Until I hear shots again. This time I look up and see Billy and Cooper Sr. standing together, while he shows him how to hold the gun.

I put my hands on my head before I run toward them. "Do you think we can hide all the weapons for today?" I ask Billy, who just smiles at me.

"Will do, lass," he agrees, ignoring me and turning and walking away from me. I turn back, running to the bride's room, and when I'm about to open the door, another shot fires through the air.

I rush, gasping for breath. "Everything is fine," I pant out when I walk into the room. I try to settle my breathing as I push my hair to the side and put a smile on my face, even though it's a fake smile. "The men were thinking of maybe saluting you guys by shooting off guns and one sort of misfired." I see the horror on Sofia's face, and I know I have to calm the situation down. "No one is hurt."

She laughs at me at the same time someone knocks at the door. "Can I come in?" a male voice says as he sticks his head in. "I come with gifts." I turn my head to look toward the door and the voice.

It's as if everything happens in slow motion. I can literally hear myself blink as it happens. My eyes fall onto the man who is coming in. I can feel the blood drain out of my whole body as he steps in, his six-foot-four frame filling the room. His black hair that felt like silk under my fingers is styled perfectly on his head. He doesn't have to look at me for me to know that his eyes are green. He's wearing tan pants with a white shirt and a tan vest; the same thing the groom's party will be wearing. Someone gasps and I have to wonder if it's Sofia, and when I turn to her, I see her looking at me with confusion on her face. It's then I realize I'm the one who gasped. It was me. *This can't be happening,* I think to myself; my head feels like it's spinning around and around at the same time that I feel the room spinning the complete opposite way. My mouth goes drier than the desert on a hot summer day, my tongue feels like it just grew in my mouth. The back of my neck slowly starts to get clammy and my fingers are tingly. Am I having a stroke? Maybe he's not here in front of me. Maybe it's my mind playing tricks on me from the sun and heat from outside. Maybe I got shot by one of the bullets.

All these things run through my mind but halt when his eyes stop looking around the room and then, finally, he's looking straight at me. "Oh my God," I declare as I put my hand to my mouth. "It's you." It's him, the man who has been haunting my dreams for the last five years. The man I met one night in a bar and went home with. The man who all I knew is I fell in love with his name. The man who is the father of my child. The minute I think of Avery, I know I have to get out of here and get her away from here. Except, I have no idea where she is. I know she's somewhere with Shelby's kids and she is fine.

The color on Stefano's face drains and he looks like he's seen a ghost. "You," he says in a whisper. I can see Sofia at the side of me, her head going from me to Stefano and back to me again. I can't even imagine what she is thinking. The only thing I'm thankful for is no one in the room besides the three of us sees what is going on. I'm about to sit down or my legs are about to give out when I hear Avery shriek. I close my eyes, trying to force her to go away. Or maybe I close my eyes, thinking if I do this, everything that is happening right now isn't actually happening. Maybe all of this is a dream. Maybe he's not right here in front of me.

"Momma, Momma!" Avery shouts, running to me and I look down at her. Her hair is pinned at the sides and she's wearing a halo of flowers. The white dress she is wearing has short sleeves and looks like there are flowers all over it. It kicks off and looks like a mini ball gown as it brushes her knees. Her little blush-pink, sparkly ballerina shoes make the outfit complete. "I get to wear a princess dress." She turns around in a circle on one foot, stumbling while she looks at Sofia and then at Stefano.

"Oh my God." Stefano gulps, putting his hand to his mouth. I have no doubt he's put two and two together. Her eyes are the same eyes he has. They have the same golden ring around them. The sound of my heart beating in my chest is filling my ears, along with the sound of buzzing.

"Stefano," I hear someone call to him. As the door closes,

my eyes go over to see a woman coming into the room. She's stunning as she saunters over to him, her long legs coming out of the split of her dress. A dress that molds her form and shows you she's got the perfect body. Her breasts look like two small balls, and if this was happening to anyone else, I would laugh. "Baby, where did you go?" she questions, slipping her hand through his. "Who do we have here?" It's a wonder I don't vomit all over the place. It's a wonder there aren't screams coming out of my mouth instead of all in my head.

He doesn't say anything to her as she looks at him with a huge smile on her face. Her blond hair is perfectly curled at the end. My eyes immediately go to her ring finger to see if maybe they are married, but it's empty.

I look at Stefano and then look back down at Avery. "Aunt Sofia," she says, "do I look like a princess?"

Sofia, whose eyes were as big as saucers not two seconds ago, smiles down at Avery and squats down in front of her. "You are the most beautiful princess I've ever seen," she assures her.

"Look, I have a crown of flowers," she brags, touching the crown on top of her head, "like a real princess.

"Momma," Avery says, coming over to me. "I have a basket full of flowers and I have to throw them." She mimics what she has to do.

The blonde laughs. "She is so adorable; what is her name?"

I look up now and add this one moment to the list of things I will never forget. "Her name is Avery."

Four

Stefano

I'm having an out-of-body experience. Either that or I've died and I'm looking down at my life unraveling before my eyes. My heart is beating so fast it feels as if it's going to come out of my chest. Even breathing feels like an elephant is sitting on me. The linen vest feels like it's too tight on my body. I swear I am now hearing buzzing noises from my ears. I listen to Jenna ask her for her name.

The minute she says her name, it's as if the angels sing. It's crazy, right? It's totally out of left field but it's as if that name settles me. "Avery," I say her name, but not in my head and more of a whisper than anything else. My eyes never leave her. "That's a beautiful name." Avery looks up at me, and I swear to God, it's like looking into my eyes. What the fuck is going on right now? She smiles at me, a smile that is half her mother and half mine. I feel like I've been kicked in the stomach. Scratch that, I feel like I've been kicked in the balls and then my stomach. I look at her and then at Addison, who looks like she's going to pass out. Her face is white, like she's seen a ghost, and I guess seeing me after five years is just like that.

"That's a pretty dress," Jenna says from beside me as she smiles at Avery, and I look over at her. For a second, I forgot she was even here. I look back at Addison, whose eyes are on Jenna's hand gripping my arm.

"Um," Sofia says, "Addison, this is Stefano." She blinks her eyes a million times a minute. "And his girlfriend." She looks at Jenna, waiting for her to fill her in because that is how much I've discussed her to anyone.

"Jenna," she says, smiling at them.

"Nice to meet you both," Addison replies, avoiding looking at me as she glances over at Sofia. They share a look and Sofia just nods at her silently and grabs her hand.

"I hate to kick you guys out, but I need to get dressed." Sofia turns to Addison and asks her, "Is it time for me to get dressed?" Addison doesn't say anything and just nods her head yes. She then looks back at me and down at my hand. "Is that for me?"

I hold up the box. "Yeah. This is from Matty."

"Thank you." She grabs the box from me and I stand here for longer than I need to, looking at Addison and then back down at Avery, afraid to walk out of the room, and then Sofia leaves. Avery smiles at me as she leans into Addison.

"I'll see you out there," I say to Avery before turning and walking out of the door. The door closes behind me with a click, and I immediately want to turn around and go back in there.

"That was so weird," Jenna observes, looking at the commotion going on around us. I look up at the sky, trying not to freak the fuck out right now. "Why don't we go and get a drink?"

she suggests to me, walking over and wrapping her arms around my neck, and I have the sudden need to step away from her.

"You go, I'll meet you there," I tell her.

"I don't want to go alone." She sings out her words. "I want to go with you. Why can't you come with me?"

"I have to go see if Matty needs anything," I say, trying not to sound irritated by her nagging, but I also feel a headache coming on. "You knew this coming here," I remind her. "You were the one who said it would be like you weren't even here."

"Fine," she huffs, her arms falling from my neck. "I'll go and get a drink and then save you a seat next to me." She smiles. "I might even save you a dance," she flirts, right before she walks away from me. I turn and look back at the door, wanting to storm back in there, but also not wanting to make a scene at the wedding.

I watch her make her way to the barn before I hightail it back over to the groom's house. I run up the steps and into the house, seeing it's Matty, Stone, and my other cousin Christopher, sitting down all drinking a beer. "Holy shit, are you okay?" Stone asks me when I walk in. "You look like you've seen a ghost." The two of them are dressed exactly like me, Matty is the only one without the vest but with a jacket instead.

I walk over and fall into the chair before my legs literally give out on me. "I think I did," I mumble and then look at Matty, who is just staring at me.

"Did you deliver the gift?" he asks me, sitting up, nervous I didn't deliver the gift.

"I did," I inform him. "Who is planning your wedding?" The question comes out without me even thinking twice, which is not normal for me. I always, always make a plan before I have any discussion with anyone.

"Clarabella, Presley, and Shelby," he replies, leaning back in the chair, taking a pull of his beer, "they work together."

"Who is Addison to Sofia?" I ask him, trying not to seem like I'm prying or even seeming like I would care who she is. But he doesn't answer me. Instead, he just glares at me.

"Off-limits," he grouses between clenched teeth. "She's a single mom." He tells me something I already know. "Don't even think about it."

"Aren't you here with a girl?" Stone laughs as he asks me the question.

"Didn't you just start dating her also?" Christopher follows up with his own question.

All I can do is ignore them. "How old is Avery?" I ask him, even though I know deep down inside me she's mine. I can't explain it, but I know. I knew the minute I locked eyes on her, she was mine.

"I have no idea, four… five… six." He shrugs.

"Have you met her little girl?" I ask him, and his glare gets even more intense.

"Are you fucking kidding me right now? You want to do this at my wedding?" he shouts and Christopher and Stone try not to laugh at his tone.

"I'm not doing anything," I say, my leg shaking up and down with nerves. "I'm just asking who they are. I just met them."

"Sofia usually has them over when I'm on the road," Matty shares. "I've seen Avery a couple of times, here and there."

"Is she dating anyone?" Christopher asks, and now I'm glaring at him.

"Listen." Matty stands up. "None of you perverts are allowed to make a play for her." He points at all three of us, and I throw in if the other two even try it, I'm going to throat punch them before they even get a word out. Actually, if they even think it, I'll hurt them.

"Relax there," Stone assures. "I'm already spoken for."

Christopher laughs at that. "Does she even know you exist?"

"Oh, she knows," Stone says with a smirk, and I'm happy they are talking about something else besides Addison.

The door opens and my uncle Viktor comes in. "It's time." Matty stands up and puts the beer down on the table in front of him. "She's coming out now?"

"No, God no," Viktor says, "but the photographer wants to take pictures with us and all of that."

"And considering there are a million of us, it's like herding cats," Christopher announces, finishing off his beer.

"They need a lot of time." Stone gets up and slaps Matty on the shoulder. "Getting married."

"It's great," he states, "you should try it."

"She doesn't even want to date him, how is he going to marry her?" Christopher laughs while Stone glares at him.

"I mean, Uncle Matthew handcuffed Aunt Karrie to the bed," Viktor reminds us, and the three of us literally groan.

"What is wrong with you people?" Matty says. "It's my wedding day; can we not talk about my aunt and uncle having sex?"

"I didn't say they had sex," Viktor defends. "You guys are perverts and your minds just went there."

"How could it not?" Stone shakes his head and walks to the door. "Why else would you use handcuffs?"

"You should see if you can borrow them," Christopher tells him, "maybe, then Ryleigh will give you the time of day."

Stone just flips him the bird. "Can we not anger Romeo by talking about his sister dating Stone?" Matty pleads between clenched teeth.

"They aren't dating," Christopher says right before walking out the door. "I think she said, 'when donkeys help pigs fly.'"

"Can we just not mess up my wedding?" Matty asks as we walk out of the house.

"No one is going to mess up your wedding," I reassure him, looking at the house that I want to go back to. Instead, I look over to the side, seeing my family starting to get together.

I start walking to them when I turn to the side and see my father walking toward me. He's wearing a light-blue suit without a tie. His aviator glasses cover his eyes, but with his face going into a huge smile, I know his eyes are a light brown.

"There he is," he says when he gets close enough to me as he takes me in a hug. I got my height from my father, for sure. He slaps my back and kisses the side of my head before letting me go. "You look good."

"You saw me two months ago." I laugh at him as he puts his arm over my shoulder. "And we FaceTime at least twice a week."

"It's different when I see you face-to-face." He lets his hands drop from my shoulders. "How've you been?"

"Okay," I reply, looking down before I look at him and confess to him what just happened. My father is my biggest supporter. He's also the one I go to anytime I have a problem, no matter what. Even when I mess up, and there have been times that I've messed up, but instead of telling you "I told you so," he calmly finds a solution. He and my mother couldn't be more opposite.

"We need to have a conversation after this," he advises me, and I literally stop in my tracks. Does he know? Did he meet Avery and know? Is he going to kick my ass for having a kid and deserting her? He must sense I'm freaking out. "Nothing bad. I met Jenna," he says, stopping as he puts his hands in his pockets. "Where did you meet her?" he asks me, and my eyebrows go up. "I'm not judging," he quickly says, "I'm just wondering where the two of you met?"

I look around and see Avery running in the distance with other kids. My heartbeat picks up, going faster and faster, and it was already going faster than normal. "It's nothing," I tell my father, because after today, the only thing that will matter to me is my daughter. Which is a strange thought since I don't think I've ever seen myself with a child. I mean, I knew I wanted to get married and start a family, but I never, ever pictured myself with a child. Especially one that was so beautiful like she is. "I need to tell you something," I start and then look over to see Matty posing for pictures. "But not here," I say, not willing to ruin his day, "but tomorrow."

"Is everything okay?" he asks, the worry filling his voice. I just nod my head because I don't trust myself to say anything with the lump filling my throat. "Okay," he agrees, "tomorrow."

He slaps my shoulder before he walks away, leaving me standing in the middle of the field. My eyes are on my family on one side and my daughter on the other. "Tomorrow," I repeat before I make my way to my family.

Five

Addison

The door closes behind Stefano, and I swear it's like everything in me just leaves. "Oh my God," I declare, trying to get to a chair before I collapse on the floor, which will make an even bigger scene.

"Oh my God," Sofia says, putting the blue box down and looking around the room to make sure no one saw what just happened. All of the women are too busy getting ready to even care what just went down.

I put my face in my hands as the door opens again, and for the second time today, I think my heart stops. I look up expecting to see Stefano storm back in here and make a scene, but instead it's Clarabella. "Okay, everyone but the bride," she announces, "it's time for pictures." I let out the biggest sigh of relief and literally hang my head when the women slowly trickle out of the room.

One of Sofia's cousins comes over and takes Avery with her, as Presley and Shelby walk into the room and take a look around.

"What is going on?" Presley asks.

"Oh my God," Shelby says, "did someone get shot?"

"Was it a horse?" Clarabella gasps. "I told them doing a gun salute was not a good idea."

"Wait… what?" Sofia says and then shakes her head. "Forget it. I need to focus on one thing at a time." She turns and looks at me. "Are you okay?" Her voice goes soft.

I shake my head, looking to see if there is any sweet tea around. If there was ever a time for sweet tea, it would be now, at this moment.

"Why wouldn't she be okay?" Shelby asks softly, coming over and sitting next to me. The tears now come out of me, but I quickly wipe them away. The four of them have been the closest thing to family I've had in five years.

"I just saw someone I haven't seen in five years," I say, and my voice cracks at the end.

"Oh, that's weird," Clarabella says, sitting down in the chair. "Who was it?"

"Five years, that's a long time," Presley states as she sits on the arm of the chair Clarabella is sitting in.

"How are they not getting this?" Sofia shrieks, throwing up her hands in the air and looking at each of the girls.

"I think I need to sit down," I say, forgetting that I'm actually sitting down.

"Oh my God!" Clarabella yelps, as if she solved the biggest mystery of the world.

"The baby daddy?"

I nod my head, and Shelby flies out from the seat beside me. "Code Purple." She starts to look around frantically. "We have a Code Purple."

"We're all here." Presley throws up her hands. "Who else are we calling?"

"We do not need a Code Purple," I say, though I need a Code Purple. Actually, come to think of it, is meeting your baby daddy five years later with his girlfriend not considered higher than a Code Purple? "This is not the time or the place." I get up and smooth down my dress. "This is Sofia's day." I look at her, and everything in me wants to fall apart, but this is her day, so I need to put my emotions away and do my job. I have to show them I can do this job. "Let's get Sofia married." I force a smile on my face as Sofia looks at me. "I need you to pretend it didn't happen."

"Okay," Sofia gives in, "but we'll have to discuss this."

"Oh, I don't think you are the only one I'll have to discuss this with," I finally say. "Did you see his face? He knows."

"I mean, are men that intuitive?" Presley asks, and I just look at her.

"Oh, he knew right away," Sofia chimes in. "They have the same eyes. It took me a total of two point six seconds to put it together."

"Well, let's hope no one else puts it together," I mumble, "especially his girlfriend."

Clarabella gasps. "He has a girlfriend, and this is information you lead with?"

"Excuse me?" Shelby butts in. "Can we know who he is?"

"Stefano Dimitris," Sofia fills them in, and now gives me the last name I will most likely have to add to Avery's birth certificate. I feel my stomach getting sick and push down the thought, *you are fine*. Well, you will be fine. It will all be fine. I don't even think I believe myself this time.

"That is a sexy-ass name," Presley says, and Clarabella hits her arm with her hand. "What? It is."

"Can we focus on getting Sofia in her dress, please?" I urge. "I'll go get your mother so we can get you in it."

"I'll go get Hazel," Shelby volunteers. "You stay here and have a shot of sweet tea. You look like someone died and then kicked your dog after telling you Santa isn't real." She takes a deep breath. "It's not a good look."

"Wow," Clarabella chides, "smooth."

"When are you guys changing into your dresses?" Sofia asks, and we all look at her. "All my bridal party is wearing lilac, and I expect the four of you to wear it also."

"But—" I start to say.

"But nothing. It's my day, and you will do what I say," she huffs as the door opens, and her mother pops her head in.

"Not to be pushy or anything, but Matty is getting antsy. He started to bounce on his heels and then your grandfather asked him if he wanted to go shooting in the woods." She smiles but you can see the panic in her eyes. "We don't think that is a good idea."

"I thought they put all the guns away!" I shriek. "Billy said he would."

"Oh, Charlotte told them if they so much as leave this area, no one is getting any food," Hazel informs us, coming in. "Now let's get you dressed."

I smile at the two of them as she leads her over to her wedding dress. "Here." Presley hands me a lilac dress. "You get the off-the-shoulder one."

"I don't know about that. I need to wear a bra ever since Avery and breastfeeding, well, they aren't praising Jesus anymore." I look at the beautiful satin gown.

"No one's are praising Jesus anymore," Clarabella deadpans. "Just put it on, you'll be fine." I walk into the bathroom and slip on the lilac satin dress. It hugs every single one of the curves I also got after I had Avery. The sweetheart neckline is attached to small cap sleeves. I zip up the dress in the back as much as I can before I have to ask for help.

"Your ass looks amazing in this dress," Presley declares. "He's going to want to eat you all up."

"I don't want him eating anything," I tell them, avoiding looking at them. "Now, you three need to get out there and make sure it's all good."

"It's perfect," Shelby says. "I just went to see, but we'll go take our seats." She comes over to me. "You've got this." I blink away the tears that are threatening again.

The three of them leave the room, and Sofia steps out, and I gasp at how gorgeous she is. "Holy shit," I say, and then my hand flies to my mouth, "you look…"

"Do you think he'll like it?" she asks me, and I nod.

"Are you kidding me?" I can't help but smile at her. "He's going to love it," I assure her, blinking away tears. "Now, why don't we get out there and get you married?"

She nods as I pick up her train and veil, and we walk out. Reed paces back and forth, waiting for her, and the minute he sees her, he puts his hand on his chest. "Don't you dare cry," Sofia hisses. "I can't walk down the aisle a blubbering mess."

"I'm not going to cry," Reed denies, but at the same time, tears are pouring down his face.

I smile at them as I hand Sofia her bouquet before turning and looking at the flower girls and ring bearers. "Okay, you guys." I squat down. "Remember, girls first and then the boys."

"I'm going to keep some flowers for after," Avery whispers to me, "so I can throw them again."

"Okay," I reply, kissing her nose, knowing her life is going to change so much.

I stand in place, making sure everyone makes it down the

aisle before I let out a big sigh of relief. It went off without a hitch. Matty was wiping away tears the minute he saw her, and I, for one, can't wait to see the pictures.

I stand in the back, trying to focus on the vows, but my eyes scan the room, looking at the back of Stefano's head. He's sitting right next to his girlfriend, and my hand goes to my stomach. I look down at my shaking hands, remembering the night I met him.

I got to the bar an hour after I said I was going to be there. It took me that long to decide to even go. I pushed my way through the people, heading straight to the back where they usually sat and saw they were definitely gone. I pulled out my phone and saw a text from Chloe.

Chloe: Went to the diner to grab some grub*.*

"Ugh." I turned and ran smack into someone's chest. Someone's very hard chest. Someone who smelled delicious. Someone who would change my life, but neither of us knew that at that moment. His hands gripped my arms. "I'm so sorry," I apologized, and when I looked up, all I could do was stare. His black hair was pushed back, and even in the dimly lit room, his green eyes captivated me. He had to be the best-looking man I had ever seen in my whole life.

"You okay?" His voice came out so smooth.

"Yeah, I'm fine," I said, stepping away from him, but then someone bumped into me, and I was thrown in his arms again. All I could do was laugh it off nervously. "I guess I'm not that fine."

He laughed, and my whole body went hot. "Let's get you to a seat, then." He ushered me to the corner where there was an empty seat right at the end of the bar.

"I really am okay," I assured him as he crowded over me. "I'm Addison." I stuck out my hand.

"Stefano." He said his name, and even then, I thought it was fucking hot.

"That's a unique name." I closed my eyes after I said it. "That sounded so dumb." I put my hands on my face, hoping he didn't see me blush.

Even though the room was booming with music and people chattering, his laughter filled the room. "You, Addison," he said to me, "are the best thing to happen to me while I've been here." I tilted my head to the side. "And go figure, I meet you on my last night here."

"So you aren't from here?" I asked him, and of course, it would be just my luck I would meet the hottest man of my life, and he doesn't live here.

"No, I was here for work," he informed me. "Have you eaten yet?"

"I have not," I replied, and he smiled at me, and his green eyes got even lighter.

"Want to grab something to eat?" He motioned with his head toward the door and all I could do was nod mine.

The sound of cheering breaks me out of my daydream as I look down the aisle and see Matty holding Sofia's face in his hands as he kisses her. Both sides of the aisle are on their feet cheering.

I clap my hands excitedly for them as they turn and start to walk down the aisle. Sofia looks at Matty as he holds her hand in his, kissing it. I feel eyes on me, and when I turn, I find Stefano staring straight at me. His eyes a dark green, unlike the time I was with him. I stare back at him for a second, and then look at the movement beside him as Jenna whispers something in his ear. "He's never going to be yours," I tell myself as I turn and walk back to the barn to make sure everything is ready.

Six

Stefano

I watch Addison walk away at the same time I feel Jenna pull my arm down. "I love that dress," she says of Sofia's dress as the couple walks down the aisle in front of us. Matty's smile is so big on his face that nothing, and I mean nothing, could wipe it away. Fuck, what it feels like to be that in love, I will never know.

I look back down the aisle toward the altar and see the boys walking down with the girls behind them. My eyes are on Avery as she walks and throws flowers in the air, then twirls. Everyone laughs at her, and I can't help but feel proud, which is the stupidest thing I have ever thought because all I've done for her is have sex with Addison. The best sex of my life, I might add, but it was after that I said no more hookups. I was never going to have another one-night stand.

"Isn't she cute?" my father says as he laughs at her throwing another petal in the air and trying to catch it coming down.

"She's beautiful," I say out loud, but in my head, I also add *she's mine*. I can't help but watch her the whole time. My eyes never leave her as she makes her way down the aisle with the other little girls. I may be biased, but she really is the most beautiful out of all of them.

"I can't wait to sit down and eat," Jenna states as she looks around at people starting to make their way out.

"Um, excusez-moi," someone says behind me, looking over my shoulder. "Did my son walk in here and not even say bonjour?" My mother mixes the French with English. She pushes my father out of the way and walks to me. She grew up in France and came to the States to go to school. She fell in love with New York and decided to stay. She was a serial dater, so much so that she created a blog and then had her very own column in a magazine. No one knew it was her until she met and fell in love with my father. Then the serial dater became the serial mom, which grew even more. She went from saying she wasn't ever going to get married to having four children and pushing for everyone to get married.

"Maman," I say in French, walking to her and bending to kiss her cheeks and give her a hug.

"Mon beau garçon." My handsome boy, she says. "Comment vas-tu?" How are you? She smiles up at me. Her dark-blue eyes light up when she puts her hand on my chest. "Ça va bien oui?" It's going good, right?

"Oui. Ça va." It's good, I tell her.

"Tu as l'air fatigué." You look tired, she tells me.

"I'm good," I reply, avoiding looking in her eyes. Something about being a parent, they know right away when something is amiss. It used to always amaze me when it happened. "Have you met Jenna?" I ask her, looking toward Jenna to change her thoughts.

"Bien sûre." Of course, she says and puts on her fake smile. Trust me, I know her fake smile. Once, when I was ten or twelve, she threatened to beat my ass in French with a smile on her face, and everyone thought she was praising me. She was not.

"Who is ready for a drink?" my uncle Matthew says, clapping me on the shoulder. "You look like you need a drink," he tells me.

"What is wrong with everyone? I'm fine," I retort, as everyone slowly makes their way out. As soon as I step out in the sun, I look around to see if I can spot Addison. "I'll be right back," I say and don't even wait until anyone says anything, and by anyone, I mean Jenna.

I walk toward the barn, hoping like fuck she doesn't follow me. I'm about to take a step into the barn when my phone beeps in my pocket. Grabbing it and bringing it out, I see an email come in.

I read the tagline as requested and put the phone back in my pocket. I walk into the barn and see a couple of people running around. My eyes roam around the room as I spot her in the corner telling someone something. She points at something and the man just smiles at her. She laughs as he turns and walks away, and I have to clench my hands into fists before I walk to her.

"Addison," I call her name loud enough for her to hear me. She turns her head toward me, the smile on her face fading as I close the distance between us. She takes a second to look around before she puts her shoulders back.

"Can I help you with something?" she asks me, not walking away from me. The minute I get in front of her, the smell of her brings back all of the memories of that night. As I look at her, I can't help but think my memories of her are way off base because she is even better than I remembered.

Oh, you can help me with something all right, my head screams as I take her in. Her blond hair is definitely longer than it was the last time. Her brown eyes are also a touch darker than they were. "Can you help me with something?" It comes out harsher than I want it to.

She looks around me and I can see her eyes are doing a scan of the room, nervously. Even her hands begin to shake. "I'm here for work," she says softly. "I need this job." The way she says those words, I have to think there is something behind it. It is said with an almost desperation in her voice. I count to ten while I think of what she said, letting her words sit before anything.

I hear voices coming even closer. "Okay, then, how is tomorrow?" I ask her. I don't know if I'm asking her because regardless of what she says, we are going to have a sit-down tomorrow.

"Um, I guess," she responds, wringing her hands before she walks over to a side table and picks up her phone. "What's your number?" she asks me, looking down at the phone the whole time.

I take my phone out of my pocket and press my code to open it. Once it's open, I click the email icon. I open the email I got before I walked in here. I press the phone number in the email. The phone rings in her hand. "What? How?" she asks shocked, pressing the decline button.

"It's what I do," I inform her. "Now, my place or your place?" Even though I don't have a "my place" right now, but I'm hoping she says her place.

"No," she snaps. Her voice goes a bit too loud, and heads turn to look our way. "Neither."

"Fine, we'll meet at a neutral space," I tell her, not wanting her to get in trouble or lose her job.

"I leave tomorrow to go back home," she says softly, her voice almost in a whisper.

"I'll text you, and we can see where we can meet." I stare at her in the eyes, the same eyes I got lost in that one night.

"Sounds good." She nods before she looks over my shoulder. "Your girlfriend is looking for you," she says before she turns and walks away from me. Her dress swishes from right to left as she quickly exits the room to go to the back somewhere.

"Hey," Jenna says as she comes and puts her arm around my waist. "You ran off."

"Yeah, I was looking for the bathroom." I say the first thing that comes to my mind, and it sounds like a bunch of bullshit.

"Oh, where is it?" she asks me.

"I got sidetracked talking to one of my cousins," I fib to her and spot a server walking around. "Can you tell me where the restroom is?"

"Through those doors." He points at the doors off to the side. "I can show you."

Jenna smiles at me before she turns and follows the guy out of the room. I let out a huge breath that I was somehow holding. "I need a drink," I admit to myself as I turn to walk and then see Avery running in my direction. Her laughter is infectious, and I could listen to it for the rest of my life.

"Hey," I greet, squatting down in front of her. Her little hand pushes her hair away from her face as she pants from running. "If it isn't Princess Avery," I say, and she smiles. "How old are you, Avery?" I ask her, even though I know the answer, but just to make sure I'm not dreaming it.

"I'm four," she states, holding up her whole hand as she tries to bend her thumb in, making me laugh.

"Who is your little friend?" My father shocks me when he walks up beside me.

"This is Avery," I tell him. He looks down at her, and then he looks back at me. He does it so fast it's like he got whiplash.

"Um..." he starts, but his voice trails off. His whole face is filled with all the questions that I have myself.

"Not now," I tell him.

Avery looks at my father, unaware of what's going on around her. "I'm a princess today," she announces, holding the side of her dress while she twirls on one foot.

I swear I see a tear in my father's eye. "You are the most beautiful princess I've ever seen," my father compliments softly, squatting beside me to get a better look at her.

"Okay, bye," she says right before turning around and rushing back to the kids she was running with.

"What the fuck is going on?" my father grits between clenched teeth, his voice very, very low. The both of us still squatting down.

"Um..." I start to say because I have no idea what the fuck to say. Not sure he would like, "I just ran into the girl I had a one-night stand with, and I have a daughter." In fact, he would probably kick my ass from here to outside the universe.

"Either I need to get my eyes checked or..." he says, pointing at Avery.

"Not here," I say, getting up.

"Then I suggest you walk out with me." His voice is tight, and I can see that if I don't go with him, he's going to grab me by my neck and drag me out of here, just like he did when I was younger.

I nod at him as we pass everyone chattering and enjoying the wedding. Some have even decided to go and sit down at a table.

We walk out of the barn and go toward the groom's house where we got ready at before. Away from the noise. When we get close enough, he turns around. "Care to tell me what the fuck is going on?" My father, who is usually cool, calm, and collected, sounds like he's about to freak the fuck out.

"I just found out," I tell him, my heart speeding up as I run my hand through my hair and then hold my neck.

"What do you mean, you just found out?" He glares at me.

I think about lying for about one point two seconds but know I can't, not with him. If anything, I'm going to need all of his help. "We had one night together," I finally say.

"Oh, for fuck's sake." He throws up his hands. Yup, exactly how I thought it would go.

"I literally just found her today," I tell him, shaking my head. If this were anyone else, I would be laughing at the whole situation, but now that I'm in it, it's no laughing matter. "When I went into the bride's suite, she was just as surprised to see me, and then Avery came in, and I was shocked. I had no idea what the hell was going on."

"Well, what about Avery?" He says her name with a softness to his voice.

"All I know is she's four, and she wants to be a princess." I smile. "And she likes to twirl." My chest fills up. "And she's fucking perfect," I say, knowing three things about her.

"This is a big deal, Stefano." His tone is softer now.

"You think I don't know that, Dad?" My voice rises. I've always been in control of everything. I've always been cool, calm, and collected, something I got from my dad. I treat everything like it's a chess game. I sit down, patiently waiting for the next move, already having my opponent's move in my head so I can come in and steal the king. But this situation is pushing me to the edge of the cliff, and I feel like I'm hanging on by the tips of my fingers.

"This isn't just a deal that you can go in, sweep up, and then leave when you're done." He makes sure I'm looking at him while he says it. As if my saying I have a daughter hasn't cemented the situation in my brain.

"Dad, I get it." I'm frustrated because I do get it, and there are questions I didn't even think of.

"You don't even own a house." He points out another reason that I am not ready for this. "You live in hotels."

"I have a condo." I roll my eyes at him.

"I have a condo." He points at himself. "That I let you stay in."

"I thought you said I get it when you die." I try to crack a joke to ease the nerves.

"Stefano," he hisses.

"Dad, I got it," I say, my voice tight. "Trust me, I fucking got it. I'm not ready to be a father. I don't have a house. I don't know what to do with a kid." I look back at the barn and see Avery standing, holding Addison's hand as they talk to Sofia and Matty. "I got it," I repeat softly, knowing that I really don't have it. "If I don't, I'm going to get it."

Seven

Addison

"What do you need from us?" Clarabella asks me when she finds me on the side, looking around the space to make sure everything is running smoothly. Shelby and Presley start to walk our way.

"I think I'm good." I smile at her, trying to get my heart to return to a normal beat. It's been beating too fast and feeling like it will come out of my chest. Either that or I will yack all over the place.

"This decor," Shelby appraises, taking a sip of her champagne, and I've never been more jealous of a person in my life. "It's spectacular. We'll have to put this online and in a brochure."

"The little touches with the tree stumps." Presley points at the center of the tables. "It's the little details like that which make it perfect."

I can't help but smile and breathe a sigh of relief. "I just hope that it's everything she's wanted. I tried to think back on everything she told me from the beginning." I glance around the room, spotting Sofia with Matty walking around, taking in everything. The smile hasn't left her face since she walked down the aisle. I'm just happy my little situation didn't put a damper on anything. The phone buzzes in my hand, and I look down to see my timer has gone off. "Okay, I need you guys to take your seats," I tell them. "It's showtime."

"It's showtime?" Clarabella asks me, confused. "I thought showtime was her walking down the aisle."

"It's time for food. Now get to your spots." I clap my hands. "Chop-chop." I smile at them at the same time I nod to the singer of the band who comes on the microphone.

"Ladies and gentlemen," she says in her smooth, soft voice, "if everyone can get to their seat, it's time to get the party started."

I zigzag through the room until I'm in front of Sofia and Matty. "Hi," I say, "it's time for the main entrance. Follow me." I motion with my head as we sneak out of the side of the barn, walking around it.

"Where are we going?" Matty asks.

"There is a secret back entrance here," I inform them. "The stairs lead to the second floor, where you guys will come out, and you'll make your way down the staircase in front of everyone."

"Love that," Sofia says, "and in case I don't tell you a million times today"—she grabs my hands—"everything is beyond perfect."

"You did good, Addison," Matty adds, putting his arm over Sofia's shoulders.

"You can't make me cry," I hiss at both of them. "Now I have to go into the kitchen." I open the side door. "Go."

"Damn, she's bossy when she's in charge," Matty teases me

as he puts his hand on the lower part of Sofia's back.

"It's the mother tone, like you done fucked up and she's going to kick your ass." Sofia side-eyes me as she walks into the door, making me laugh.

I wait for them to both enter before I turn and make my way to the kitchen. I pull open the door in the back and hear Luke yelling out commands. "We have four minutes!" he shouts to them as he walks behind the long silver table. White plates are already placed on it. "I want the plates looking perfect."

"How's it going?" I ask him, wringing my hands with nerves.

"Horrible." The minute he says that, I feel the blood drain out of me. "Oh my gosh, I'm kidding. Relax."

"What the H E double L is wrong with you?" I hiss at him, putting my hand on my forehead.

"Relax," he assures me, "I've got this." He earns himself a glare as my phone buzzes in my hand. At the same time, I hear all the cheers, so I know they just made their entrance.

"We have two minutes," I tell him, and he snaps his fingers.

"One minute, people," he announces, walking toward his staff. "If I say two minutes, they might get lazy." He winks at me, and I see everyone is doing something.

The first course goes off without a hitch and I stick my head out for a second to make sure Avery is okay. The best thing I did was make sure the kids had someone to take care of them. Luckily for me, someone from Matty's side and Sofia's side stepped up to the plate.

I slip out of the kitchen, walking over to the head server, who is standing by the wall with his hands behind his back. "How is it going?"

"Smooth," he tells me. "Almost time for the second course."

When I push open the door to the kitchen, I clap my hands. "Next service is ten minutes out."

The sounds of pots and pans fill the kitchen as the voices go higher and higher as the pressure is on.

"What are you doing?" Presley storms into the kitchen, followed by her sisters.

"Um," I say, not sure exactly what she's asking, "working?"

"You did this so much better than we would have," Clarabella declares to me, her eyes shining, and I wonder if she's being sincere or if she's gotten in the sweet tea. Either way, I'm taking it as a compliment.

"No, I didn't." I shake my head. "And it's not over until the last person leaves. You taught me that." I point at Shelby.

"Yes, you did, and now it's time for you to come out and enjoy it with us." Shelby grabs me by my hands, pulling me away from the kitchen. "You have given your orders. If they need you, they know where to find you."

"I don't really think," I start to say but then stop when I see Sofia push open the kitchen door. Her face is in a scowl, so I stop moving my feet.

"Oh, you better get your ass out here and help me celebrate my wedding," Sofia orders, pointing over her shoulder.

I look at the four of them. When I applied for the job, I was hoping I would get it. Even in the interview I felt like part of the team. The way I came in and they took me under their wing. They accepted Avery without batting an eye. They accepted me with all the baggage I had. They did more for me in the short time I was with them than my family did my whole life. "Fine."

I smile at them as we walk out of the kitchen door. We walk toward the table, and I look around, stopping in my tracks. My eyes focus on Stefano squatting down in front of Avery, next to the dance floor. He must feel my eyes on him because he turns his head and looks our way.

"Oh my God," Clarabella says in a whisper beside me.

"Is that…?" Shelby now tries to ask the question but stops.

"Oh my God, she has his eyes," Presley observes, her hand going to her mouth, "and smile."

"I know," I finally say.

"How did you not know?" Shelby looks over at Sofia.

"How was I supposed to know?" Sofia hisses back at her. "Do you think I walked around staring into his eyes. I've met him twice."

"Didn't you go on vacation with them for two weeks?" Clarabella asks her.

"Again, I didn't walk around looking into his eyes." Sofia glares at them. "How was I supposed to know that his tall, dark, and handsome Greek-slash-French cousin was her baby daddy?"

"He's Greek?" I ask shocked, and see Presley and Clarabella roll their lips.

"And French," Shelby points out before turning back to Sofia. "Does he speak both?"

"I know he speaks French for sure. He was talking to his mother in French," Sofia informs us all, "like pure French."

"That is so hot," Clarabella says. "The only thing I know in French is voulez-vous coucher avec moi ce soir?"

"Who doesn't know that saying?" Sofia folds her arms over her chest. "It's universal."

"How did you not know this?" Shelby asks me.

"It didn't really come up." I throw my hands up.

"You know what did come up?" Clarabella looks over at me. "His dick."

"That came up, for sure," Presley chimes in.

"You told me it was the best sex you ever had," Sofia reminds me.

"It's been a while," I tell them, not bothering to mention to them that when I finally had sex after him, I felt way off. It was the last date I ever went on. "Can we stop talking about this?" I finally plead, not really wanting to picture his dick any more than I have been.

"What are you going to do?" Shelby asks quietly beside me.

"We are going to get together tomorrow and talk." I let out a huge sigh.

"Can I come with you?" Presley asks, and all I can do is shake my head.

"Okay, ladies, people are starting to look at us," Shelby says. "Let's get out there and pretend that you just didn't meet your baby daddy after five years."

"Easier said than done," I retort, following them to my seat beside them, which is at the other end of the room. I avoid Stefano the whole night, sticking to my seat. Only when Avery finds me, rubbing her eyes, do I get up.

"I'm going to head out," I tell the table, and the three of them get up. "I'll be fine."

I walk out of the venue with my head down, hoping no one, or better yet, Stefano doesn't follow me. I make my way over to the little house I have for the night, slipping the dress off Avery before sliding out of my own dress.

I don't sleep the whole night, and when Avery wakes up, I feed her quickly and head out of town. The two-hour drive home feels like it takes five hours. Grabbing all of our bags, I walk up the stairs, heading to our apartment. I try to balance all the things while I wait for her to make her way up the stairs. "My legs are tired," she complains to me as she takes each step with both feet, instead of one at a time. My hands burn as I try to hold on to the bags before they slip out of my hands.

"It's hard being a princess," I huff as we finally make it to our front door. A bag slips out of my hand the minute the next-door neighbor's door opens.

"You're back," Mrs. Drummond says, walking out. "How was it?"

"I was a princess," Avery declares. "Can I show her my dress?"

"In a little bit," I say to her, opening the door, and she walks into our place. "Mrs. Drummond, I have a meeting this afternoon, so would you be able to watch her for a couple of hours?" She has been my next-door neighbor for the past year, and she loves Avery like her grandchildren. They just live far away, so she is always happy to spend time with Avery.

"Anytime, dear. Bring her dress over so she can try it on," she says with a huge smile.

I walk into the house, making my way to the bedrooms and dumping off the bag, then going back. My nerves are fried at this point. I try to get settled, but I just can't, so I grab my phone and pull up his contact I stored last night when I couldn't sleep.

Opening the text messages, I type.

Me: Hi there.

I stare at it for a second and then erase it. My stomach feels like it's going to come out of my throat. "Just text him if he's free."

Me: Hey, it's Addison, are you free?

I'm about to press send when it dawns on me. "Are you crazy?" I ask myself. "What if his girlfriend sees it?" I look at his number. "I'm just going to call him." I press the green button and I freak out after it rings once, hanging up. "Oh, he must have missed my call." I put the phone on the bed beside me. I rub my face with my hand, my eyes burning from not sleeping all night. The phone rings beside me, and I jump out of my skin, looking over and seeing his name on the screen. "Don't answer it," I tell myself, but my hand doesn't listen.

"Hi," I greet, trying to act nonchalant as if this isn't killing me deep down inside.

"You hung up." His voice is light and makes my stomach get flutters.

"No," I lie through my teeth, "it went to voicemail." I close my eyes, hoping he believes me.

"Did you leave a message?" he asks me.

"Um, yes." I close my eyes.

"No, you didn't."

"No, I didn't," I finally admit. He laughs softly, and my vagina decides she wants to come out of hibernation.

"Anyway, I'm home, and I got someone to watch Avery." I try to change the subject. "So, I have an hour, are you free?"

"I can be." I hear rustling in the background and wonder if he's still at the farm or in a hotel. "I'm at Matty's house now," he says, and I spring off the bed.

"What?" I ask, shocked.

"Where do you want to meet?" He avoids my freak-out.

"How about we meet at Luke's—" I start to say.

"I'll be there in ten minutes," he agrees without skipping a beat.

"Great. See you there." I don't say anything else because he hangs up the phone.

I don't bother looking at myself in the mirror because if I see how horrible I look, I won't even think of going.

I grab Avery's dress from last night and find her on her bed sleeping. I walk out softly, going next door and knocking on the door. Mrs. Drummond opens a second later. "She's sleeping," I tell her.

"I'll come over there," she replies, grabbing her phone and following me out.

"Thank you so much. The princess dress is on the couch when she wakes up."

I walk down the steps and turn right, heading over to Luke's. It's a five-minute walk, but every single step feels like there's cement in my shoes. I pull open the door to Luke's and step in, taking a look around to see if he's here or not. The tables are mostly empty, which isn't a surprise since it's two in the afternoon. After the lunch crowd and before the dinner rush.

"Hello." The hostess comes over. "Are you dining in or out?"

"Um, in," I say, "for two." I hold up my hand with two fingers sticking up. My hand shakes like a leaf.

"Right this way." She smiles at me and turns to walk toward the table.

"Is it possible to get a booth in the back?" I point over at the booth where we usually eat when we come here since it's close to the kitchen, and Luke frequently joins us.

"Sure." She zigzags through the empty tables to the back and puts the menus on the table. "Your server will be right with you," she tells me as I slide into the booth, facing the door.

My hand taps the table as I look around, the nerves are eating me up. "I should get a drink," I say, holding up my hand and then quickly putting it down. "What if he thinks I'm an alcoholic raising his kid?" I don't have a chance to think anything else because the door opens and my head turns to face it. He walks in, his black hair pushed back, a white T-shirt showing off his toned arms, and with his aviator glasses on his face. The only thing coming out of my mouth is, "Damn."

Eight

Stefano

I walk into the restaurant with my palms sweaty and my heart racing so fast I feel as if I ran here instead of taking Matty's car. The hostess stand sits empty, and when I step up to it, I look around to see if I find her. Most of the tables are empty. My eyes go to the bar, seeing one guy sitting there. I'm about to take out my phone and text her when I hear a woman's voice.

My head flies up to see the woman walking toward me and to the back of the hostess stand. "Are you dining in or out?"

"I'm meeting someone here," I say, looking down at my phone. I'm about to call her when I look up, and I spot her looking my way. She holds up her hand at me. "Found her," I tell the girl as I walk toward Addison. The nerves are running through me. All night I kept thinking about this talk right here. I tossed and turned all night, never settling. Asking the questions in my head over and over again. But now that it's here, now that I'm going to be able to ask the questions, my mind is drawing a blank. Maybe it's seeing her again that is throwing me off course.

She's sitting at the table all the way in the back. I zigzag through the tables, coming to the booth she is sitting at. "Hi," I greet her as I slide into the booth in front of her.

"Hi," she returns softly.

"Have you been waiting long?" I ask her, putting the phone down on the table.

"No." She shakes her head. "I just got here." I can tell she's nervous. Her hands are on top of the table, crossed together as her thumb beats against her other thumb.

She looks like she's about to say something to me when the server comes over. "Hi there." I look up at the server. "Can I get you guys anything to drink while you look at the menu?"

I look at Addison, who smiles at the server. "I'll have a water." She then turns to me.

"I'll have the same," I tell the server, although I think I need a shot of whiskey or something. But the last thing I want her to think is that I drink regularly.

"I'll be right back," the server says when she turns around and walks away. Returning right away with two glasses of water.

"So I guess you have questions," Addison begins, looking at me.

"I do," I answer her and see that she takes a deep inhale.

"Okay, then let's start at question number one," she urges me.

"When is her birthday?" It's the first thing I thought about when I met her. That and then all the birthdays I've missed with her.

"September twentieth," she replies softly. "She was born at twenty-nine weeks." I can't help but gasp at that information.

"Is she okay?" I ask, which might seem like a silly question considering I've met her and she's perfect.

"She is now," she reassures me with a smile. "It was rough at the beginning. She was born at two pounds one ounce." My heart beats so fast in my chest, you would think I'm in the middle of a cardio workout instead of sitting down having a discussion. "She was in the NICU for over a month." My head spins at this information. I never expected it was such a hard start for her at the beginning. "She's up to normal height and weight as of her last visit."

"She looks perfect," I finally say, and she nods, agreeing with me. "When did you find out you were pregnant?"

"About six weeks after. I was in the middle of finals, and I wasn't really sure until I ate pizza and then threw up all over my bed. I was also exhausted, more so than regularly. I fell asleep once sitting in a chair." She laughs, her hand holding her glass of water. She spins the glass around and around. I know she's nervous, and I know she's doing anything she can to move her hands. I want to lean over and grab her hand and tell her that it's okay. But instead, I sit in front of her and listen to her tell me the story. "Then I went out and bought a test and when that one came back, I thought it was defective." She taps the table with her finger. "So I went to the doctor and turns out it wasn't defective and I was, in fact, with child."

"How was your pregnancy?" I think of the questions I wrote down in my notes on my iPad last night once I got to Matty's. All the questions I wrote down are now forgotten, so I'm going by the seat of my pants now.

"It went well. I was tired until the second trimester. I craved peanut butter and Nutella day and night." Something inside me sinks as I think of her doing it all on her own. The guilt of not being there is even stronger today as I listen to what she went through without me.

"What have you told her about me?" This is the question I wanted to wait until the end to ask, but with the way my head is spinning, everything is coming out in a different order. To be honest, it was the only question I now want an answer for. I don't care about anything else except for this one.

"I told her you went to work," she answers, and I laugh.

"For four years?" I joke with her, and she smirks. The nerves I've had in my body slowly leave me. Sitting with her, I find the calmness of it. It's crazy that I didn't have anything on my agenda two days ago. My whole life was just work, and now it's shifted.

"I mean, she's four, so she really doesn't get the whole time thing. I know, once she gets old enough to understand, I'll have to come up with something else."

I nod at her as the server comes over. "Have we had a chance to look at the menu?" she asks, ready to take our order.

"I'll have kale salad," Addison orders, and the server looks at me.

"I'll have the same," I answer, and she nods and walks away.

"You eat kale?" she asks me as she grabs her glass of water.

"No, I hate it." Her mouth just hangs open. "It was easier than looking at the menu.

"Is there a father figure in her life?" I ask the question, and the whole time my stomach sinks just thinking about it.

"There is none," she confirms, sitting back. "It's just me and her." I don't know why I feel a sense of relief from that statement. It makes me feel even more like a selfish asshole.

I nod my head. "I want to meet her and get to know her," I finally say, not even sure of any other questions I have, but this is the most important one.

"Of course," she says without thinking about it. "It was never my intention to keep her from you." She looks down at her hands and then looks back up at me. "It was the first one-night stand I ever had," she admits, her voice going low as she looks around to see if anyone is listening to us, or even close enough to hear the conversation. "You were leaving the next day, and I just figured it would be less awkward than you waking up and asking me to leave." She shrugs.

"I wouldn't have asked you to leave." I stare into her eyes.

"What would you have done?" She asks me the loaded question.

"I have no idea," I tell her honestly. "Who knows? I would have at least gotten your number."

"That would have saved us a whole bunch of problems." She smiles sadly, and I know there is more to that statement than meets the eye. The server comes back with two bowls, placing one in front of Addison and another one in front of me. I look down at the bowl of green, and she must see the grimace on my face because she laughs out loud. It takes me back to the night in the restaurant, right before I asked her to come back to my place.

"Thank you," Addison tells the server before she walks away from the table. "It's good, try it."

"I know what kale tastes like. It's an acquired taste, and I have not acquired it," I admit to her as she grabs her fork and starts eating.

"How did your parents deal with you having the baby?" I ask her, and she avoids even looking up.

"They weren't fans of my decision," she says, "but it was never a decision in my head."

"I guess they've changed their minds now." I pick up the fork and play with the kale in the bowl.

"I guess so," she replies before taking a bite of her kale.

"Well, you've met my family." I chuckle.

"I have." She smirks and tucks her hair behind her ear. "All four hundred of them."

"I need to tell them." I try the kale, and just like all the other times, it's as gross as it always was. "This is... I can't," I say, pushing the plate away from me.

"Oh my," she exhales.

"Oh my for the kale, or oh my for me having to tell my family?" I grab the glass of water as I force down the kale.

"A bit of both." She laughs, and her eyes light up a bit.

"Well, my father knows," I tell her, and her fork falls out of her hand with a clang. "He put two and two together when he saw me talking to her."

She puts her hand on her head. "Does he hate me?" Her voice goes so low, if I wasn't sitting in front of her, I wouldn't have heard her.

"No." I shake my head, my voice coming out tight. "He doesn't hate you. Me, on the other hand, he was ready to kick my ass for leaving you."

"Did you tell him that I didn't tell you? Well, even if I wanted to tell you, do you know how many Stefanos there are in the world?" I just stare at her. "Twenty-four million hits from Google."

"You searched just my first name?" I ask her, trying not to laugh.

"That's all I had. I tried to think of other things but well..." She looks down. "I didn't really remember them, and it was six weeks after, so..." She shrugs.

"After I meet her, I'd like my parents to meet her and then we can ease the rest of the family into it." Her eyes go big. "I mean, Matty has already met her. And, well, my uncle Matthew will want to meet her for sure."

"That sounds reasonable. I won't ever keep her from you or your family." Her voice trails off, and I know she wants to say something else, so I wait. "I just ask that you don't parade women in front of her." She swallows hard. "I get that you have a girlfriend, and eventually, she is going to meet her, but before she does, I would like to meet her."

"That sounds reasonable," I admit to her, "and if you get a boyfriend." She nods her head. "How about I meet her first, and then we can set up a date for her to meet my parents?"

"That sounds good," she replies, and now she's the one pushing the kale around in her bowl.

"How about tomorrow?" Her eyes fly to mine, shocked. "We can do dinner." To be honest, I would have done it right now, but it's getting late, and I'm not sure if I was pushing things.

She takes a deep inhale, putting down her fork. "I guess there is no good time for this, really."

The server comes over and picks up the plates before asking us if we want anything else. We both say no, and she walks away. "Where do you want to do it?" I ask her.

"We can do it at my place, in her environment," she states. "I think that would be the easiest."

The server comes over and puts the bill down, and I snatch it up before she gets to it. "I got it," I tell her. "What is her favorite food?"

"Pizza," she says, "Eggos, the blueberry ones and not the chocolate chip ones. White bread not wheat, even though it's better for her. Bananas and strawberries cut up together, she loves that. Burgers, she likes burgers with cheese, no veggies or sauce. Fries, well, because who doesn't like french fries. Twice-baked potatoes with bacon in it because without it, it doesn't taste the same."

"That is a long list," I say, taking my wallet out and putting my card down for the server.

"It's even longer, but those are the most important ones," she says, slipping out of the booth. "I've got to go. She's with the neighbor, and it's almost dinnertime."

"Okay, I'll touch base with you tomorrow, and we can work out a time."

"Sounds like a plan." She nods and walks away from me. I watch her walk out of the restaurant. She's wearing blue jeans and a white T-shirt with flip-flops. As she walks away from the door, she does it with her head down. The burning starts to form in the pit of my stomach, thinking maybe I upset her somehow. I'm about to go after her when my phone rings, and I look down and see that it's Jenna.

"Hello." I answer after the second ring.

"Hey," Jenna greets. "Whatcha doing?"

"Just headed back to Matty's house," I inform her, nodding at the server who has come over to process my card.

"How long are you staying out there?" This morning, I hightailed it out of the hotel, leaving her with a plane ticket at the airport. We were supposed to be there for three days, but I said I had a work emergency and had to bail. She was not happy at all.

"Um," I start to say and then nod at the server, who gives me a copy of my receipt. I slide out of the booth and head outside. "I haven't decided yet." I tell her the lie instead of saying my daughter lives here, so now this is where I'll be living.

"What?" she shrieks.

"Listen, Jenna," I start out saying, and even I inwardly groan at my tone. "I don't think this is going to work out."

"Excuse me?" she retorts, shocked. "What are you talking about?"

"I think it's best if we just be friends." I swear if any of my female family members were here, they would kick me in the balls. "I have a lot going on, and I need to focus on that."

"Incredible," she huffs out. "When did you come to this decision?" she asks me but then doesn't give me a chance to reply. "You were distant the whole weekend."

"I'm sorry, I didn't mean to—" I don't finish the sentence because she snaps.

"Fuck off!" she shouts, and then I hear nothing. I look down at the phone and see she ended the call.

"Okay, then," I say, putting the phone in my back pocket as I walk over to the truck and get in. "Time to make a plan." I look out of the window, knowing exactly who I have to call next.

Nine

Addison

The sound of soft bells wakes me up and I roll over in my bed. My hand reaches over to stop the noise. My head feels like it weighs five thousand pounds, while my eyes refuse to even crack open. This is what I get for staying up all night, replaying the conversation I had with Stefano in my head. Even when I finally fell asleep, all I did was dream of him. For the past five years, I would dream about him on and off, but now that I've seen him again, nothing can compare to being in front of him for real. I don't know how I do it, but I press snooze and seven minutes later the bells ring again. I know I have to get up. I slowly crack open one eye before turning off the alarm. I throw the covers off myself before I slip back to sleep. Walking out of my room to the kitchen, I press the button for the coffee machine. I stand here in front of the Keurig with my eyes closed as the machine puffs out steam, and then the smell of coffee fills the room. After the coffee spits out the last drop, I add a splash of milk to it. I take two sips of coffee before I make my way to Avery's room. Before this apartment, we shared a room and a bed. It was the most I could afford, but she was young and didn't know better. I'm thankful she didn't see the struggles I went through when she was younger.

Her bedroom is painted white, something I couldn't change because the landlord wouldn't let me, but everything else is pink, including her pink toddler bed I bought. I found the mosquito net at the dollar store, and with a little bit of YouTube and Pinterest, I turned it into a canopy bed. It was the best I could afford. I tiptoe into the room and see she is sleeping on her side, with the covers pushed to her feet. I slip into her bed with her, pulling her to me. I kiss her soft cheek as she softly snores in my arms. "Good morning," I coo quietly to her. She groans in my arms like she does every single morning. The only thing my girl isn't is a morning person. From when she was a baby, she was the best sleeper in the world. The doctor said it was because I was so calm during my pregnancy. I just went with I was lucky. "How did you sleep?"

She sticks her butt out as she stretches. "Good," she mumbles as she cuddles into me. "I dreamed of a castle." I can't help but laugh quietly because this is her answer every single day.

"A castle." I act surprised. "How cool is that?"

"And I was a princess." I gasp, looking down at her. Her eyes go big as she nods her head. "With a crown."

"Oh my goodness." I kiss her nose. "Well, Princess Avery, it's time to get up." I turn to get out of her bed. "What do you want for breakfast?"

"Pancakes," she replies, and I smile down at her.

"Get dressed." I point at the clothes I put on her bed last

night. I rush through making her pancakes, and we walk out of the house five minutes later than I wanted to.

"We've got to hurry," I urge her as we walk down the steps toward the front door. The heat hits us as soon as I open the front door and step out. "It's going to be a hot one."

Opening the back door of the car, I hold her hand as she steps in and attempts to buckle herself in. I finish for her. "It's hot," Avery grunts as I turn on the car.

"It'll cool down in a second," I tell her as I start the car, waiting a couple of minutes for the heat to leave the car. The drive to the daycare takes me six minutes since I caught all the green lights. I grab her backpack from the passenger seat before opening the back door for her. We walk in hand in hand, some kids scream her name as we walk by her class to her hook. I hang up her backpack before squatting down in front of her. "Tonight, Mommy has a friend coming over," I inform her. I was supposed to tell her at breakfast, but every single time I tried to, the words wouldn't come out. I wonder if it's because I knew she would ask me questions, and I didn't know what to answer. Either way, it's now or never. "So we are going to have pizza."

Her eyes go big, usually we have pizza night on Fridays, so this is a very special treat for her. "With french fries?"

"You bet," I say. "Give me a kiss." She leans in to kiss my lips. "Have a good day." I get up and hold her hand as I walk her to the classroom door.

The teacher is there waiting for her. "Happy Monday," she greets me, and all I can do is smile at her.

"Happy Monday," I say to her as Avery runs into the class and toward her friends. I wave before walking back out and heading to work. I zone out mostly everything as I think of what is going to happen tonight. My head is already throbbing, and it's not even nine o'clock. Grabbing my purse before walking up the steps to the office, I take my keys out to open the front door of the little bungalow they built with five offices where the bedrooms would be. I'm always the first one in since they were kind enough to work around the daycare's schedule. I get to work by nine, and I work until four. It's perfect, and I'm so grateful. I step in and press in my code for the alarm before looking around the living room and dining room that have been converted to the waiting area. It's filled with pictures of past events they have done.

I put my purse on my desk before walking around to the kitchen in the back of the house. I look out of the window, seeing the side of the barn. Or at least what looks like a barn. Once you get inside, you'll find rustic wooden floors and exposed wooden beams that can be dressed up. It can fit up to five hundred and fifty people. Right behind the barn is a kitchen where the caterers can set up.

I'm about to grab a cup of coffee when I hear the front door open and then close again. I walk out of the kitchen toward my desk. "What are you doing here?" I ask Sofia, who is standing next to my desk.

"I work here," she says, laughing as the front door opens and Clarabella comes in.

"Is there a meeting I didn't know of?" I ask, seeing Presley walk in, followed by Shelby.

"She called a Code Purple," Presley reminds me, pointing at Sofia.

"Aren't you supposed to be on your honeymoon?" Clarabella huffs, looking at Sofia.

"Are you crazy?" she asks Clarabella. "She just found her baby daddy." She points at me. "Who slept in my spare bedroom last night!"

"What?" I ask, shocked.

"Oh, this is going to be good," Presley singsongs, clapping

her hands. "Let's go to the conference room."

"Do we really have to?" I ask them, and the sound of their laughter fills the room. "Yeah, I knew even as the words were leaving my lips it was a silly question."

I follow them to the back of the house and into the conference room. "Okay, let's hear it," Shelby demands, pulling out one of the chairs around the round table.

"Well, I don't know what to say, we met yesterday afternoon," I share, pulling out my own chair and plopping down in it.

"And?" Clarabella prompts, as she sits down next to me.

"Well, he's her father," I say, "and he is going to meet her tonight."

"Holy shit," Sofia says.

"I know." I throw up my hands. "How do you tell your kid this is her father?" I look around the table at all of them shaking their heads, not sure what to say.

"If it's any consolation," Sofia adds, "I turned out fine." I roll my eyes.

"What did you tell her about her father?" Shelby asks softly.

"That he was at work," I tell them and the whole room again laughs. "What was I supposed to tell her?" I look around the table. "Your momma had a ho moment and boom you were born?"

"You are not a ho, nor did you have a ho moment. It was two people who had needs." Clarabella tries to make it sound better. "Two consenting adults."

"Who didn't even share last names," I add in.

"When you spin it like that," Presley waffles, "it does sound bad."

"Presley," Shelby snaps at her.

"What? It does." She looks back at me. "Sorry."

"What if he doesn't like the way I parent her?" I admit my

biggest fear to them. It's also the question that kept me up half the night.

"Um, fuck him," Shelby declares.

"Yeah, that." Presley points her thumb to Shelby. "You did the best you could with what you had, and Avery is perfect, so there isn't anything that will happen like that."

"Well, when is he going to be telling everyone else?" Sofia asks. "Because I was waiting all night for him to say something, and he didn't even say a word. I mean, he came home, went to the bedroom, and stayed there all night."

"No idea. I was, like, freaking out, so he decided we should tell his parents first and then slowly…" I trail off.

"Have you met the family?" Sofia gawks at me. "There are no secrets in that family. They pretend they will keep secrets and then one person quietly tells another and then boom there are five different text chains that you are a part of."

"Can we focus on what the hell is going to happen?" I pinch the bridge of my nose.

"You are going to go for dinner and then it'll all be okay," Shelby tries to reassure me.

"Sure, let's pretend," I mumble before I get up. "I'm going to go and get lost in my work," I inform them, "and pretend I'm not having dinner with my baby daddy tonight."

"Good luck with that," Clarabella voices to my retreating back.

"Ugh, I know," I grumble to myself as I walk back to the kitchen and grab a cup of coffee before attacking all the emails. Mondays are always a bit hectic because of the weekends, but I finally walk out of the office at five after four. Even though I was busy, I felt like every single hour was a lifetime.

When I finally pick up Avery and get her home, I start the bath. "We're going to wash up before dinner," I tell her, walking over to her dresser as I look through her clothes.

"Can I wear a dress?" she asks me and I nod my head, walking to the closet and seeing the four dresses she has. I call them her Sunday best clothes. She takes a quick bath and is getting dressed when my phone rings.

I rush over to the kitchen table, grabbing it out of my purse. His name flashes on the screen. "Hello."

"Hi, it's me," he says to me, "Stefano."

"Yes, I know; it says your name when you call." I laugh at him.

I hear him chuckle. "I'm outside." My head whips to the balcony door and I quickly walk over.

"Outside where?" I ask him, my feet stuck to the floor.

"Outside your place." It's his turn to laugh.

"What?" I shriek before I walk over to the balcony door, unlocking it, and pulling it open. Stepping outside and looking over the railing, I see him standing in front of the door. He's wearing a pair of jeans and a black shirt. The aviator glasses on his face hide his green eyes.

I quickly back up and out of sight. "What are you doing here?" I say quietly, so he doesn't look up.

"Well, you didn't text me," he replies, and I close my eyes.

"I was going to text you in a bit," I admit to him as soon as I calmed myself down.

"Can I come up?" he asks me. *No,* my head screams, *you can't come up here.*

"Um, sure," I say, walking back inside and toward the front door. "We are apartment four," I tell him right before I press the buzzer.

Ten

Stefano

The sound of the buzzer makes me take a step toward the glass door, pulling it open. The door clicks open as I step into the apartment building. The staircase is on one side while brass mailboxes are on the other. Putting my aviator glasses on top of my head, I take the six steps up that lead me to apartment one and two before turning and walking up more steps where I get to another landing, but this one only has one door with the number three on it.

The closer I get to her apartment, the more nervous I get. I spent the better part of the day looking at houses. It was the most surreal experience of my life. Choosing a house, knowing that I'm going to have a child grow up in it. I was worried about the school district. I was worried about parks in the neighborhood. I was even worried about the fucking crime rate in the area. It was as if, overnight, I became my uncles and it suddenly all made sense. All of their overbearing craziness they do, I understood it all.

I take a deep inhale as I come up to the next landing, seeing her door with the number four next to the door that is number five. I stand in front of the brown door and literally psych myself up. "You've got this," I tell myself. "She's four, how hard can it be?" I take one more deep breath before I knock on the door.

I can hear the sound of little feet running on the other side of the door, and a smile just fills my face. "Who is it, Momma?" I hear her voice. "Is it pizza?"

"I don't think so," Addison says, "but we should see who it is."

"Look inside the hole," Avery shouts, "in case it's a killer!"

I shake my head, chuckling at the way she said the word. "Go get dressed," I hear Addison say to her before I hear her little feet running away from the door. The sound of the locks opening makes my heart speed up a touch faster, my hands get even more sweaty as I hold the bags in them. The door swings open and I see Addison with a smile on her face. "Hi," she says, holding the door handle. She's wearing black dress pants that hug her curves and stop at her ankles, her feet are bare. The white button-down shirt flows around her and is tucked into the pants. She looks so professional, and I wonder if she's as nervous as I am. "Welcome." She moves aside for me to step inside.

"Thank you," I say, nodding at her as I walk in and stand on her little carpet at the door, "for having me." I take a look around at the small apartment that is neat and tidy, but bare and minimal. She has a small two-seat couch with a TV stand with a tiny television on it. The kitchen and dining area are right on the other side of the room.

"What do you have there?" Addison asks me as she closes the

door behind me.

"I brought her flowers," I say, holding up the flowers I picked up right before I got here. "I got pink flowers since they looked like princess flowers," I tell her, nervously holding them up for her to see them.

"Those are very pretty," she admires, with a smirk on her face.

"I also bought her a couple of things." I hold up the two bags of toys I bought her today. "Some toys and some princess things."

Addison comes over and puts a hand on my arm. "Are you nervous?" she asks me, and I chuckle nervously.

"I have never been this out of my comfort zone before in my life," I admit to her. "I spent a full two hours at the toy store going aisle by aisle. Picking up things and then putting them down. Then going back over again." I shake my head. "I'm sure at one point the salesgirl thought I was lying about buying anything because she just left me there."

"Whatever you chose, I'm sure will be amazing," Addison assures me, and then I hear the small feet running out from one of the bedrooms. Her hair is flying everywhere as she runs to the front door, her dress swooshing around her legs.

"I know you," Avery states from beside Addison, her arm wrapped around her leg as she sizes me up. "You called me the prettiest princess in all the land."

"You do know me," I say nervously, but excited she remembers me. "I brought you flowers," I say, handing her the bouquet and realizing it's maybe a bit too big for her. "I got pink because I think they look like princess flowers."

"Momma, he brought flowers for me," she whisper-yells, making me laugh out loud.

"I see, why don't you say thank you," Addison tells her.

"Thank you for the princess flowers." Avery smiles at me.

"I'll take those and put them in a vase," Addison informs me, "so your hands aren't full." I hand her the flowers and she gives me a smile of encouragement.

"What is in the bags?" Avery asks, pointing at the two bags I'm carrying.

"Well, I went to the store, and I saw a couple of things that reminded me of you." I smile at her. "I got you a couple of presents."

"You bought me presents?" she says shocked, as she looks from me to the bag and then back to me, then looks at Addison, who is standing in the kitchen opening the cupboard on top of the fridge to grab a vase. "Momma." Avery walks over to her. "Is it my birthday?"

"It is not your birthday," Addison tells her, putting the flowers in the vase. "Sometimes people buy you presents just because, or if they are coming to see you."

"Oh," Avery says before skipping back to me, "it's not my birthday."

"I know," I tell her, squatting down, "but it's the first time I've visited you, and I thought I would bring you a little something."

She claps her hands, and her face fills with a megawatt smile. "Okay." She jumps up and down. "What is it? What is it?"

"Well, you are going to have to open it up and see," I tell her, handing her one bag first.

"Open this one first," I tell her and she gets on her knees as she pulls open the bag.

Her little hands work the bag down from the box, and she gasps right before she squeals. "Momma," she yells over her shoulder, "I got princess shoes!"

Addison looks at her and then looks at me. "What do you mean you got princess shoes?" She comes over and squats down next to Avery. "Oh my!" she exclaims when she takes in the pink box. Inside the big box are six small boxes and four of the boxes have different colored shoes. One is gold, another silver, then a pink and a blue pair. In the top two are three different types of crowns and then some plastic earrings, rings, and plastic bracelets. "That is a lot of princess things."

"If she has them, we can always go back and exchange it," I assure her, and I see Avery shaking her head side to side fast.

"I'm almost afraid what is in the other bag," Addison mumbles as Avery comes back over to me for the second bag. I give the bag to Avery, who struggles to bring it to Addison, dragging it half the way. "What's in the bag?"

"Stuff for me," Avery says, moving the bag away from another pink box with the word princess written on the top of it. She opens the box, and if I thought she squealed before, it's nothing like it is now. "Dresses," she proclaims, her whole face lighting up, and I don't even care how much they cost me or that I spent over two hours picking them out. I would do it over and over again just to see that joy on her face. "Momma," she says, taking out the yellow princess dress, then grabbing the light-blue one. "Look!" She hands her the dresses she took out of the box before she grabs the silver one and then the pink one.

"Each dress comes with its own hair stuff," I point out to Avery, but she's already taking it out of the box and trying to put the bandanna on her head.

"Momma, can I wear one now?" she asks Addison, even though she's grabbing a dress.

"Sure," Addison says, "but what do we say to Stefano?"

"Thank you, Mr. Stefano," she says, standing up and jumping in place. "It's my favorite."

"You are very, very welcome," I tell her as she grabs the pink dress, running to her room to change and then stopping.

"I forgot my shoes." She comes back and grabs the pink pair before running to her room.

"This is a lot of princesses," Addison says, looking at the two boxes.

"Yeah, I put back the princess vanity set," I admit to her, and her eyes go big. "I didn't know if she had it or not." I shrug. "I figure you can never have enough clothes or shoes. Or at least that is what my mother always says."

"You were right on that," she agrees, standing up. "We should tell her."

I nod at her. "Do you want to wait and do it while we eat?" I ask her, and she looks over her shoulder.

"How about we order the pizza and then break the news to her," Addison suggests, picking up the bags and walking over to Avery's room, putting them inside.

I stand and open my phone, ordering three pizzas since I don't know what she eats on hers, with fries and some chicken wings. I also order a cheeseburger in case she doesn't like the pizza. "I ordered the pizza. It should be here in twenty minutes."

"Sounds good." Addison nods at me as she wrings her hands in front of her.

"Where do you want to do this?" I ask her, looking around to see if there is a more comfortable place to tell her.

"The couch is good." She points over at the brown couch, and I walk over to sit down on one end. I look at the pictures hanging on the wall while Addison calls Avery.

I hear the sound of clicking and clacking, and when I look up, she is walking out of her bedroom with her pink dress on, with a red bandanna in her hair and gold shoes. She has one of the plastic earrings on the side of her ear and she is wearing every single bracelet that came with the set. She has five rings on two fingers. "Look at my dress," she urges Addison as she turns slowly in her plastic shoes.

"You look amazing, now come sit down." Addison motions with her head toward where I'm sitting. "Mr. Stefano and I want to talk to you."

She walks over to me clicking and clacking her shoes the whole way. I suddenly really feel sorry for the person who lives under her. I sit at the edge of the couch as she comes over and sits next to me, leaving a little space for Addison. Instead of sitting next to her, she kneels in front of her. I have never in my life felt like this. Ever. My whole chest feels like it's being crushed, yet it also feels like it's going to explode.

"Look at my ring." Avery holds up her hand to me. "Thank you for buying me presents."

"You are so welcome," I tell her.

"Honey," Addison starts, and I can see she is blinking away tears as she sits back on her feet. "Do you remember when you asked if you had a dad?"

"He's at work," Avery says, and my heart sinks at the way her voice is, "very far, far, far, far away." If it was any other time, I would have laughed at her exaggeration.

"He was at work," Addison says and looks at me. I can see her swallowing the lump in her throat.

"Well, you see," I start, turning to her, thinking of ways to say what needs to be said. "I was really busy." I stop talking because none of this makes any sense to me.

But Avery just looks at me, tilting her head to the side. "Are you my dad?"

I swallow down the lump in my throat before I say the words. "I'm your dad."

Eleven

Addison

I hear Avery ask the question, and my heart speeds up so much in my chest, I can't even describe it. I try to swallow, but the lump has formed in my throat and nothing happens. Then I try to say something, but when I open my mouth, nothing, and I mean nothing, comes out. I blink away the tears forming in my eyes, but then Stefano looks at me and then back at Avery, saying the three words that will forever change this moment. "I'm your dad." I feel as if I'm having an out-of-body experience as I look at Avery while she listens to his words. This, this moment right here, this is the moment I've dreamed about ever since she asked me about her dad. I should be happy, but there is a little bit of sadness to this moment.

Avery sits there in her new princess dress and looks up at him with matching eyes to her father. "Did you get lost?" Her voice comes out soft.

Stefano chuckles at her question before he puts his arms around her. "A little bit." He looks at me next. "But I'm here now."

"Are you going to visit?" I can't even imagine what she is going through. I hope this moment is a moment she will always remember.

"No." He shakes his head, and my whole body feels like it's drained. I thought I was ready for this conversation. I played it over and over in my head so many times over the past four years, but it's nothing like I imagined. "I'm going to live here." I don't know who gasps out in shock first, me or Avery, who now jumps off the couch.

"You can sleep in my bed." She grabs his hand, pulling him off the couch. "Come see my room."

"Um…" I voice to his retreating back. He laughs, looking over his shoulder but goes with her as she pulls his finger toward her bedroom.

I get up from the floor but don't follow them. Instead, I sit on the couch, and my head hangs forward. "I wanted a princess bed," Avery starts to tell him, and I look toward her bedroom, "but Momma said maybe when I turn five." I sit back on the couch, putting my head back.

"That sounds like a good present," Stefano replies.

"I don't think you can fit in my bed," Avery finally declares to him, and all he can do is laugh.

"No, I have my own house," he replies as they come back out of the bedroom. The sound of her plastic shoes echoes throughout the room.

"Do you have a princess bed?" Avery asks him, and he shakes his head.

"Not yet, but I think I will soon," he tells her and I stand, hoping my legs don't give out on me.

"We should get dinner," I start to say when my doorbell rings.

"That should be dinner," Stefano states, walking to the door and pressing the button. "Who is it?"

"Delivery for Stefano," the man replies, and he presses the button but doesn't move from the door. He waits for the guy to knock on the door and then looks out the peephole.

"You know who it is," I tell him, and he just looks over at me.

"And I wanted to make sure," he says, opening the door just enough for him to grab the food and then he closes it back with his foot.

"Who's hungry?" he asks, and Avery tries to jump, but she's afraid her shoes will come off.

"Me!" she shouts, walking over to the round dining table in the middle of the living room/dining room. "I'm very hungry."

"Why are there three pizzas?" I ask as I make my way toward the table. He puts the three boxes on the table and then takes the brown bag that is on top of the boxes off.

"I didn't know what toppings you like on it," he admits, a bit flustered, "so I got one that is just cheese." Taking the first box off the pile, he goes on, "Then a pepperoni, and I got one that has everything."

"I like cheese," Avery says as she tries to get onto her chair. One of her plastic shoes falls to the floor. "Did you get french fries?" she asks him, looking up at him.

"I did," he confirms to her and all I can do is stand here, stuck in my shoes as if there is cement inside them.

"Yay!" Avery claps her hands.

"I'll get the plates," I finally say, walking over to the little kitchen counter and opening the cupboard. The four flat plates are piled next to the four soup bowls that sit next to the four small plates. I grab three plates and turn back around to put them on the table before walking over and grabbing three forks and two knives.

"You have to cut my pizza," Avery tells him as he opens up the first pizza box, "'cause I can't use the knife yet, or I'll cut my hand off."

I close my eyes, really wishing she would stop repeating the things I've told her. "I'll cut your pizza," Stefano says softly to her. "Which one do you want?" He looks at me as I pull the chair out that faces him and I sit down.

"Anything is good," I reply, my mind still reeling this is happening, that he is actually here and it's not part of a dream.

"Momma," Avery calls me. "Can I have some water," she asks me, "in my pink cup?"

I get up and walk over to the dish rack near the sink, grabbing her pink sippy cup. "Um, would you like some sweet tea?" I ask him over my shoulder.

"Is it special sweet tea?" he asks, and it makes me chuckle. "If so... no."

"It's not Billy's sweet tea," I assure him. "We keep that at the office." I turn to put Avery's pink cup on the table and then two glasses before walking to the fridge and grabbing the jug of sweet tea and the pitcher of water.

I sit down and the table has never been so full of food before. "Um, we should clear some room." Stefano looks up at me. "How about I move the pizza to the counter?" I grab the three boxes of pizza, picking them up and turning. "There, that is better."

I sit down and look over at Stefano, who is cutting Avery's food as if he's been doing it for her whole life. "This looks good, Momma," Avery says to me. "I love pizza."

"It does look good," I agree, waiting for him to finish cutting her food before starting to eat.

"This is good," Avery says, picking up a piece of pizza with her fork. "The best pizza ever."

"I'm glad," Stefano replies, as he cuts a piece of pizza for himself and pops a piece in his mouth. "Did you have fun at school today?"

"Daycare," Avery corrects him. "I go to school when I turn five."

"Oh," Stefano says.

"She went to preschool," I fill him in, "but it's summer, so it's daycare until September when she starts kindergarten."

"I'm going to school," Avery tells him. "They don't have naps at school."

"You don't like naps?" Stefano asks her and all I can do is cut my pizza in my plate and push it around. My stomach is in my throat after today, and I'm afraid if I do eat, it'll just come right back up.

"I like naps sometimes," she tells him, "but sometimes I don't like it, but they don't make me nap if I don't want, they give me books."

"That's good," Stefano returns, eating up every single word that she is saying. "Reading is good."

"It makes me smart," she declares, then looks at me and smiles. "Right, Momma?"

"Yes," I reply, nodding at her. I don't know what else they talk about because I'm in my own head.

"Momma," Avery says, "I'm done."

"Okay." I look at her plate and see she ate it all. "Go brush your teeth and get your pj's on."

She nods at me and starts to go down the hall before she looks over at Stefano. "Will you be here tomorrow?"

"I will." He smiles at her and she smiles back at him.

She slips back on the plastic shoe that fell off her before. Only when it's on does she go to the bathroom. I hear her dragging the stool to the counter. "Are you okay?"

"Yeah," I say, turning back to him, "just—"

"Oh, I know." He leans back in the chair; the black shirt pulls against his chest. His green eyes are a bit darker than they were when he got here, but it's also because the light is dim. "That was—"

"Brutal," I fill in for him as I finally drop my fork.

"I thought I was going to throw up," he admits to me and I can't help but be a little relieved.

"Good," I say to him, and his eyes go big. "At least it wasn't just me."

"Have you told your parents about me?" he asks the question, and it shocks me for a minute. I think about lying to him, but it'll only be a matter of time before he knows the truth.

I look over to the bathroom door, hearing the water running before I tell him, "I don't speak with my parents." I want to say, after all this time, it doesn't bother me, but it does. I think it will always bother me.

He looks at me shocked, and I know he's going to ask me why, so I just tell him, my voice going very low. "When I found out I was pregnant and told them." I look down at my plate, not wanting to look at him when I say the next part. Except my pride gets the best of me and I lean back and put my shoulders straight. "It was either get rid of it or do it on my own. So I'm doing it on my own."

His jaw goes tight and I see his hands ball into fists on the table, his eyes moving back and forth as he looks into mine. "Mommmmmmmm, I'm done!" Avery shouts from the bathroom. "Can you come and help me?"

"I should get in there and wipe up the water she must have spilled all over the place." I get up. "I'll come back and clean up."

"I'll clean up," he offers, getting up. "You go take care of that." He motions with his chin for me to go to the bathroom. I walk away from him before he sees how much this whole day has affected me. "Did we brush our teeth?" I ask when I walk into the bathroom and step into a puddle of water.

"I did," she confirms, looking at me and showing me her teeth. "My dress got wet." She looks down at the pink dress.

"It did," I say, grabbing a towel and putting it on the water puddle so she doesn't slip. I sit on the edge of the bathtub before I pull the dress off her. "I'm going to hang this," I tell her of the dress. "How about we take off all the jewelry?" I grab her hand, taking off the rings and putting them on the counter before I grab a washrag and wash the sauce off her face. "Did you like the pizza?"

"It was good," she replies, not the least bit fazed that she met her father for the first time.

"It was," I agree with her as I take the bandanna off her head and grab the brush to brush her hair. "Go get your nightgown on," I tell her and she hops out of the bathroom and toward her room.

I hang her dress on the back of the door and finish cleaning up the bathroom when I hear her yell, "Stefano, do you want to read me a story?"

I close my eyes and push away the little tinge of sadness I have because it's always been me putting her to bed. It's always been me telling her the bedtime story. It's always been me and now I'm going to have to share her. "Of course I want to read you a story," I hear Stefano say, and I have to be happy he wants to do all the things. I have to be happy he didn't fight he was a father. I have to be happy he didn't just walk away from us without looking back. I walk out and turn off the bathroom light, seeing all the food has been put away and the dishes washed and in the dish rack.

I walk over to her bedroom door, leaning on the doorjamb while he sits on her small bed, his feet sticking out of the end of the bed, his back to the wall as he reads her *Cinderella*. She's on her side and already sleeping, but he doesn't stop until he reads the last word. He closes the book and looks down at her.

"She's asleep," I tell him and he just nods his head.

"Can I kiss her?" he asks me, and I can't help the tear that rolls down my cheek. "Or will it wake her?"

"You can kiss her," I say as I quickly wipe the tear away. He bends over and kisses her cheek. Getting up and tiptoeing out of the room, little does he know she can sleep through a party.

"I'm going to get going," he says softly as we walk back into the living room and toward the front door. "I'll call you later and we can talk."

"Okay," is the only thing I can say because I have no idea what else to say. "Sounds good," I agree as he walks out the door.

"Lock up," he urges, waiting at the top of the stairs. "I'm not leaving until I hear the lock."

"I thought it was rude to close the door in your face," I reply, a tad annoyed, "but if that's the case." I close the door and lock it. "Goodbye!" I shout to the closed door.

"See you tomorrow, Addison," he replies back to the door. I just put my head to the wood, closing my eyes, wondering what in the hell am I going to do.

Twelve

Stefano

I wait for her to say something else, and when I've been here longer than a few minutes, I jog down the steps. My head spins the whole time, and I mean the whole time. Even getting into the car I don't turn the music on, I don't call anyone, I sit in the silence and hear their voices over and over in my head.

Did you get lost?

I don't talk to my parents.

I had to choose.

I honestly don't know how I make it back to Matty's house. I park the car and put my head back on the headrest and take a huge exhale before opening the door and making my way to the front door. Opening the door, I hear the television coming from the family room, and instead of just going upstairs to clear my head, I walk over to the family room. Her parents threw her out of the house when she needed them the most. Because of me.

I look into the family room. "Who else is here?" I ask, not sure if anyone else followed them home. With my family, you just never know.

"Just us," Matty answers, sitting up, probably taking in the look on my face. Or maybe the fact that I'm shaking. Making my way into the room, I sit down on the couch and put my head back and rub my face. The voices from the television are shut off. "Are you okay?" Matty asks, his voice filled with worry.

I open my eyes and look at them, seeing Matty sitting up while Sofia just lounges next to him. "You know?" I ask Sofia, and all she does is roll her eyes at me.

"I think the question you should be asking is, how the hell did anyone else not know?" She sits up now and looks over at Matty, who now has a confused look on his face.

"What's going on?" he asks, looking at me, then back at Sofia.

Sofia doesn't say anything, instead she looks at me and waits for me to say something. "Um," I start, but I'm not sure what to say. I sit forward, folding my hands together. "Avery—" I start to say but then Matty gasps and jumps out of his chair.

"You?" He points at me before he puts his hand on his mouth, then putting both on top of his head. "How?"

Sofia laughs at him. "Well, if he has to tell you how." She winks at him. "I don't know how we are going to have a baby, especially since we just did that before he got home."

"Okay, eww." I jump off the couch. "Was it here?"

"No," Sofia assures me, getting up and I look back at the seat I was just sitting on. I'm almost about to sit back down when she adds in, "Well, not this time." Her laughter fills the room.

"Okay, everyone needs to stop talking," Matty demands as he points at me. "You, explain."

"Should I get something to drink?" Sofia asks, and Matty just glares at her but all she does is laugh at him.

"That look doesn't scare me, Matthew Petrov." She points at him. "So direct the look at him. He was the one who did it."

"Out with it," Matty orders me.

"It was one night," I finally say, my feet moving as I pace their living room, back and forth in front of them.

"You don't do one-night stands," Matty reminds me, and I groan.

"Well, obviously I did," I exhale. "It was after that one time I said I will never have another one-night stand. I had just finished my first-ever merger, and I was flying high." I run my hands through my hair. "She bumped into me at a bar, and then we went to grab something to eat, and she just, fuck, I don't know. She just made me forget my rules."

"Can we circle back to how you didn't see?" Sofia looks at Matty.

"How was I supposed to see?" Matty puts his hands on his hips. "Now I see it, but you think I walk around with a picture book, and I'm like do any of my cousins look familiar?" He throws his hands up in the air. "Oh, you have no father for your daughter. Here, take a look at him. Does he look familiar?"

"Can you be more dramatic?" Sofia asks, laughing at him, and he tilts his head to the side. "Okay, wrong question." She holds up her hands.

"Anyway," I say, looking back at Sofia, "what can you tell me about her parents?"

It's Sofia's turn to glare at me. "Nothing." She folds her arms over her chest. I know she is not going to tell me anything when it comes to Addison. I know this because she's loyal to a T, and her loyalty will be with Addison before it is with me.

"You know what I do, right?" I ask her, and this time, it's me putting my hands on my hips. "I can find out everything in two minutes flat." I stare at her.

"Then why haven't you?" She asks me the loaded question I have been asking myself since I found out about Avery.

"Because I wanted her to tell me," I admit to her, "and I felt like I was invading her privacy."

Sofia gasps. "How are you related to this family?" She points at Matty, who rolls his eyes at her.

"We are all not like my uncles," he retorts, "or your grandfather." He smirks at her.

"She just told me she raised Avery on her own." I fill Sofia in on the little part that she gave me. The statement made my blood run cold in my body. The statement that when she walked away from the table, I thought I would break the glass in my hand from how hard I was squeezing it.

"She did, and she did a great job." Sofia almost glares at me.

"No, she didn't do a great job," I correct softly, and I talk fast because she looks like she is going to throttle me. "She did an exceptional job, I know that." I shake my head. "I just don't get it."

"I don't really know the details," Sofia says softly. "All she told me was they haven't spoken to her since she walked out and said she wouldn't get rid of her baby."

It's then that Matty grunts, "What the fuck?"

I ignore him because if he is feeling even a quarter of what I felt, it's a lot. "How long has she been working for you guys?" Surely, that question isn't invading anything.

"Not that long, but she's busted her ass the whole time." She stands with her shoulders back and I'm almost thankful, knowing even if I wasn't here, she had someone who would go to war for her and for Avery.

"Okay." Matty holds up his hands, sensing we are going to go toe-to-toe. "What does this mean?"

"What do you mean?" I ask him because his question is loaded.

"Well, you have a kid," he points out, and I don't know why, but I can't help feeling proud, especially since she's the most amazing kid I've ever met.

"I do." I smile at him, and if I could puff out my chest, I would. "I need to get a house."

I grab my phone out of my back pocket. "I have to call your mom." I thought I would be able to get a house on my own, but after searching and driving around for the past two days, it's clear I need help in that department.

"Are you finally setting roots?" Matty asks, and I throw my head back and laugh.

"You've been in the South too long," I say, then look over at Sofia. "Is there anything I should know?"

"Is there a specific question you are asking?" Sofia counters but then holds up her hand. "Doesn't matter, I won't tell you."

"Great." I shake my head. "Good talk."

"Don't you 'good talk' me, Stefano," she hisses. "I'm not the one who had sex without a condom."

"We used protection. Do you think I would be that careless?" I throw back at her. "Look at Michael and Jillian, it's not one hundred percent." I mention my cousin Michael, who had a one-night thing with Jillian, only to find her four months later when he went to pick up Mia and Emma.

"You think?" She smirks at me, and I just shake my head.

"Go to your room," Matty urges me. "When are you telling everyone?"

"The question you need to be asking is, did you tell your girlfriend that you are now a father?" Sofia asks me. I don't answer her that she is a non-factor. Instead, I answer Matty.

"I don't know. Why?" I ask him.

"Because when you do, they will all be descending," he teases, making me laugh. "It's going to be a Bat Signal to end all Bat Signals. Then everyone, and I mean everyone, is going to descend."

"I'll let you know," I assure him before I walk up the stairs to the spare bedroom. Pulling up her number, I think about texting her instead of calling, but something in me just makes me press the blue phone button. I look down at the phone and put it on speaker as I kick off my shoes and throw myself on the king-size bed.

It rings three times before she answers in a whisper, "Hello."

"Did I wake you?" I whisper back into the phone.

"No," she replies, and I hear the sound of sheets rustling. "I was just checking on Avery to make sure she was okay before heading to bed." Her voice goes up a touch.

"Can you meet me tomorrow for breakfast?" I ask, holding my breath, hoping she says yes.

"I don't know," she answers. "I have to have her at daycare, and then I start work by nine."

"What about lunch?" I ask her, hoping she says yes to this.

"I try not to take lunch," she admits, "so I can leave early and get Avery."

"Why did you sneak out that morning?" I want to kick myself the minute the question comes out of me. It was a question I knew I would ask her eventually. It was the question I've asked the universe time and time again when I would think about the beautiful stranger who made me forget all my rules. The beautiful one who made me laugh like no one else, and the one who made me go from zero to a thousand with just one look.

She lets out a deep breath. "It was the first time I ever had a one-night stand." I don't know if I should be happy about this or not. "I was mortified you would think I did it often."

I close my eyes at the way her voice dipped at the end. "Did it matter?"

"To me, it did," she says. "I wasn't like that. I wasn't that person." I want to tell her I know she isn't. I knew that night she wasn't that person, and even if she was, it didn't matter to me. "I went back to the hotel six weeks later." I gasp in shock at her declaration. "Told them what room you were in and everything, but they wouldn't give me your information." I sit up in bed, my heart beating a million miles a minute as it rises to my throat, and I feel like I'm going to throw my phone at the wall.

I'm shaking that she did that. I'm shaking she put all of her pride aside to look for me. I'm shaking because it was my job to protect her and Avery, and I didn't do my job. I'm shaking because she probably went to look for me out of desperation, especially after her parents kicked her out. I'm shaking because now I'm going to do everything in my power to make her whole again, even if I have to destroy people to do it. I don't tell her this. Instead, I whisper, "I'm so sorry."

Thirteen

Addison

*M*y eyes close as soon as I hear him whisper the words, and a lone tear falls onto my pillow. "Addison," he says my name in a whisper, but this time there isn't just one lone tear. Now the tears are streaming down my face. "I'm so sorry."

Today has been, without a doubt, one of the best and also one of the hardest days.

"You don't have to apologize." I try to get my voice back to normal as I wipe the tears from my cheeks with the back of my hand.

"But I do." His voice stays just as low as it was before. "I have so much to apologize for that I don't think there is ever going to be enough time in the day." He stops talking for a second. "I know this is not going to sound like it's the truth." His voice is higher now. "But I never had a one-night stand either."

I laugh through my tears, making the sniffling less conspicuous. "You don't have to say that." I turn over in my bed, looking out the window I don't have blinds on. Looking out into the dark night, I see the twinkling of stars in the sky.

"It's the truth." I hear rustling coming from his side of the phone, and I wonder if he's hiding while he talks to me. "I've never thrown caution to the wind. You were the first time I didn't think things through."

I blink as I watch the stars in the sky. "Um, thanks." I chuckle. "I think." What does one say to that? Do I tell him he was the first time in my whole life I threw caution to the wind? Do I tell him the night with him is a night I think of every single time Avery does something new? Do I tell him I think about him every single time things get rough, and I don't think I can do it or that I'm not doing a good enough job? Do I tell him all these things? Instead of telling him those things, I stay on the safe side. "I think we need to sit down and discuss how this is going to go."

"I would like that," he says, and I have to give it to him. Ever since he has found out about her, he has never wavered. He has never run away; he has stood there ready to embrace everything that comes with her.

"Can you meet me tomorrow at four?" I sit up in my bed, my heart speeding up, knowing over the next couple of days, some big changes will be coming my way. I just hope I can handle them. "I'll get Avery, and we can maybe go for ice cream or to the park." I quickly change it, not wanting him to think I just randomly take her for ice cream instead of having her eat dinner first. This is uncharted territory for me to have to think about what he thinks about what I do with her.

"I'll come and get you," he quickly adds, not even bringing up the fact about the ice cream.

"It's easier if you meet me," I tell him, trying not to sound like I don't want him picking us up. "I have the car seat and all of that." I close my eyes as soon as I say it.

"Okay, do you want to go out and eat?" he asks me, and the pit of my stomach starts to burn.

"We are eating out on Saturday when we go to the fair," I reply, knowing I really can't afford to eat out twice in a week. I think we would survive, but there is a budget, and I stick to it.

"Okay," he says, "I can ask Matty if I can make dinner here." If he were in front of me, he would be able to see how my eyes just almost come out of my sockets.

I sit up in bed, flustered, thinking about him cooking in Matty and Sofia's house. "How about you just come here for dinner?" I want to bite my tongue as soon as the words come out of my mouth. Why couldn't I just leave it be that we would talk at the park? *Why do you constantly have to say things you shouldn't?* my head yells at me.

I'm about to take it back and suggest we just talk while Avery plays when he says, "That would be amazing."

I inwardly groan that he accepted my invitation. "But I have class at seven thirty," I quickly add so he knows there is a time limit for this.

"Class?" he asks me. "What do you mean you have class?"

"Well, I'm trying to get my college degree," I reply, and I don't know why I feel a bit embarrassed even though I know I shouldn't.

"But you were in college when we met?" I don't know if he's asking me the question or just remembering.

"I was but..." I let my voice trail off, trying to come up with words that won't point the finger at the real reason I didn't end up finishing. I don't regret any of the choices I've made, especially when it comes to my life now. Things happened for a reason.

"You dropped out," he adds what I didn't really want to admit to him.

"I sort of had no choice," I admit. Not wanting to drag this out, I give him what I would normally not share. "Here is the thing with my family," I say, looking down at my hands, wondering how I can spin this story to not make it look like my family is a bunch of assholes, but well, they are. There is no beating around the bush. "My father comes from old money that he inherited from my grandfather, who also inherited it from his family. He was raised in a way where things were either right or wrong. There was no middle ground. Old family values, I would not be the one to tarnish the family name. He would not be the laughingstock of the family because he had a daughter who couldn't keep her legs closed." I laugh, pretending it doesn't bother me.

"When I told them I wouldn't have an abortion or get rid of it, things changed in a way I never thought they would. I mean, these were my parents. I knew they were mad, but I figured they would come around. They didn't." I blink away the tear that comes, screaming at myself, *I will not shed a fucking tear for them.* "It seemed that all payments were stopped, and I didn't know. I owed a little over fourteen thousand dollars for the following year. When I called my father, he didn't answer me, and my mother ignored my phone calls and even my text messages." I thought I had buried how I felt about it, but having to tell him, all the memories of back then come out like the box has been opened again. "I couch surfed for two months." I don't add in why I had to couch surf. Who wants to admit that their own family put them out on the street? That they stopped paying their rent and got them evicted? "Luckily for me, when I started school, I got a part-time job, and my parents would give me an allowance that I didn't always spend. So while I worked full-time, I was able to save up for my own place at the three-month mark. Right when I turned six months." He doesn't say anything to me. All I hear from his side is him hissing. I smile sadly.

"It all worked out. I have an amazing job now, and hopefully, I can get some clients of my own."

"I have no doubt you'll get them," he encourages me, and it's been a long time since someone has been in my corner encouraging me. The feeling is almost foreign to me at this point.

I hear the sound of feet coming my way before I see her standing in the doorway. "Mommy." She rubs her eyes with her fist. "Can I have some water?"

"Of course, angel face." I toss the covers off me. "I have to go," I say into the phone.

"See you tomorrow," he says softly.

"See you tomorrow," I repeat before I disconnect the phone, tossing it on my bed before I make my way over to Avery and stop in front of her. "Did I forget to leave your sippy cup next to your bed?" I ask her, knowing with everything that happened with Stefano tonight, my whole nightly routine was shook up.

"It's not there," she mumbles to me.

"I'll go get it, you go get back into bed," I tell her. She turns and walks slowly back to her bed as I make my way to the kitchen. I grab her pink sippy cup from the dish rack before walking over to the fridge and pulling it open to grab the jug of water. The pizza boxes are stacked on the bottom shelf, filling it up. He moved everything around to make sure that it all fit. I don't even look in the brown bag next to the boxes. I just grab the water jug, fill up her cup, and close the top. I take a sip of the water through the straw to make sure it's on properly before I walk back to her room.

She's back in bed in the fetal position. "Avery," I say her name softly, wondering if she's still awake or if she fell back asleep.

She stirs the minute I say her name, looking up at me. "Yeah," she mumbles before sitting up in the bed. I sit down next to her and hand her the cup. She takes it in her hand and brings it to her lips with closed eyes. The pizza must have been really salty because she almost finishes the whole cup in one go. She hands it to me, trying to catch her breath before lying back down and pulling the covers over her. I walk back to the fridge and fill the cup back up before going back over to her and placing it beside her pillow like I do every night. The sound of her soft snores fills the room.

I lean down and kiss her cheek. "Love you," I tell her softly, before I walk back to my bedroom.

Grabbing my phone, I pick it up and put it on the bedside table before I slide into bed again. I'm just laying my head on the pillow when the phone rings, and I see it's him again. "Hello," I answer softly.

"Hey, sorry, it's me again," he says, and he sounds like he's out of breath.

"Yes," I reply, not sure why he's calling me again.

"I'm going to tell my parents." He comes right out and says it as a declaration. I almost laugh because he sounds so serious and nervous all at the same time.

"I figured." I can't help but chuckle now.

"I kind of have to tell them before Matty lets it slip." He lets out a big exhale. My hands get sweaty realizing that Matty knows. I figured he would know because of Sofia, but knowing he knows is just cementing that this is actually happening and it's not all in my head. "If I don't tell my mother, and she finds out from Matty, she's likely to castrate me."

I can't help but laugh out nervously. "Might as well tell them, then." I put my hand on my stomach as it decides that it's going to go straight up to my throat like a wave in the middle of the ocean.

"I'm sorry you went through all that alone," he says to me, his voice going soft, and I close my eyes again, and I breathe out through my mouth softly. "I don't know how, but I'm going to make it up to you."

I shake my head. "There isn't anything to make up for." I open my eyes and look over to the doorframe where she just stood not too long ago, her small hands rubbing her eyes. All I can do is smile. "I would do it all over again for her." My voice trembles. The silent tear escapes. "She's the best thing I've ever done. Hands down, the best thing that I've ever done."

"Thank you." His voice sends shivers down my body, which is crazy since the last time I felt like this was the first time he leaned over and kissed me. There in the middle of the diner, with people coming and going, no one paying attention to the two people in the corner. No one knowing that night would change everything.

"For?" I ask him, not sure what he's thanking me for.

I know I'm also not ready for what is to come. I'm not ready for his words to come out. There is nothing that can prepare me for what comes next. "Being the best mother to our kid," he says with a chuckle. I picture him smiling with a smirk that I've seen for the past four years growing on our daughter, always mesmerized she got it, even though she never met him. It was a piece of him she got without knowing. "She's the best, and it's because of you."

Fourteen

Stefano

I know I should tread lightly and go at it slowly, but I don't know what it is about Addison that just makes me forget everything I have instilled in me. Every single rule I have in place is just suddenly erased and there are no rules when it comes to her. No one-night stands, that was crossed off the list. No strings attached, keep things at arm's length. But again, with her that night all I could do was push all those little nagging comments to the back of my head. All I wanted was to kiss her. There in the middle of the worst diner food I had ever had, all I wanted to do was hold her face and kiss her. I kept ordering food only to drag out the time we spent together. I kept ordering the food until I finally got the courage to ask her what I was dying to ask her the second she bumped into me and looked into my eyes. I honestly think the world stayed still for that moment. "She really is the best kid," Addison agrees, and I can even hear the smile in her voice.

"Okay, I should call my parents and get it over with." I take a deep inhale. "Wish me luck."

"Hope it turns out better than it did with mine," she says. I know she's trying to make a joke out of it, but my hands clench into fists. From the little she told me, my blood is boiling, and I know I want to sit down with her and for her to tell me exactly what happened. However, couch surfing for two months was enough to make me see red or black or whatever color someone sees when they are about to lose their shit.

"See you tomorrow," I say and quickly disconnect her. As soon as I hang up with her and go to search for my father's name, I quickly go back and add her number to my favorite list so that no matter what happens, she can always get through to me.

I then go back and press the camera button for my father. The sounds of ringing fill the room as my face fills the screen. It takes three more rings for the little circle to spin and connect in the middle of the screen. It takes a minute before my full face is now pushed to the corner and my father's face fills the screen. "Look who it is," he greets me, leaning back on the couch. He's wearing a basic gray shirt and most likely sweatpants, his black hair pushed back, and his beard a little bit longer than it was three days ago when I saw him.

"Hi," I say, kicking off my shoes before sitting with my back against the headboard in the bed. "Where is Maman?"

"She's right here," he says and turns the phone so I can see my mother sitting in the corner of the U-shaped couch with a book in her hand. She's wearing a loungewear set that she just makes look fancy. Her hair is loose and draped over one shoulder, her face is without a stitch of makeup. "See."

"Maman," I say in French, and she looks up, her face filling with a smile so big her blue eyes light up.

"Mon chéri." My sweetheart, she answers in French, putting the book down beside her and sliding over to my father's side. He moves his arm so she can snuggle into him. He drapes an arm around her shoulder before kissing the side of her head. "Tu es où?" Where are you?

"I'm at Matty's," I tell them both.

"What?" my mother asks me, shocked. "Pourquoi?" Why? she asks me, and all the words get jumbled in my mouth.

"Um." I suddenly feel like I'm sixteen again, and I just messed up and have to break the news to my parents. Like the time I skipped school and decided I would forge my father's signature, but they caught me and called home about it. My sister, Karrie, gave me the heads-up before I walked in. So instead of letting them yell at me, I came clean to them as soon as I walked in. Of course, I acted like the lie was secretly making me guilty, which they fell for or maybe they could have smelled the bullshit but let it slide. "Do you guys think you could come down here this weekend?" I ask them both. The nerves in my body make me jump off the bed, and I slowly pace the room back and forth.

My mother looks at me, trying to decipher what I just asked her. It's as if she knows something is up but can't put her finger on it. She stares at me for a couple of minutes before she answers me, "Why?" The look goes into a glare, and she sits up as she waits for it. It's the mother instinct; she knows shit is about to hit the fan. When I was growing up, I would think it was a special gift she had. I've learned she just knew better than we did.

"How do I say this?" I think about how to say the next part. I could always tell them I need to see them, but my mother isn't one who just will let that slide. She needs to know everything now. "No easy way to say this." I look at my father, who just closes his eyes for a second longer than he should. My mother again picks up on the detail and looks at me, then at my father, and then at me again. "I'd like you to meet your granddaughter." Fuck, that was easier than I thought it would be, well, at least for me to say it.

The screech that comes out of my mother isn't something I was expecting. "She's pregnant? You've known her two weeks!" she yells. "C'est pas possible?" It's not possible, she mumbles in French. "C'est un blague? Tu plaisantes j'espère?" This is a joke. She looks at my father and then back at me, and this time, she grabs the phone from him. "Stefano," she says my name through clenched teeth, "tell me that you are not stupid enough not to wear protection? You have been dating her a month."

My eyebrows pinch together, and it finally sinks in that she thinks it's with Jenna. "Oh no, not her." I shake my head.

"What?" She jumps up off the couch. "Is this a poisson d'avril trick?" April Fool's joke, she asks my father, who grabs the phone from her.

"Vivienne," he says her name softly, "calm down." He takes her hand and pulls her down on the couch next to him.

"Calm down?" she hisses back at him, and even I grimace at the way she asked him that. "Calm down your *son*." She emphasizes on your son, and I have to roll my eyes. Isn't it always the case that we are one parent's child when we fuck up? "He just told us we have a granddaughter."

"I heard," my father says calmly as always. I get the calm from him, for sure. "Why don't we listen to the rest of what he has to say?"

"D'accord." Fine, she hisses at him. "Who is the mother of this child?"

"Addison," I say, and I can't help the way my chest heats up at her name. I can't help but to be filled with pride at who the mother of my child is.

"Addison?" my mother says her name, blinking a couple of times. "Wait, the one who planned the wedding?"

"Yes." I nod my head and stop moving as I wait for it.

"But?" She shakes her head, and then I see it when it finally dawns on her. The gasp comes out of her as her hand is lifted slowly to her mouth. "The princess girl?" she asks me and then looks over at my father. "Why are you not saying anything?" she asks him.

"Merde," my father replies, using the French word for shit. Before we were born, he knew a couple of words, but then when we started learning, he learned with us because he wasn't going to be left out of conversations. Also, because he thought my mother was always plotting something with us without him knowing, and she usually was. "Mon amour." My love, he says to her, and she springs up again.

"Oh, don't you, 'mon amour' me," she hisses at him. "Tu le savais et tu ne m'as rien dit." You knew and you didn't tell me. "Ridicules, j'en reviens pas." Ridiculous, I can't believe this. "Imbécile." Imbecile.

My father gets up and puts the phone down on the coffee table. "Ma belle." My beautiful, he says. "Can we just listen to what he has to say?"

"You do not even start, Markos." She shakes her head and sits down in front of the phone. "You knew this big secret, and you didn't think to tell me?" She shakes her head at him and starts mumbling French words that I'm not even getting for how low she is saying them. But it doesn't sound like anything good. "You kept this from me?" she asks him. "How could you know this huge secret and not tell me?" My father opens his mouth to say something, but she holds up her hand to stop him. "How could you do this?" Again, he says something, and she side-eyes him, and he closes his mouth and then glares at me. "And you," she hisses at me. "What the hell is wrong with you?" I don't even bother answering her because she's not one to be toyed with until she gets it all out of her system. "We bought you condoms for you to use." She throws up her hand in the air. "It's a monthly subscription." She then trails off, mumbling all the bad French words.

"Are you done?" I ask her, and even my father shakes his head.

"Ne me cherche pas, Stefano Dimitris." Don't you start with me, she hisses at me, and she uses my full name, which anyone knows is never a good thing. Never. "Am I done?" she mimics my question.

"Do you want to meet her or not?" I ask her, my tone tight as I think she might say no. I don't know how the fuck I will explain this to Addison. I can't even imagine what she is going to say if my parents say no. Them saying no is really not an option.

"What kind of a stupid question is that?" my father shouts out. "Do we want to meet her or not?" He then looks over at my mother, waiting for her to say something.

"On arrive demain." We are coming down tomorrow, my mother declares.

"Her parents are going to think we raised a bouffon." I have to laugh when she calls me a bouffon, but then I look down, trying to ignore the comment about her parents. I think about if I should tell them about her parents or not. It takes me over a minute of not saying anything for my father to pick up on the silence.

"What's the matter?" I think about lying to him about what is bothering me, but I also know my parents will want to meet her parents to show them that I'm not an idiot. I also know I don't want her to feel bad about it.

"Her parents kicked her out." My words come out crystal clear, and the silence of the room just makes the words echo more.

My father's hand comes up and he slams his hand down on the coffee table, the movement making the phone shake a bit. "Stefano," he hisses out my name.

"Dad, you don't think I know this?" I ask him, sitting on the edge of the bed as I hang my head down. "I feel." I blink away the stinging of tears, but for the first time, I let them out. "I don't even know what I feel, it's like this burning in my stomach," I tell them both and my mother uses her thumb to wipe away the tears that are coming out of her eyes. "And then my chest is tight and I feel like I'm going to throw up every seven seconds," I say breathlessly.

"It's called love, you dumbass," my father says softly. "We are coming down tomorrow," he reiterates what my mother just said. "We'll take them out."

"You can't," I tell him. "She said they are already eating out on Saturday."

"Stefano." My mother grabs the phone from the table and makes sure I can see her whole face. "You call her and tell her that your parents are taking her out because we owe her a lot more than a meal." The glare and tone are something I'm not going to argue with, especially after what just happened.

"Fine." I take a deep inhale. "I'll see you tomorrow, I guess."

"Idiot," is the last thing my mother says before she hangs up on me.

I toss my phone to the side and look up at the ceiling before I rub my face with my hands. I then lean forward, putting my elbows on my knees and hanging my head. It's maybe five minutes before I hear the sound of footsteps running up the stairs. I look at the door, hearing a knock for one second before the door opens, and Matty stands there in shorts and no shirt. "You told your parents?" I just stare at him. "The Bat Signal has been unleashed."

"Well, it's been five minutes," I say, looking at my watch, "the family is slacking, if you ask me."

Matty laughs and shakes his head. "I just got four messages from Uncle Max and Matthew asking if they have rentals in the area."

"Say no," Sofia yells from somewhere in the house, "they can stay with us!"

"Are you insane?" Matty yells over his shoulder. "Don't you dare even speak that out loud, they might have Spidey senses." He walks out of the room. "This is going to be fun," he states right before he closes the door behind him.

I pick up my phone, wanting to speak to only one person. I pull up her name, and instead of calling her, I text her. If she's sleeping, I don't want to wake her.

Me: Can you talk?

I look down at the phone and see the gray bubble with the three dots pop up before my phone pings with a text.

Addison: Haven't we spoken enough?

Fifteen

Addison

I press send on the message and put the phone down, but the phone rings softly beside me. I can hear his laughter fill the phone as I bring it to my ear. "Hello."

"Am I bothering you?" His laughter is still coming through. I don't know why, but his laughter makes me smile.

"Well, it's been about twenty minutes since the last phone call," I reply, sinking into the bed.

"I called my parents," he says, and everything stops. I don't even think I'm breathing at this point.

"Oh," I say.

"Yeah, they are coming down tomorrow."

I immediately sit up. "What?" I say in a whisper, but it comes out in a yelp.

"And asked if they can take you out for dinner to meet Avery."

My heart, which is normally beating in my chest, is now beating so freaking fast and hard I feel like it's about to come out of my rib cage.

"Ummm," I start, closing my eyes to get my heartbeat to normal as my ears now start to buzz. "I don't need to be there." I put my hand on my head, thinking that maybe I'm going to faint or maybe I have scarlet fever.

"What?" he shrieks. "Of course you have to be there."

"Ugh." I put my hand on my stomach. "I don't know. I don't do well with parents." My head is just about ready to explode. This is too much; this is all just too much. "I mean, look at my own." I laugh bitterly, trying to joke about it, but the pain still hurts, even after all this time. The emptiness is still there. The fact they haven't even tried to get to know Avery just breaks my heart because she's the best, but I also know it's their loss. They don't deserve her awesomeness in their lives.

"You need to come and maybe protect me from my mother," he declares, and I am not rolling my lips to stop from laughing at him. His tone is both equally scared and panicked. "She is not pleased with me."

I don't even know why, but the words come out without me knowing. "Okay." I give in. "I'll go. Now, I need to get to bed or else there will be bags under my eyes tomorrow, and that isn't the look I want to have when meeting your parents for the first time."

He chuckles. "Addison, you could be wearing a potato bag and war paint on your face that is dripping down, and you'll still be the most beautiful woman in the room."

My heart stops. Completely. "Good night, Stefano," I say before I hang up on him and put my phone on do not disturb. I'm not doing this with him. He has a girlfriend, and I'm not the one who is going to walk in there and just steal him away. I'm not that person. "We have a child together, so I'm going to have to be nice to him, but that's it when it comes to Stefano and me," I huff, putting my phone on my bedside table. *But isn't he sexy?* my head screams out. *Remember when he did that thing with his tongue?* I put my hands on my ears. "I'm not listening to you anymore." I turn over and close my eyes but that makes it even worse because now all I can see is me ripping his shirt off him while he places me on that hotel desk no one actually works on. His hands roam up my legs that are spread with him standing in the middle of them, our mouths devouring each other. My eyes spring open. "That didn't help anything." I turn onto my back before turning over on my side. "He's in bed with his girlfriend right now," I tell myself. "Yeah, so shut the fuck up and go to sleep."

I don't know how long it takes me to fall asleep, but the next day, I have to literally peel myself out of bed. I spend more time than I should picking an outfit, knowing that after work I'm going to see him. We get into the car with seconds to spare and only when I pull out of the parking lot does Avery start to ask me questions, "Momma, is Stefano really my dad?"

I glance in the rearview mirror, seeing her look out the window. "What do you mean?"

"He said he's my dad," she says, her feet going up and down, "so now I have a dad."

"Well, you always had a dad," I tell her, gripping the steering wheel.

"But now I can tell people that my dad ate dinner with me." I pull into the parking lot and put the car in park. "So if Ms. Terry asks me what I did last night, I could say I had dinner with my dad."

"Yes." I look over at her. "You can say you saw your dad." She nods her head at me as she unbuckles her seat belt before jumping down from her booster seat. I open my car door and then open hers. She jumps out of the car and holds my hand as we walk into the school. The minute we walk in, she takes off to her classroom door.

"My dad came to see me," she announces as soon as she sees her teacher, who looks at her and then at me. The shock is all over her face, especially since I told them her father is uninvolved in her life. "He brought pizza, and he got me princess dresses."

"Oh, that sounds like fun," Ms. Terry says.

"Okay, come give Momma a kiss," I say, squatting down, and she comes over to me.

"Will Stefano come and see me again?" she asks me, and I just nod my head.

"We are going to the park after school, and he's going to be there," I tell her, and she jumps up before running back into the class. I avoid looking at anyone before I walk back to my car. Even when I get to work, I walk in, head straight to the kitchen, and start the coffee. Unlike yesterday, there is less fanfare this morning.

Shelby comes in not long after me. "Morning," she mumbles to me as her phone rings in her hand.

Clarabella is the next one in with a car seat. She huffs as she comes in and the door closes behind her. "Have kids, they say." She blows the hair out of her face. "It'll be fun, they said."

I roll my lips when I look at her and see she's literally leaking through her silk shirt. My eyes must go big, and she looks down. "I'm like a cow," she says, putting the car seat down with the baby still sleeping. "I swear, he cries, and it just pours out of me. The other day I just thought about him, and it was dripping everywhere."

"Ew," Presley states, coming in the door at the moment, "you're leaking." She points at her, and Clarabella just gasps.

"Really?" She looks down. "Wait, your shirt doesn't leak milk?" She rolls her eyes. "Watch your nephew while I clean up."

"Clean up in aisle ten." Presley makes a joke at Clarabella's back. She just lifts her hand high in the air and flips her the bird. "Good morning," she greets, picking up the car seat and bringing it with her.

I turn around and start the emails. I have a whole list of questions I have to ask Sofia when she gets in. The time flies by, and when I hear the door open, I expect it to be Sofia. So when I look up with a smile, it quickly disappears when I see Stefano walking in. He's wearing black jeans and a white short-sleeved shirt that makes his arms look bigger than they were yesterday. He pushes his aviator glasses on top of his head, the smile on his face filling it when he sees me.

"What are you doing here?" I don't even move from my chair because I can't. It's as if all motions have left my body.

He holds up the brown bag I didn't see in his hand. "I brought you lunch."

My mouth opens to say something but nothing comes out, I just close it and then open it again. But, in that little bit of time, Clarabella comes out from the back and the front door opens and Sofia steps in.

"I just left you like ten minutes ago, so how are you here?" she huffs at Stefano.

"First off, I left you guys an hour ago," he corrects, "and second, your shirt is all buttoned wrong." She looks down and laughs.

She quickly fixes it and glares at him. "What do you want?"

"I brought Addison lunch," he says, walking toward my desk and my legs finally decide it's okay to stand.

"Interesting," both Clarabella and Sofia say at the same time before crossing their arms over their chests.

"Nothing is interesting." I walk around my desk toward Stefano, the smell of him making my mouth water and my stomach twinge which makes a certain part of me tighten. "Thank you," I say, grabbing the bag from him.

"See you later." He smirks at me and then a smile fills his face. I want to punch him in the face, but I also want to climb him like a tree, so the two parts of my brain are working at the same time.

"Yes," I grit between clenched teeth, then bite down before I say something I shouldn't.

He turns and puts the glasses on. "Ladies, have a great day." He pushes the door open, and when it slams shut behind him, I close my eyes.

"Oh my God," I hear Sofia mumble, but all I can do is shake my head.

"It's nothing." I avoid even looking at them before heading back to my desk.

"It's not nothing," Clarabella declares. "It's lunch from Luke's."

"If he got her a whole combo, you know he means business," Sofia adds.

"If he even got her a drink, he's been thinking about her the whole day." Clarabella looks at her, then at me. "Open the bag," she demands of me.

I open the bag, and my eyes scan a sandwich, a bag of chips, a little something else that looks like a dessert, and a bottle of tea. "It's a bag of chips, and I think, a dessert."

"You're lying," Sofia scoffs and takes a step forward, but I close the bag before she gets too close, making them both laugh.

"It's a phase." I say the only thing I can say. "He just found out he has a daughter." My hand trembles as I put the bag on my desk. "He'll move on as soon as everything gets settled." The words feel like acid in my mouth. He's going to leave in a matter of time, and I'm going to have a heartbroken girl to deal with.

"He's buying a house," Sofia states, and just like that I'm more surprised than I was five minutes ago. "Apparently, that is a huge deal."

"But—" I start to say, my head spinning. "But he is a city guy." If I could bang my head on my desk, I think I would bang it over and over again. Just like they do in the cartoons.

"People can change," Sofia reminds me, "look at me."

"You grew up in the South," Clarabella throws out, laughing. "Look at me, she says," she makes fun of her.

"On a farm," Sofia counters, throwing her hands in the air. "This is as city as it can get." She tilts her head to the side. "Buckle up, buttercup, and welcome to the family."

Sixteen

Stefano

I walk out of her office, the door slamming behind me, and I immediately want to go back in there. I know showing up threw her off. I knew the minute she looked up and saw me that she was not expecting me. I also knew I was going to bring her lunch, especially when she said she doesn't eat to save time and leave early. I didn't even know what she ate but I asked for the most popular item, so that is what she got.

My phone buzzes in my back pocket and I take it out to find a text from Matty.

Matty: Batmobile lands in ten minutes. Where are you?
Me: On my way.

I get into the car and put the phone in the cupholder when another text comes in.

Matty: You went to take her lunch?

Me: Yes, why?

Matty: Why? Why do you think? The question is why did you take her lunch?

Me: She has to eat. I can't text, I'm driving.

Matty: You have my car. I know damn well you can voice text. Pussy ass, just get here. I don't want to have to deal with the whole family when they aren't even here for me.

I don't bother even answering him because I'm at the private airport in a matter of four minutes. I get out of the car and look around to see Matty standing by the chain-link fence that encloses the area. "Why does everything take four minutes to get to?"

"Small town," he mumbles, looking up from his phone. "The most I'm in my car is fifteen minutes and that's if I'm downtown." He's about to say something else but stops when we see the plane slowly coming to a stop near the fence. The phone buzzes in both our hands.

Matthew: We have arrived.

I look at Matty, who looks at me. "Does he think we can't see the plane?" He chuckles as the plane shuts off and the side door of the plane opens.

"Wait, I didn't know he was coming," I say, looking at Matty, who just shakes his head and chuckles. The door to the plane opens and the stairs come out. My father is the first one to stick his head out and walk down the four stairs before my mother joins him. He always walks out first so he can hold her hand once she gets to the last step. I look behind her to see her best friend, my aunt Karrie, get out followed by my uncle Matthew, then my uncle Max, and finally my aunt Allison.

"Oh my God," I exhale to the six of them once they reach the gate and the door opens. "Is anyone else in the plane?"

"No," Matthew says from behind my father, throwing his

head back and laughing. "Viktor was going to come but he had something."

"You know he doesn't go anywhere without me," Uncle Max says, "and usually I would opt out, but this." He shakes his head and laughs. "I'm not missing this."

"I'm here to make sure that everyone is safe and in case I'm supposed to bond anyone out," Aunt Allison states. "Grandpa Cooper spoke through clenched teeth." She raises her eyebrows at me. "He's expecting a phone call."

"I thought—" I start to say to my father as he walks to me and slaps my shoulder, followed by my mother, who just glares at me. I bend to kiss her cheek, and she kisses me softly, even though she is pissed at me.

"That was your first mistake," Matty mumbles from beside me, "you thought." He smirks at me and is shocked when Matthew slaps his shoulder. "Ouch. I didn't do anything wrong. He's the one who, you know." He then puts his hands together and looks like he's rocking a baby. I push his shoulder to tell him to shut up.

"Did you think she wasn't going to call me?" My aunt Karrie moves my mother to the side to stand in front of me. "I'm her best friend." She smiles at me and I lean down and kiss her cheek. "Who else do you think is going to reel her in?" she asks me, and I didn't even think about that part of it.

"I could have done that," my father states, which makes everyone but Aunt Karrie laugh.

She glares at my father. "We all know the way you reel her in." She folds her arms over her chest. "I don't think sex is something anyone is going to want to watch."

"Jesus," Matty says, putting his hand on his stomach. "It's a good thing I didn't have lunch." That earns him a glare from my mother. "Sorry, Tatie." He uses the French word for aunt to make her soften toward him. Everyone knows if my mother is mad at you, all you have to do is try to speak French, and she suddenly forgets what she is mad about and is happy you are trying to connect with her. Well, everyone but her children, that is.

"We are going to have to all reel it in." I look at my mother.

"We are a lot to handle." I look at everyone and do a circle with my hand. "But she hasn't really been around many people, so baby steps." I start to get nervous for Addison. The last thing I want is for her to be nervous or uncomfortable. If I see she's shutting down, I'm getting her out of there, and I'll deal with the consequences after.

"Let's go see the house," my father urges, and I nod at them. It's a good thing Matty came with his other truck because both truck beds have luggage. I don't have the energy to ask how long they are staying; from the looks of things, it'll be at least a week.

My parents come in the truck with me and my aunt Karrie while the rest go with Matty. We pull into the driveway and my father whistles. "This is—"

"This is a home," my mother declares, opening the back door of the truck.

"I like it," my uncle Matthew says with his hands on his hips as he takes in the house.

"How is the crime rate in the area?" my uncle Max asks as he pulls out his phone. "I'm going to just enter the street name and I'll be able to tell you."

"Aren't you glad you called everyone?" Matty teases, slapping my shoulder before walking up the steps to the front door.

I take out the key from my pocket and open the front door, stepping in, sliding the first door closed. "Most of the doors are sliding," I explain, sliding open the second door.

"Great," Matthew observes, "this way when she is pissed at you, she can't slam the doors."

I nod at him as we walk into the foyer area and the circular staircase is in the middle.

"This is nice," my father notes, looking around. "How many bedrooms?"

"It's five bedrooms," I reply. My father whistles like it's a lot of house for someone who just lived out of a suitcase for most of the time. "I know."

"Is she moving in?" my mother asks me as she walks to the side where the kitchen is.

"I have no idea," I answer honestly. My goal would be for us to live here, but I think I should discuss it with her before I tell my family.

"Well, didn't you make a plan?" my uncle Matthew asks me.

"It's been two days," I tell him.

"Exactly," Max counters, putting his hands on his hips. "How don't you have a plan?"

"It's a shock for anyone, I'm sure." My aunt Allison smiles, giving me an encouraging smile.

"Either way, I want to make a room for Avery," I inform them of the only thing I'm one thousand percent sure of.

"Yes." My mother nods her head. "I'm already on it." She smiles at me and I know she was already on that yesterday as soon as I got off the phone with her.

We walk around the house and go outside, where we talk about putting in a pool, because what kind of a monster doesn't have a pool for his child. My phone beeps, and I look at the group.

"I'm going to go and get Avery and Addison," I say nervously, then look at my parents. "I'll text you when it's time to meet." I look at my father, trying to tell him that it would be better going at it slow. He just nods at me as I turn and walk out the door.

I make it to the ice cream shop before them. I park the car and get out, walking over to the little picnic table in the shade to wait for them. I look to the side where a giant soccer field is in front of a huge jungle gym where kids play in different spots. Some kids are trying to cross the monkey bars while the other kids are screaming as they go down one of the slides.

Older kids are off to the side where there is even a basketball court as they start a game. I start to get really nervous as the seconds tick by, and I look down at my phone every thirty seconds because it feels like it's been forever. My eyes roam the area, and then I spot them walking toward me. Addison is wearing tan pants that hug every fucking curve she has and a tight black sleeveless shirt showing off her slender arms. The neck is in a circle, and you can see her clavicle. The clavicle I bit into the second I slid inside her as she sat on that hotel desk that no one uses. My cock gets immediately hard, but I shake my head, looking down and then up again toward the both of them. Addison holds Avery's hand while they talk, or better yet, as Avery tells her a story. Her free hand goes crazy in the air as she tells her the story. I can't help but smile when I look at them. I also can't help but feel settled. It's the strangest feeling I've ever felt in my whole life.

Addison must sense someone looking at her, and when she looks up, our eyes meet. "Look." I see Addison's mouth move as she points at me, and Avery lets go of her hand and runs the rest of the way to me. I get up from the picnic table and squat down, waiting for her.

"I told my friends I have a dad." The way she makes the declaration, you can hear the happiness in her voice. She says it, pushing the hair out of her face, and all I can do is smile as I take her hand and pull her into me to hug her as if I've been doing this always.

"How was your day?" I ask her when I let her go but then

look up at Addison, who just smiles down at us. "Shall we get ice cream?"

"Yes!" Avery shouts as she jumps up and down.

"I think that's a yes," Addison says, smiling. "Just a little one, we still have to eat dinner," she tells her, and I think Avery will agree to anything she says.

"I want the unicorn one," Avery says to me in a whisper-yell, "please."

"We will take a small unicorn one," I tell the girl, then look at Addison, who just shakes her head. "I'll have a vanilla cone," I tell her, even though I don't really like ice cream. I know I must keep my hands busy or they'll shake.

I grab the ice cream cone with a small scoop on top of a waffle cone. It looks like it's pink and blue but also yellow and orange. I grab my cone and pay her before returning to the table. I sit on the bench in front of Avery and Addison.

"So," I say, taking a lick of my ice cream, "my mom and dad came to visit me." I look at Avery as she licks her ice cream, her nose even getting some. "And they would like to meet you."

Avery looks at me. "You have a mom and dad, too?" I look at Addison, who just blinks and looks down at her purse. She fidgets with the zipper for a second before I turn back to Avery.

"I do," I tell her. "Do you want to meet them?" I ask her, really hoping she says yes, because I don't know what I'm going to do if she says no, thank you.

"Okay," she agrees as if her world won't be turned upside down.

"Okay," I say, breathing a sigh of relief that I didn't have to beg her to meet them. I smirk and then look up at Addison, who nods at me as if she knows the struggle I'm going through.

In the two seconds I look at Addison, Avery loses the battle on the ice cream. When I look up, her hands are covered in melted ice cream, her chin has drips of it, and somehow, she even got it on her forehead. "Can I go on the slide?" she asks Addison, who grabs the cone from her and gets up to toss it in the bin.

"Let's clean you up first," she suggests, opening her purse and taking out a white plastic container. She opens it and pulls out what looks like a tissue, but I finally get a look at it and see it's a wet one. She wipes her face off and then her hands before she kisses her nose. "One time on the slide, and then we go," she tells her, and Avery nods at her before she runs off.

"Are you okay?" I ask Addison, who nods at me.

"I guess so," she exhales. "I don't know how I'm supposed to be or feel. My main concern is Avery."

"My concern is both of you," I tell her, and she is about to say something when Avery comes back.

"Did you see me?" she asks me, getting on the seat next to me. "I went the fastest."

"I did," I lie to her. "The fastest I've ever seen," I tell her, and she nods at me.

"Let's skedaddle," Addison says, making me laugh.

"Skedaddle." I roll my lips. "That's a word I haven't heard in a while."

"Well, the last time I said let's bounce," Addison tells me as we start to walk to the restaurant, "she thought I was going to bounce her head."

I laugh as Avery slides her hand into Addison's and mine. I don't even have any words to say, I can only look down at our hands that are together. "What is the name of this street, Momma?" Avery asks her.

"Main Street," she tells her quietly.

"I've never been to a town that had a Main Street before," I add in, and they look at me like I have five heads. "Usually, I'm in big cities." I look at Addison now. "Why did you choose this town?"

"Um, it seemed like a perfect place to raise her," Addison replies as she swings Avery's hand, making her giggle. "Plus, I didn't know anyone here, so no one would bring up certain people." She avoids saying her family. "It was a clean start for all of us." I know it's not the time and place, but I also have little patience. I also know it's only a matter of time before I snap and either ask her about it or go behind her back and find out. I would rather not do the latter, but I also know I have to protect my family, which now includes her.

I look up and see my parents standing outside the restaurant. Talking to each other, my father picks up my mother's hand that is in his and kisses her fingers. Her other hand holds a big bag and I cringe inwardly, not knowing what is inside. "Also, my uncles might come as well," I mumble to her with no time to spare. She doesn't have time to say anything. She just looks up at me like a deer in headlights. "Here we go."

Seventeen

Addison

The closer and closer we get to Stefano's parents, the harder and faster my heart beats. The more my hand starts to sweat, the more my knees start to shake. "Here we go," I think I hear him say, but the buzzing in my ears takes over.

"There they are." I look up toward where the man's voice is coming from and my feet literally feel like they weigh six thousand pounds. He looks over at us and he smiles a great big smile, and you know it's genuine because his eyes light up. It's Stefano's dad, Markos, as he was introduced to me at the wedding. I didn't know back then he was my daughter's grandfather, which made it so much less awkward than it is now. He lets go of the woman's hand, who I know is Vivienne, because she came to me at the wedding to let me know that she wasn't drunk and asked if I could get her some sweet tea. She said all of this in French until Zara came along to fill me in.

"Oh mon dieu," she says in French, and I start to panic, not knowing what she said. *What if they hate me?* My head screams at me so loud I about have a panic attack in the middle of Main Street.

"Hello," Markos says when we get close enough. The buzzing in my ears just get louder and louder, and my stomach lurches to my throat.

"Hi," I say softly as Avery lets go of my hand, no doubt because I was squeezing it too tight.

"Bonjour," Vivienne says to me. Her blue eyes are almost crystal blue. She comes over to me. "It's nice to see you again, Addison," she says and hugs me, making me stop breathing altogether. "Thank you for meeting us," she whispers in my ear and the tears now sting my eyes to come down. She lets me go and then squeezes my hand, blinking away her own tears before she turns away and looks down at Avery. "Hello, ma puce." She smiles at Avery, who just looks at her with her eyebrows pushed together. "That means beauty," she tells her and Avery now smiles big. "I heard that someone is a princess."

The word is like music to Avery's ears. "It's me." She jumps up. "I'm the princess." She points at herself.

"Well, a princess has to have a tiara," Vivienne declares, turning to hold out her hand to Markos, who hands her the blue bag.

It has engraving on the side but I can't read what it says. I think it's some sort of fancy writing. "What is going on?" I look over at Stefano, who smiles at me, but his smile is sort of broken when he sees her move the white tissue paper aside to take out whatever is in the box.

"My mother is... how do I put it." He thinks for two seconds before adding in, "Extreme."

I look back over at Vivienne, who pulls a blue box out of the bag, with the emblem also stamped on top of the box. "This tiara," she says, turning the square box in her hand, "is from Buckingham Palace." She opens it before she turns it around so Avery can see and so can I.

In the middle of the box, a fucking tiara sits on a white satin pillow. My mouth hangs open as I look down at a diamond fucking tiara. "Is that?" I don't even know what I'm asking because nothing else comes out. The tiara has diamonds all around it as it works in a pattern, and even little diamond flower shapes are scattered around it.

"Yup," is the only thing Stefano says, nodding his head.

"Oh my," is the only thing I can say when she takes it out and places it on Avery's head. The diamonds shine in the sunlight, and in the middle of the peak of the tiara is a diamond hanging and swinging side to side while Avery looks at me.

"Momma." She gasps, trying to whisper but failing miserably. "I'm a real princess." She points at her head. "Look at my tiara."

I look at her and again the only thing I can say is, "Oh my."

"Can I wear it to school?" she asks me, and I look at Vivienne, who looks at Avery as if she hangs the moon and the stars. She takes her in as she blinks away the tears in her eyes. It's a look I wish my own mother had for my child, but somehow this might be even better.

"I think it should be worn on special occasions." *And by that,* I say in my head, *I mean never out of the house.* I can't even begin to think of how much that cost them. A tiara from Buckingham Palace, my head feels like it will explode.

"Is today a special day?" she asks me, then looks over at Stefano when he answers.

"Yes, today is a very special day." He squats down beside her. "This is my mom and dad," he explains, looking at his parents at the same time Avery looks at them. "That is my dad, Markos, and this is my mom, Vivienne." He smiles at Avery. "You get to meet your grandma and grandpa."

"Umm, excuse me," Vivienne says, holding up her hand. "I will not be a grandmother." My stomach sinks so fast, but only until a smile fills her face. "I'll be Glammy like a glamorous grandmother," she says to Avery. "If you want, you can call me Glammy Vivienne or just Vivienne. It's as you wish, ma puce." She then turns to look at Markos.

"And he can be GILF."

My eyes go huge and I think I'm going to choke on my saliva. "Oh my God." It's as if there are no words in my vocabulary except for those three.

"What is a GILF?" Avery asks me, and I don't even know what to say.

"We are not calling him GILF," Stefano scolds between clenched teeth, then looks at Avery. "It's a French word," he says to her and then looks at me, asking for help, but sadly I'm of no help right now. All I can do is look at the tiara that sparkles in the sun.

Vivienne gets up and walks over to Markos, putting her hand on his chest and looking up at him. You can see the love in her eyes. "I'll call you GILF," she whispers to him before she leans in and kisses his lips.

"Can we not right now?" Stefano hisses as he gets up and puts his hands on his hips.

"Shall we go inside, then?" Markos suggests to us.

"Yes, let's do that," Stefano says.

"Avery." Vivienne holds out her hand to Avery, who goes to her without question and slips her hand in Vivienne's. "Do you want to go shopping with me? We can go and buy princess dresses to match the tiara."

"My dad bought me plastic princess shoes," Avery shares, "and dresses."

Vivienne laughs at her and then silently glares at Stefano. "Isn't that nice?" she says sarcastically. "But how about we get you some sparkly shoes to match the tiara?"

I watch them walk into the restaurant but don't follow. Instead, I stand here with my eyes closed. "Are you okay?" Stefano asks me, and my eyes open to look at him.

"I should be," I mumble to him, "but I am not. I am one thousand percent not okay." I shake my head. "She bought her a tiara." I put my hand on my head to stop it from exploding. "That might be the most expensive thing in my house."

He puts his hands in his pockets, and I see him bite down, the vein in his head looks like it will pop just a bit. "We need to talk about that also," he says, his tone is tight. I tilt my head to the side, waiting for him to say something else. "I found a house and would like you and Avery to come and look at it with me."

This is too much. I thought yesterday was too much. I was wrong. I was so, so wrong.

"You bought a house?" I don't know if I'm asking him or if I'm telling myself this.

"I did." He nods at me.

"It's been two days." My hand falls from my head to my side. In two days, he's learned he's become a father. Bought princess clothes for our daughter, informed his parents—who flew in right away, so their airline tickets must have been super expensive—and now he's bought a house. It takes me more than one day to decide on a pair of shoes, and this man has bought a house in two.

"When you know, you know." He takes a step toward me. His hand comes out of his pocket and he slips it in mine. The heat of his hand runs through my veins, all the way to my stomach.

I'm in shock or I would have moved my hand out of the way. Imagine if his girlfriend saw us standing in the middle of the street holding hands. "Let's go sit down before my mother does or says something that we will have to awkwardly explain to Avery after."

I don't say anything because he pulls me slowly with him into the restaurant. I walk in, my hand is still in his, and the first people I see are Sofia and Matty, standing next to the table filled with people. My eyes go to Avery, sitting in the middle of the table talking to everyone, the tiara still on her head as if it was made for her.

I take a few steps into the restaurant, and Sofia notices me. She comes over to us, her eyes going from me to my hand still in Stefano's and then to Stefano. "I'll save you a seat," he says before Sofia gets close enough, his hand slips out of mine, and a cold draft runs through my fingers.

I watch him pass Sofia as she glares and then looks at me. I don't know why, but I could cheer out loud that she is here. My body sighs in relief when she stands in front of me. "You didn't think I'd let you go into the lion's den without backup, did you?" She laughs at me. "Also, you look like you are going to pass out," she says with a smile, but I can see the panic in her eyes as she looks around, probably for a chair for me to collapse into.

"Ummmm," I say, my tongue feeling like it's swelling in my mouth.

"Momma," Avery calls my name, and I look toward her. She is in Markos's arms as he holds her. The look on his face is utter and complete love. I know she will be able to do anything with him and he will let her. "Look, this is how you wave as a princess," she tells me as she holds up her hand and slowly waves side to side.

"Is that a diamond tiara?" Sofia leans in and asks me in a

whisper.

I nod my head. "It is." I look at her. "It's from Buckingham Palace," I say, my mouth going a million miles a minute. "Came in a blue embossed bag with matching box, sitting on a white satin pillow." I blink now, and if this was anyone else, I think I would be doubled over laughing hysterically. "From Buckingham Palace, how does one even get that?"

Sofia rolls her lips. "Is this a Code Purple?" She looks around.

I hear the hollering, laughter, and claps when I look over at the table and see Avery standing on her chair, looking over at everyone in the restaurant as she practices the wave. "What is higher than Code Purple?"

Eighteen

Stefano

"Okay, when are you going to FaceTime me?" my father asks me, or more like, it sounds like he's a child. "I didn't talk to her last night because your mother hogged the phone call."

"I'm getting to the house now. How about you call me back in ten minutes?" I say to him, and he just smiles and hangs up.

I shake my head getting out of the car and walking toward her building's front door. It's been a week since I found out I was a father and in that week my life has done a one-eighty. I lived out of a suitcase, more or less, now I have a house with clothes hanging in the closet. I have furniture delivered daily, thanks to my mother and my aunts. I just finished Avery's room and tomorrow I'm going to invite them over to see it.

I pull open the door and start walking up the steps to her apartment. Every single night I show up for dinner and the three of us eat as if we've always done it. I even went out to buy a car seat so I can go and get her from school. I haven't actually gone, but I'm working up to it. Today I get to take her to the fair and she is so excited.

I knock on the door and hear the sound of feet approaching it. I squat down to see her when she opens the door. Her eyes light up when she sees me. "It's my dad!" she shouts over her shoulder.

"Hello," I greet her, opening my arms for her, and she literally launches herself into them. I kiss her neck as she hugs me, and the phone rings in my back pocket. "That's for you," I say, pulling the phone out of my pocket and seeing my father's name trying to FaceTime me.

"I said ten minutes," I scold when his face comes onto the screen and he scowls at me, "it's been two."

"Where is she?" he asks me, and I turn the phone so she can see him. "There she is, my princess."

"Hi." She waves her hand, then stops and waves it like they taught her at our dinner. It was crazy and out of control, but it was one of the best nights ever. When my uncles introduced themselves, she turned to me and said, "This is my dad." I don't know what else was said, because all I could do was stare at her in awe. The dinner went on way too long, and I felt really guilty when Addison missed her class. I made it up to her last night when I let her do her homework while I took Avery out after dinner to get ice cream.

"I'm going to the fair," she tells my father, taking the phone and walking into the house with it. Another thing, my parents talk to her every single day. Without fail they call and FaceTime her.

"Who is she on the phone with?" Addison asks when she steps out of her bedroom wearing light-blue jean shorts and a white cropped tank top, and my cock drains all the blood from my head. Her long hair is loose and over one shoulder. "Um, hello?" she says, looking at me, and all I can do is gawk at her.

"What... sorry?" I ask her, trying to clear my brain. "What did you ask?"

"Who is she on the phone with?" She points at Avery.

"I'm on the phone with GILF," Avery states, then shakes her head. "Grand-père," she says the two words that are supposed to be grandfather in French.

"What did I say about using that word?" I hear Addison and close my eyes. "Also, can I have a word with you?" She looks at me, and I feel like I'm in trouble as she turns and heads into Avery's room.

I follow her, and the whole time, my eyes are on her ass that goes side to side, with the bottom of her hair swaying. "I got this today." She points at the bed, at the massive box sitting on it. "What is this, you ask?" Addison doesn't even wait for me to answer. "It's a care package from your parents." I'm about to gush when she holds up her hand. "She got an iPhone and an iPad." She picks up the two items. "And then she got earrings that I'm going to pretend are not diamonds, but I know better. They sent this by courier. Who sends diamond earrings by courier?"

"Um," I start to say, "I'm sure they had a tracking number."

"Stefano," she snarls between clenched teeth, "she's four and has an iPhone."

"I don't know what to say." I put my hands on my hips. "What's the going age for a phone these days?"

"Momma," Avery calls, coming into the room, "Glammy needs to talk to you."

"Ask her," I whisper to Addison, who glares at me, and fuck, do I want to throw her down and kiss the fuck out of her.

"Hi," she greets, taking the phone. "We got your box. It's too much."

"Oh, nonsense," my mother says. "We sent her the iPad and phone so we can FaceTime her or she can FaceTime us." I shake my head and put my hands up because I don't know what to say. My mother talks to Addison for a couple more minutes before she hangs up and we head out to go to the fair.

The drive there takes less time than it does to find parking. I go around and around in circles on the gravel, trying to get a spot. It's jam-packed, and I finally find one that looks like it's in the middle of trees. I get Avery out of the car and then hold her hand as we walk through the parking lot toward the fair.

Avery squeals her delight as we get closer and closer to the noise, where tickets are being sold at a white hut. "What do you usually get?" I ask Addison, who is fishing into her back pocket for her money.

"I get tickets," Avery says, "but only for rides."

I don't even know what she means, so when I get to the counter, I look at the girl, who asks me if I want tickets or a bracelet. I look over at Addison, who is looking at Avery and telling her something. "What's the difference?"

"Bracelet gets you on all the rides unlimited times, and the tickets are—" she explains to me.

I don't even let her finish. "I'll take three bracelets," I tell her and hand her my black credit card. She rings it up and then hands me my card with a paper to sign.

"There is an ATM beside the games that don't take cards," she tells me as she hands me the three bracelets.

"Here," I offer, handing the bracelets to Addison, and Avery gasps.

"We got the bracelets," she says and I just look at her. "We never get the bracelets." I look at Addison, who ignores looking at me as she puts the bracelet on Avery.

"Shall we go in?" I say as I put my card back in my pocket. We walk in and turn to the left, where people are all cramped together as they play games to win big stuffed animals. Squealing is going on as I look around at the different games.

"We don't play games because it's too much money," Avery explains to me. My head whips to look over at Addison, and she looks like she wants to crawl into a hole.

"It's just that—" she says, and it clicks. She couldn't afford to do this, which is why she never bought the bracelets.

I swallow down the lump in my throat and ignore the sinking of my heart. "Well, today is a special day, so you tell me what you want to do."

Avery doesn't know what to say. All she does is look at Addison. "Let's go play that game." I point over to the first game I see with people sitting down and shooting water from a gun into a clown's nose.

"Okay," Addison says as she takes a deep inhale and we walk toward the seats.

"Stefano," she says my name and I just shake my head.

"No," I snap, a bit harsher than I want it to be. I walk to Addison and lean down and whisper in her ear. "Let me do this," I say softly when her breath hitches. "Please, for her."

"Okay," Addison relents to me, and I don't tell her that tomorrow we are going to sit down and have the big awkward talk. Now is not the time. Instead, I slide my hand into hers, and our fingers slip into each other's as Avery holds her other hand, pulling her to the game.

"We need two," I state, holding up my hand once we get closer. "Sit," I urge Addison as I point at one of the empty seats, then sit down and put Avery on my lap. "You hold this," I tell her of the silver gun in my hand.

The guy comes over, and I pull a twenty-dollar bill from my

back pocket. "Here." I hand it to him. "I don't know how many times that is, but keep it," I tell him, and he smirks and then looks at Avery.

He doesn't even wait for the rest of the seats to fill up before he starts the game. I put my hands on hers as I point at the nose. "And go!" he shouts to the two of us before other people sit down.

She presses down, and I wait for the water to come out before moving it to the clown's nose. The guy starts to talk, but all I can focus on is the little fucking duck moving up to the top of the bell. I've never wanted to win anything as much as this before in my life. Avery is so focused on the water going into the nose, she doesn't even hear the bell ringing, and when she does, she looks up and sees the red siren on top of us.

"We won!" Avery hollers, jumping up and clapping her hands. The guy comes over and smiles at us.

"We have a winner!" he announces. "You can choose anything from the bottom row." He points at the small animals on the bottom.

"How many for the one on top?" I point at the huge ones hanging.

"Takes about twenty times," he says to me.

"Okay, let's do it again," I tell him. It takes us about thirty times since people come and fuck up my plan, but after about an hour, Avery stands there as the guy hands her the biggest stuffy they have. Her eyes light up so much that I would have paid double the hundred it cost me.

"Momma," she says, "I got a big one."

"I see," Addison murmurs as she wipes the tear away from her eye with a huge smile.

"This is the bestest day ever," Avery chirps to me as she puts her hand in mine and we walk over to the rides. We spend all day and end up eating lunch and dinner there. We even sit on the grass to wait for the fireworks starting at ten. She sits next to me with the big bear as her backrest.

I put her on my shoulders when we get up and head to the car because she's tired and her feet are going to fall off, according to her. She gets into her car seat, and I'm not even in drive by the time she falls asleep. The car ride is quiet as Addison puts her head back on the rest. When I pull up to the house, I look over at her. "You get the bear. I'll get Avery."

She nods at me and we literally drag our feet up to the third floor. I walk in and head straight to her room. Placing her on the bed, I take off her shoes and socks. She doesn't even stir when I put her pj's on her.

"She's out for the count," I say when I walk back out seeing Addison drinking a glass of water by the counter. The only light on in the house is the one beside the couch. "I'll get going." I point at the door, even though I don't want to go.

Addison follows me to the door and I open it right before I turn back and see her. "Thank you," she says, standing by the door as I step outside, "for today." Her hand comes up to hold the handle of the door. "She is never going to forget it."

I turn to face her. "It was my pleasure," I reply softly to her. "It was one of the best days I've had in a long, long time. Actually, every single time I'm with you guys, it's the best time of the day."

She looks down, not sure what to say, and I know I should leave. My head is saying one thing, but my heart is the one in charge here. I take steps toward her to close the distance. She looks up at me. "The only thing that would make this day even more perfect," I say to her, my head bending, "is kissing you." It's the last thing I say because my lips are crushed to hers.

Nineteen

Addison

I don't know if it happens in slow motion or not, but all I see is Stefano in front of me. All I can see is his green eyes, which were light all day, but now in the semi-darkness of my entryway, they are a deep green. The scruff on his face is a bit longer than usual, but all I could do all day long was wonder if it would prick my lips when he kissed me or if it would be soft. I spent the whole day trying not to fall in love with him because how could I not? The way he treats me and our daughter, my heart is no match for him. I know I have no right to him. I know I have to stop the ridiculousness of this and remember he goes home to another woman every night. I know I should put that thought front and center, especially when it's dark and he's close to me, and the smell of him just makes my stupid body forget it all. My hand grips on to the door handle tighter and tighter as his body gets closer and closer to mine. His head lowers to mine and my head screams out *No,* while my body moves in closer to him. I think my breath hitches right before his lips smash onto mine, but I'm not sure.

I'm not sure of anything at this moment. The only thing I'm sure of is this kiss is one million times better than I remembered it was. His hands reach out to grab my face, and I swear my body melts into him as his tongue slides into my mouth. I don't know if I moan into his mouth or if my mouth swallows his moan, either way my whole body awakens for him, just like it did five years ago. He tilts his head to the side to deepen the kiss, our tongues going around and around. I'm lost in this, lost in the kiss. Lost in the fact, even after all these years, his kiss still cuts me off at my knees. Lost in the fact I think I could kiss him for the rest of my life and still get butterflies when he's around. *But he's not yours,* my head screams. My eyes flicker open, right before my hands go to his chest, and my eyes close for one more second before I push him away from me. "That was a mistake," I say, my hand coming up to my mouth as my fingertips touch my lips that can still feel his lips on mine. "That was a big mistake."

All he does is nod his head and leave without saying anything. I don't bother watching him walk down the steps, instead I close the door. The sound of the click echoes throughout my apartment and I'm sure the staircase. I lock the door, another sound that seems louder than it ever was before. My head falls to the door as I close my eyes, and I can still picture his eyes right before he kissed me. It was the same look in his eyes all those years ago. "He's with someone," I tell myself before I push off from the door and go to the bathroom.

I turn the water on in the sink, avoiding looking at myself in the mirror. The guilt of me kissing a man who is with someone isn't a look I want to see. I turn the shower on, stepping in and putting my head back so the water can run down my face. Even when I get out of the shower, I avoid looking at myself as I slip on my shorts and tank top.

I peek in on Avery, who is out for the count. Today has been the most she's ever done at the fair. She must have done that teacup ride ten times in a row, happily showing the girl her bracelet each time. I bend to kiss her forehead. "I love you," I whisper to her, and all she does is turn over on her side.

I tiptoe out of the room toward mine and slide into bed. My lips still tingle from the kiss. "Asshole," I hiss when I lie down and think about the kiss I shouldn't be thinking about. "He just kisses me," I blurt out. "You let it happen also." I'm about to argue back to myself when the beep from my phone makes me turn to look at the side table where it came from.

I just stare at it as another beep comes in, this time I reach out and grab the phone, seeing it's a text from Stefano.

Stefano: *Are you up?*

I don't know why I answer him. I should just put the phone down and ignore it.

Me: *No.*

I'm about to turn on the *do not disturb* when the phone rings in my hand. Seeing his name pop up just gets me angrier that he's put us both in the situation. Maybe he's used to doing things behind his girlfriend's back, but I'm not going to enable him. I press the green button. "Hello," I answer, waiting for him to say something.

"Hi," he says, letting out a huge deep breath, making my stomach get all these damn flutters. Why is him breathing out such a turn-on?

"Listen." My voice comes out a little higher than I want it to, and you can definitely hear the pissed-off tone. "I am all for you being a dad to Avery, but that is where it ends with us."

I wait for him to say something to apologize for putting both of us in this awkward place, but instead, he shocks me with his question. "Go on a date with me?"

The shock quickly leaves and it's replaced with rage, and I sit up in bed. "Excuse me?" I ask him because what if I think he asked me out but instead he asked me to take Avery out?

"Go on a date with me?" he repeats the same question, but this time I know I heard right.

"Are you insane?" I snap out. "I am not going to date a man who is dating someone else. This isn't *Sister Wives*." I shake my head. "The audacity."

"Addison," he says my name softly, "I'm not dating anyone." His words stop me from cursing him out.

"What?" I ask, shocked by this news. "When?" I toss the covers off me and get out of bed. The nerves are running through me so fast that sitting down is going to drive me crazy, so instead I just pace my small bedroom.

"When we first met to talk about Avery." His voice is soft and all I can do is sit on the bed.

"Why didn't you say anything?" I close my eyes, wishing I knew this before he kissed me so I could have—I don't know—made it last longer. Maybe jump his bones at my front door. Maybe climb him like a monkey and never let him go.

"You never asked," he replies, and I take the phone away from my ear and put it on speakerphone.

"What was I supposed to ask you exactly?" I chuckle nervously. "Oh, hey there, did you tell the blonde who chased you around all night at the wedding that you're a dad?" I wish I had an off switch when it came to my mouth and being nervous.

"I don't know," he huffs "maybe because you care," and all I can do is gawk at the phone.

"You made me think I was the other woman," I hiss at him.

"Do you know how bad I felt?"

"I'm sorry, I never meant for you to feel that." His voice is so soft and sounds so sincere, I have to close my eyes before I do something stupid like ask him to come over. "Go out with me on a date. I want to date you, Addison. Like a real date. Like a woman and a man go out together, even though they already have a child."

"No." I shake my head.

"Okay, fine," he sighs. "I would like to have you and Avery over for lunch tomorrow." I'm about to say no to that also, but then his voice catches me off guard. "I want to show you and Avery the house."

"Fine," I finally give in. "But just a visit."

"Fine," he relents, "for now." I can't help the smile that fills my face, and I'm happy he can't see it. "I'll text you the address. Come over as soon as you guys wake up and we can make breakfast together." I just nod my head. "I'll see you tomorrow, bright and early," he says, his voice sounding like he's smiling. "What time does she usually get up?"

"Depends. It could be six a.m., or it could be nine. It's Russian roulette on the weekend," I tell him. "I'll text you when she wakes up."

"Sounds good," he says and I'm about to hang up. "Sweet dreams." His voice dips right before he hangs up.

I stare down at the phone, my head once again spinning because of him. "He broke up with his girlfriend," I tell my dark room as I put the phone down on the side table. Getting back into bed, I quickly fall asleep. When I feel little fingers on my face, my eyes flicker open, but then I jump when Avery just stares at me, scaring the shit out of me.

"Morning, Mom," she says, as if I didn't almost have a heart attack. "I'm hungry."

"What time is it?" I mumble as I turn over and grab my phone, seeing it's seven thirty. I also see Stefano has already texted me.

Stefano: I'm up.

I check the time stamp and see it was at 7:00 a.m. I wonder if he set the alarm or just woke up. I see another one from six minutes ago.

Stefano: I forgot to give you my address.

I stretch out and then reply to him.

Me: Just got up, give us thirty.

Stefano: I'll be here waiting for you guys.

I look over at Avery. "Let's get dressed and go for breakfast," I tell her and her eyes open big. She jumps out of bed and rushes to her room to get dressed and then comes to find me in the bathroom while I brush my teeth.

I toss on a pair of beige linen shorts and a white spaghetti-strap top. I'm lucky that before my parents cut me off I was always shopping and buying clothes. Sure, the clothes are somewhat outdated, but some pieces are still good. Avery opts for a princess shirt with matching shorts that Vivienne sent to her last week. I draw the line when she walks out with her tiara on her head. "Is today a special day?"

"Not today," I inform her, and she pouts. "But you can wear it all day once we get home." Which seems to satisfy her. We walk out of the house and I punch in the address, and when we turn onto his street, I know all of a sudden, we are in a different tax bracket. I know because I grew up in a similar house, maybe a touch bigger. But definitely in a neighborhood where we knew everyone had money. My eyes almost pop out of my head when the GPS tells me I have reached my destination. I'm about to tap the phone, thinking there is a mistake, but the front door opens and Stefano steps out onto the porch. He's wearing blue shorts with a matching blue shirt. He walks down the steps with no shoes on, coming to my car. "This house is a mansion." I gasp, right before he opens the back door.

"Hi," he says, bending to kiss her neck as he unbuckles her seat belt. "Good morning." He kisses her again. "I just put bacon and sausage in the oven."

"I like pancakes," Avery says to him as she gets out, and he picks her up to carry her. I slowly get out of the car, trying not to freak out at how huge this house is. "Whose house is this?" I hear Avery ask him as he walks up the stairs. "You live in a mansion." He just chuckles at her.

"No, I don't," he denies as he opens the front door and then places her down on her feet before turning to wait for me.

"That's what Momma said." She throws me under the bus, and I gasp.

"I did not." I try to lie, but my daughter is shaking her head.

"She did." She points at me, then turns around. "This is nice."

"If you want, you can go upstairs and see if you can find the room I made for you," he suggests as I step in. A spiral staircase sits in the middle of the house, and I about groan, of course it comes with a spiral staircase. "Be careful," he warns her as she walks up the stairs.

He turns to look at me when she gets to the top and turns to walk toward an open door. "Hi," he repeats to me, closing the distance between us before he wraps an arm around my waist, pulling me even closer to him. My heart starts to speed up. "Thanks for coming." Every single word that I've ever learned is thrown out the window. I have no vocabulary in my body, none. "We have to talk. We do." I don't know if he's asking me or telling me.

"We do?" I say and then I'm interrupted when I hear Avery squealing and then running to the railing.

"There is a princess bed!" she shouts, looking through the

spindles. "It's a big princess bed with a dresser and everything." She looks at Stefano. "Can I play with the toys?"

"You can do what you want. It's yours," he replies, and she squeals right before she runs back into the room.

"Come and have some coffee. We can talk before she comes back downstairs." He drops his arm around my waist and slips his hand into mine. "I'll give you the tour after," he tells me as we walk past what looks like an office, and on the other side, I think, is a dining room, but all there is are hanging lights with no table.

I stop in my tracks when we walk into the kitchen that has a little table off to the side, but there is a huge island in the middle of the room with six stools tucked under. But it's the attached family room that makes my feet stop. It's what I always thought my family room would look like. It's what I've always dreamed my family room would look like. Definitely not like the family room I grew up in, where everything had a place, and you were afraid to touch anything. Where pictures were displayed because of who was in the pictures and not because it was a nice picture. No, this room is where you know it's okay to curl up on the couch. Where you can sit and have a movie night with throw blankets. Where you can lie down and take a little nap.

A huge couch sits in the room that can seat a lot of people, with a big square table in the middle facing a fireplace. A big-screen television is hanging above it. "This is—" I start to say as he lets go of my hand and walks into the kitchen. "This is perfect," I tell him softly before I smell the coffee, turning to watch him put another pod in the coffee maker.

"Where do you want to sit?" he asks me, grabbing the milk from the fridge and pouring a bit in each cup.

"The couch, if it's okay," I say, trying to hide how badly I want to sit down and curl my feet under myself.

He walks toward the couch with both cups of coffee and waits for me to follow him before he hands me a cup and I sit down, but not the way I want. I take a sip while Stefano faces me. "Do you know what I do for work?" he asks.

"I don't." I just look at him, placing the cup of coffee on the big wooden table. I look for coasters in the middle, where a big square tray holds remotes and a notepad, but nothing else.

"I'm a forensic accountant," he says, putting his own cup on the table, so I don't feel as bad.

"What does that mean?" I tilt my head to the side and he leans back onto the couch.

"They hire me to investigate financial inconsistencies, misappropriation of funds, and irregularities with the company, and to investigate fraud and cybercrimes," he tries to explain it to me. "I work for private companies also and, well, the government—but I can't discuss that."

"How?" My curiosity is piqued.

"A computer is not the sacred place people think it is," he says with a smirk. "People use those things without a second thought, thinking that things can be deleted." He folds his hands together as he sits forward. "News flash, they can't." He grabs his cup of coffee and takes another sip. "So I go in and find out what's wrong, and they either change it or people get fired." He shrugs. "But then sometimes the board of directors calls me in and asks me to see if everything is up to par and, well, no one likes when I show up."

"How did you even get a job like that?"

"It started when I was younger." He smiles. "I started hacking into things here and there."

"What does that mean?" I ask him, knowing there is something more to that.

"Well, one year, I think it was Stone, he was failing math, and he asked if I could change his grade. So, I hacked the system and his forty-nine got changed to a seventy-nine." I gasp.

"Did anyone find out?" I ask him.

"Yeah, the teacher did when his parents didn't show up to have a meeting with them." I put my hand to my mouth. "Obviously, I didn't only change his grade, I changed a few, so they chalked it up to a system error."

I shake my head. "That's interesting." I pick up my cup of coffee.

"I guess it is, but I'm not going to lie, I shit the bed when I found out that they called in the authorities to see if anything else was compromised. My thug life was short-lived," he confesses, his voice soft, but then laughs. "I mean, I did hack the internet when my cousin Franny had a sex tape." My mouth hangs open. "And then Uncle Matthew needed some info on someone. What I'm saying is, I need you to be honest with me."

I put the cup of coffee down, finally realizing what he is saying. "Or you'll find out yourself." I swallow down the lump in my throat. There really isn't anything for him to find out that he doesn't already know, except for the fact my credit score is shit and I'm in debt up to my eyeballs, but I'm slowly working my way out of it.

"In not so many words." He makes sure he stares in my eyes when he says the next part, "Or I'll have someone do it from my team so I don't feel guilty."

"Someone from your team?" I ask him and he nods his head.

"Yeah, a couple of guys from the same class as me decided to open a firm and, well, now we are the most sought out firm in the world. There are different divisions in the company. We started with just the three of us, and now we have over one hundred people working for us." He looks down and then looks up again. "I'm sorry for leaving you to do it all by yourself."

My hand flies out to put on his arm, the way his voice cracked rocks me to my core.

"You didn't know."

"But now I do, and it's time to do my share," he declares to me. "You don't live the high life, and I can't even think about the struggle you had without hating myself. So, I need you to be honest with me." He blinks away the big tears. "And tell me about what you owe."

"I've got it under control," I reply, not really sure what else to say. "Now, I do." I avoid looking into his eyes as I hold the cup and look down in it. "But it wasn't always like that."

"I want to know," he nudges, and for the first time I finally let someone in.

"Well, after I made my stance that I was not going to give up the baby or terminate my pregnancy, all financial aid from them stopped. My allowance didn't come one month and I was like *whatever*, but then I got a nice notice from the school that I owed them for the tuition, which was fourteen thousand dollars." I shake my head. "And then, if that wasn't bad enough, when I went to the doctor the month after, I found out my health insurance wasn't going to cover Avery. For the first time in my life, I was literally alone." I see his hands clench into fists. I'm back to feeling the despair like I was that day. I felt like I had nowhere to turn, feeling like the world would swallow me up. Every day I got up and wondered how I would go on, but I fought for everything we have. I worked my ass off, and it's finally coming back to me. "And then she was born premature, so there was six weeks in the NICU." I wipe away the tear. "But I'm on a payment plan," I say, proud of myself. Proud that no matter how my parents told me I would fail, I didn't.

"How much?" he asks the big question.

"It doesn't matter." I finally look up at him. "It's fine now.

We're doing okay."

"How much, Addison?" he repeats, and this time his teeth are clenched.

"It's not much," I try to lie, but then his words play back in my head, *I can find out anything.* "It's a little over three hundred thousand."

Twenty

Stefano

I listen to her as she says how much she owes. I hear the sadness in her tone and I also see she is trying to keep it all together. I can't even fathom how she did it for four years all by herself. All of this happens and all I want to do is throw something against the wall and kick my own ass for not being there. I lean forward off the couch to the notepad in the middle of the coffee table. Picking it up, I spot the check under it I started to write before she even told me the total. I grab it and then look over at her. "I'm giving you this," I tell her and she looks at me confused, "and if you don't take it, I'm going to have it deposited in your account."

I hold out the check for her and all she does is look down at my hand, the top of the check with her name on it, and also for the amount of four hundred thousand dollars. "I can't take that," she squawks, and her eyes go big as she hides her hands behind her back.

"Fine," I say, putting down the check by her coffee cup. "I'll pay all your bills. Either way, you will be getting that money."

"I don't need it," she says to me, and I side-eye her with a glare.

"I don't care," I tell her. "After everything…" I try to calm down my heartbeat and the way I just want to lash out at everyone, me included. Her family, her fucking family is going to pay for what they did to her, for leaving her without anything. Who does that? Who? "Everything you went through, it's never going to be enough."

I fold my hands together but all I want to do is lean in and kiss her again. "Why are you being like this?" she asks, frustrated when she finally realizes she is not going to win. There are things she will win, but it's not this.

"Because it was my job to take care of you two." I look into her eyes, hoping she sees how much her story killed me to listen to. "And I failed." The lump forms in my throat. "Miserably."

Her hand flies out from behind her, landing on my forearm. "You didn't fail anything." Her voice starts out low but then rises by the time she says the rest. "You didn't even know."

"But now I do." I lean in a touch. "I know now, and I promise you that you will never, ever have to worry about that again." I move even closer to her so I can taste her lips on mine. Her tongue comes out to lick her bottom lip, and I want to trace her tongue. My cock goes so hard it hurts. "Never again." I'm about to kiss her when we both hear footsteps coming our way.

Addison jumps back from touching me and nearly flies off the couch. "Are we going to eat?" Avery asks, walking into the living room. "My stomach rumbled."

"Yes," I confirm, getting up, hoping my dick isn't popping

out in my shorts and she points it out. "Let's see if the bacon is ready, and then we can get some pancakes going." I clap my hands as I walk around the couch, as far away from Addison as I can, because getting closer to her will make my cock jump out even more.

"You have a big—" Avery says, and the blood immediately drains from my whole body, thinking she is going to say penis. I don't even know why my head went there but it did. "Kitchen."

I literally let out a sigh of relief. "You think so? Well, then, you should see Glammy and Grand-père's," I inform her as we walk to the island. "It's really big." Her eyes go huge. "I got you a stool," I tell her, walking over to the wooden thing my mother told me to buy her so she could stand next to me safely. Apparently, all my cousins have it, who knew. "Okay, let's make pancakes." I grab the bowl. "Momma." I look up at Addison. "We are going to make breakfast for you."

"I can help." She is about to take a step to us and I hold up my hand and shake my head.

"You will not. You sit down, drink your coffee, and relax."

"Yeah, Momma," Avery repeats, "relax." She then looks at me. "Do you have chocolate chips?" She tries to whisper to me but her voice is nothing like a whisper.

"I do," I whisper back to her. "Should we do chocolate chip pancakes?" I ask her, making her eyes go big, and she smirks at me as she nods her head. Side by side we make breakfast, well, she helps make the pancakes. I do the stove but she does help with setting the table. I can't even put into words how I feel sitting down at the table with them.

After breakfast, we go out into the yard where I show her the tree house my parents bought for her. She runs toward the tree house, her hair flying behind her, yelling that it says her name on it.

Addison and I follow her, the both of us not sure what to say. "This is incredible," Addison finally says, looking at me.

"Not as incredible as her mother," I mumble, but I know she hears me because her cheeks get a touch pink, "or that kiss we had last night."

She's about to say something when Avery comes running out and grabs her hand, pulling her toward the tree house. I stand here as she shows her everything in the house. When the clouds start to roll in, Addison tells her it's time to go. Avery isn't the only one who groans about that. I walk them to their car and Avery pouts the whole time. "Be good and I'll come and see you tomorrow, okay?"

"Okay, but don't go in my house," Avery tells me of her tree house and it makes me laugh.

I close the door to the car, standing in front of Addison. "Thank you for today," she says as she wrings her hands together nervously.

"You're more than welcome." I try to draw it out longer. "You are also more than welcome to stay for dinner and even breakfast." I wink at her and she just shakes her head laughing. "Did you take the check?"

"Stefano," she groans my name and all I can do is smirk at her as I close the distance between us.

"I like hearing you say my name," I tell her, then lean in even more, "but I love hearing you moan it more."

She pushes my chest away as she laughs even harder. "Goodbye," she says, opening the driver's door.

"No kiss?" I question, right before she closes the door and the back window opens.

"I'll kiss you," Avery says to me, and yup, totally done for. My heart explodes in my chest as I stick my head in the window and kiss her cheek and then her neck. "That tickles." She squeezes her neck closed.

"Call me when you get home," I tell her and watch her drive away. I stand here until I can't see her anymore and then go back into my house. Walking inside, I see the check still on the table and shake my head. "Stubborn woman," I mumble before I make my way to the kitchen, put things away, and clean up before grabbing my laptop. I get lost in my work and only when my phone rings do I look up.

I see that it's Avery FaceTiming me. "Hello," I greet once her face fills my phone.

"Hello, Dad," she says. She doesn't really call me Dad or Daddy often, but when she does it warms my soul. "I'm going to bed."

"Going to bed?" I gasp before I turn my head to see it's after seven. "Did you eat dinner?"

"Yes, Momma made grilled cheese," she tells me and I smile. "Momma, Dad is on the phone."

"What phone?" I hear Addison ask from somewhere in her apartment.

"Mine," she states, walking to her mother. I see she is getting dressed, I get a glimpse of her leg and her lace panties before she squeals and grabs the phone from Avery.

Her face fills the phone. "And this is why it's not a good idea for a four-year-old to have a phone," she hisses.

"I mean, she could have called me with your phone." I make the argument, and all she does is glare at me. "Go put our girl to bed and call me back," I tell her and she's about to say something to me. "I like that color of lace," I declare. All that earns me is her teeth grinding together.

"Say good night to your father." She hands the phone to Avery.

"Good night, Father," Avery says, "I love you."

"I love you, too," I say softly and then the phone goes dead. I wait thirty minutes before I call her number.

"Hello," she mumbles and then I press the FaceTime button. "Why are you FaceTiming me?" she asks me but accepts and her face fills the screen.

"What are you doing?" I ask her, seeing she is on the couch.

"Homework," she tells me. "What can I do for you?"

"Two things," I say, holding up one finger. "One, you forgot the check." She rolls her eyes. "And two, will you go out with me?" I just look at her. "Why don't you just think about it?"

I wait for what seems like forever but is just a couple of seconds. "Okay, fine, I'll think about it."

I can't help but smile at her. "Are you free next Saturday?"

She laughs. "I thought you said to think about it?"

"I did." I laugh. "But I have to start planning."

She laughs at me. "What if I say no?"

I smirk at her, my heart speeding up fast, my cock getting hard for her. "What if you say yes? I have to be ready."

She shakes her head, but the smile on her face is beautiful. "Goodbye, Stefano."

I look at her, wishing I could kiss her again. "Good night, li'l momma." I wink at her, and she rolls her eyes before she hangs up.

I immediately call Matty, who answers after two rings. "What do you want?" He doesn't even say hello.

"Can you watch Avery next Friday night?" I tap my leg nervously, not sure what I'm going to do if he says no.

"Sure, why?" My fist secretly flies in the air.

"I want to take Addison out on a date," I tell him.

"Aren't you dating Jenna?" he snaps. "I swear to God, I'm going to kick your ass and then call Uncle Matthew."

I gawk at my phone. "What the hell is wrong with you? Do

you think I would ask her out if I was still dating Jenna?" I don't even wait for him to answer me before I continue, "Idiot. What do you take me for?"

"Didn't you just meet your four-year-old daughter?" he retorts, laughing.

I don't even bother answering him, I hang up on him, and then text Addison.

Me: I got a babysitter for next Friday, is that good?

I don't want to bother her while she's studying, but I can't wait. The phone buzzes in my hand, and I see it's her.

Addison: I didn't say yes yet.

Me: But you didn't say no either. Would it be okay, or do you have to work?

Addison: I don't have to work.

I smile that she still hasn't said no.

Me: Okay, good, so one thing less to worry about

Addison: I've got to study.

Me: Call me later, if you want.

I pull up the text to my father right away.

Me: What should I do for a first date?

The sound of thunder fills the room, and I look up in time to see the lightning follow another couple of booms. The sound of rain hitting the window fills the room, and my leg starts moving up and down when I see the little gray bubble with the three dots come up. It stays like that for more than two minutes before my phone rings. I press the green button, and then my father's face fills the screen. "Hey," he says, smiling at me, and I see my mother is there. "What does she like to do?" my father asks me, and all I can do is shake my head, shrugging.

"I have no idea." I look at both of them. "That is why I'm asking you."

"Well, at least you know she likes you if she had sex with

you," my mother observes, and all I can do is close my eyes. Also, she is not wrong.

"Okay, well, I'm not having sex with her." Yet, I leave out because no one should be talking about sex with their mother. But then again, no one is my mother.

"And why not?" She throws her hands up. "I fell in love with your father because of all the sex we had."

"And the fish," my father chimes in. "She really started to love me when I gifted her Elsa, the fish."

My mother gasps. "I broke up with you because of that fucking thing. Who gives a woman a fish?" She shakes her head.

"You loved that fish," my father says as my phone pings with Avery's name.

I sit up as thunderclaps fill the room, along with the flash of lightning. "I have to go. It's Avery." I don't even wait for my father to say anything.

Her face fills the screen, and I can see she's in a dark room. "Daddy," she whines, her voice soft, and I swear I can see tears streaked on her face. My whole body goes numb and stiff at the same time. I toss my laptop to the side and run to the door before she even says another word. "We have no lights." I run around the fucking house, looking for my fucking keys and finally finding them in my bedroom.

"Where is Mommy?" I ask her and she jumps when thunder claps again.

"She went to check—" she says. "I'm scared." My whole body goes cold. I run out of the house, the wind and rain hitting me, and I have to shield my eyes.

"Hey, look at me," I tell her as I get in my car and pull out of the driveway, the wipers going as fast as they can to clear the rain off my windshield, but it's coming down too hard. The bright white line of lightning flashes in front of me while Avery cries softly. "I'll be right there," I soothe her as I try to go as fast as I can safely. "Look at me, baby girl. I'm going to be right there," I tell her, and then the line goes dead.

"Avery!" I yell her name, and when I call her back, it tells me the person is unavailable. I pull up in front of her house and run out faster than I've ever run. I swing open the door, and the heat hits me right away. "Fuck," I hiss as I take two steps at a time until I get to her door and knock fast and hard. "Addison!" I shout her name, "Avery!"

The sound of the door unlocking somehow makes me feel a touch better. She opens the door, and I pull her to me. "Stefano," she says. "You're soaking wet." She laughs at me, my heart beating even faster. "What are you doing here?"

"Avery called me," I explain, walking in and feeling the heat run through me. "Avery," I say her name, and she comes running to me as I squat down. "Where is your iPad?"

"On the bed, there is a red light in the middle," she tells me. "I was scared."

"She called you?" Addison asks me. "But why?"

"I was scared," Avery repeats softly.

"You ready to go?" I ask Avery and then look over at Addison. "Come home with me?" I don't even know if I'm asking her or telling her.

"We're fine here," she says. "The lights will be back on soon."

"I have the room, and it's getting really hot in here." She can't deny it's an oven in here. The windows are open, and towels are on the floor to soak up whatever water they can. "Come with me."

"Fine," she huffs, "let me grab some things."

I just nod at her as I pick up Avery in my arms, ignoring the fact that I'm wet and now so is she. "Am I going to sleep in the princess bed?" she asks me, and I smile. I don't say anything because I can't. My heart, which would come out of my chest, is now lodged in my throat as she wraps her arms around my neck. I literally can't say anything. I have never been so scared in my life. I had no idea what I would do if I got here and they were not here. I can't even imagine.

Addison walks back out of her bedroom with a small bag in her hand. "Okay," she says as she walks toward the front window and closes it, "shall we go?"

We are all soaking wet when we get in the car and back to my house. "I'll take her and change her and get her into bed," Addison says, but I don't let her out of my arms. I carry her to the bedroom. I turn on the lights and hear the gasp behind me.

"What in the f—" Addison starts, stopping as she looks around the room. The pink, four-poster, canopy queen-size bed sits in the middle of the room. The pink satin bedding shines as the pink tulle hangs from the four posters.

"My mother," is all I can say as I put Avery in the middle of the pink carpet.

"Don't," Addison warns, rushing forward with her arm out, "she's going to get the carpet wet."

I laugh and shake my head. "Doesn't matter," I reply, walking over to the pink dresser with diamond buttons for the drawer handles. "Glammy got you some clothes." I pull open the drawer, and another gasp comes out of Addison. I look back over my shoulder as she spots the corner of the room where there is a white plush rug with different pink pillows against the wall, where a round circle of pink silk drapes down around the pillows. "It's a reading corner."

"A reading nook?" she says, shocked. I peel Avery out of her wet clothes, tossing them to the side where Addison steps to pick them up. I put pink pj's on Avery and get her into bed.

"Night," I say to Avery, kissing her neck, "I'm going to put on a little light." I walk toward the side of the room and turn off the lights, but then the twinkle lights come on as if they're stars in the sky.

"Jesus," Addison says, looking around, "do those lights stay on all night?"

"They're sort of motion censored," I say, and she shakes her head.

"Of course they are," she mumbles as we walk out of the bedroom.

"Where do you want to stay?" I ask her when we are standing in the hallway, and she shrugs. "You can sleep in the guest room." I point at the room on the left. "Or you can stay in my bed." I smirk at her, winking one eye, and I can see her try to hide her smile. She pushes my shoulder, moving to the side to walk away from me. I grab her hand before she walks away from me, turning to pull her to me. I don't think about anything else but kissing her. My lips crash down on hers. She gasps right before my lips touch hers, giving my tongue the access it needs to slide into her mouth. My hand drops hers to wrap around her waist and pull her to me. Her chest crushes on mine as our tongues go around and around in circles. I kiss her now like I wanted to kiss her this morning, our tongues fight with each other but this time she doesn't push me away. Her hands go to my hips, and my cock fights to get out of the wet shorts. I deepen the kiss for a minute before she steps away from me. "Okay, Stefano." She looks at me, her eyes darker than before. Her head pulls back a bit. "I'll go out with you."

Twenty-One

Addison

I watch the clock turn to four before I get up from my desk, smoothing down my skirt. My hands are all clammy with nerves as I walk to the back of the house where I know everyone is in their office. Every single step toward the chattering of voices gets my heart beating faster and faster as it echoes in my ears. My hands nervously shake as I get closer and closer. I know they were supposed to have a little meeting this afternoon about possibly bringing in someone else to help. I stick my head into the conference room, seeing the four of them sitting around the table going through the applicants who have been applying all week long. "I'm headed out," I say, avoiding eye contact with each of them, smiling quickly before hightailing it out of there.

"Okay," Clarabella says, leaning back in her chair looking at me.

"Have a great night," Presley calls, and I can hear her snicker right before she adds in, "On your date."

"You guys know?" I shriek, walking into the room, putting my hands on my hips, and looking at all of them as they all roll their eyes at me. This last week has been me dodging them and their questions. Every single time they walked in the room, I picked up the phone and pretended I was talking to clients. It did help I was also very busy this week seeing new clients. I managed to book four of the five I saw, so deflecting was easy. But I guess I wasn't that good at deflecting.

"How can we not know?" Sofia crosses her hands on the papers in front of her. "I'm babysitting."

"Who said it's a date?" I fold my arms over my chest. "It could be the two of us going out to discuss co-parenting."

"Is it?" Clarabella asks, her eyebrows going up. "How did he phrase it?"

"Well," I start to say, trying to think of a lie, but I'm the worst when it comes to lying. I can't do it to save my life. "He said, let's get together to talk." I avoid looking at everyone as I glance at the ceiling and around.

"Did he?" Shelby asks, and when I look at her, I see her folding her lips. "Is that what he said?"

"Well, more or less," I finally stutter and Clarabella shakes her head.

"So he didn't ask you to go on a date with him?" Presley accuses as she taps her pen on the desk.

"Ugh," I say, throwing up my hands. "Yes, yes, he did."

The four of them clap their hands together to cheer. "So are you going to wear sexy panties, in case?"

Yes! my head screams, but I shake my head from side to side. "In case what?"

"Oh, come on," Clarabella chides, "you have to ask yourself

if it is as good as you thought it was."

"I might have, maybe," I admit to them, "but I just can't sleep with him."

"Why not?" Shelby asks me, her eyebrows pinching together. "You are both single adults."

"Yes, but it's more complicated now." I spit out the words I've been telling myself since last week when he kissed me.

"You sleep over at his house almost every night," Sofia states, shocked. "Are you telling me that you sleep in separate beds?"

I gasp. "How do you know?" The words are a whisper. Ever since my place lost power, we have been spending quite a few nights there. The next night, we somehow still didn't have electricity because a tree fell in the middle of the road and knocked down a pole, so I took his offer up to sleep at his place. Then when the power did come back on, the house was an oven. Even being in it for a couple of minutes, we had sweat pouring down our faces, so again we slept over. I even did my class there last night in the office, and when I finished, Avery was already asleep, so I caved to staying again. But tonight, I am going back to my place.

"We live around the block," Sofia reminds me. "We went out on a date two days ago, got home after one, and your car was in his driveway."

"I didn't have power," I defend quickly, "and he offered."

"What else did he offer?" Clarabella winks at me.

"I'm leaving." I turn around. "I'll see you when I drop off Avery."

"Don't forget to shave!" Clarabella hollers before she laughs.

"And wear panties you are okay being ripped off you," Presley adds, and I turn to look over my shoulder at her. "What? If you have been sleeping at his house all week long and haven't given him anything, that man is walking a fine line and he's about to snap so… Poof." Her two hands come up in fists and then open. "Gone." She is not wrong. The two of us have been playing this game of cat and mouse, and I, for one, am ready to snap. At this point, I don't even know who is the cat and who is the mouse, but something has to give. It's the little touches while we prepare dinner; it's the kisses right before I go to bed. It's the fact I know he's sleeping so close to me. It's him getting up in the morning and coming down without a shirt on, showing me at least one thing has changed since the last time. His abs are so much more defined, which is saying something since he had an eight-pack the last time. It's the way he's with Avery. It's the way that he slides his hand into mine when we walk out the door, even just to go to the backyard. It's the way that he'll sit on the couch and watch mindless television with me just to sit next to me. It's the way he set up his office, so I can study, and keeps Avery busy. It's everything that he's done since he found out about her.

"Have a great weekend," I mumble to them as I make my way over to my purse, grabbing it and leaving work.

"Be safe!" I hear Presley shout.

"Yeah, yeah," I mutter as I make my way over to my car. I pick up Avery from daycare, who is going on and on about going to Sofia's house. I should be happy that she is the friendliest kid I've ever met. She is so social and never once is shy about anything.

My phone rings the minute I walk into the house, and I look down and see it's Stefano. "Hello," I answer, my stomach feeling like I'm going to throw up from all the nerves.

"Hey." His voice sends shivers up my body. "What time will you be over to drop off Avery?"

"Where are we going?" I ask him, and he just laughs.

"I told you it was a surprise." He laughs again.

"Okay. What should I wear?" I ask him and his laughter stops.

"If I tell you nothing, what will you do?" His voice comes out so low that if he was in front of me, he would see my cheeks get all pink.

"I'll be at Sofia's at six," I tell him, not answering his question. "Bye." I hang up the phone and go over to my bedroom, opening up the closet.

"What screams I want to have sex with you, but I don't want you to know I want to have sex with you?" I ask the hangers in front of me. I move one hanger at a time, contemplating what I'm working with. The only thing I have that is even remotely sexy is the light-green skirt I bought through one of those Instagram ads one night. I grab a white, silky, sleeveless, tank bodysuit that goes very low in the back.

I take a shower, making sure everything is cleaned up. I can hear them laughing in my head. "If I get into an accident and they have to cut off my clothes, do they want to see that? No." I try to avoid looking at myself in the mirror because deep down inside, I know the reason I did that was just in case. I let my hair loose, using my hands to shake out the curls, and opt to just add some mascara to my lashes.

I slip on the tank body suit, clipping the two snaps together before I slide on the skirt. It is tight on my hips and goes down to my midcalf in the back, but the front is cut up to the middle of my thigh. My whole right leg is out, and when I walk, the other leg comes out, too.

"You're pretty, Mommy," Avery says when she comes into the bedroom.

"Thank you." I smile at her before slipping into see-through, low chunky heels.

At five thirty, I grab Avery's bag and my clutch purse I planned for tonight as we make it down to the car. I try not to second-guess every single thing as I drive over to Sofia's.

I pull into the driveway and see Stefano is already there. I open the back door, and Avery jumps out as I grab her bag. She runs in ahead of me to the front door, ringing the bell and then looking over her shoulder at me.

The front door is pulled open by Sofia, who smiles down at Avery, and then looks at me and her mouth hangs open as her eyes go big. "She came to play." She puts her hands over her head and claps them.

"I want to play!" Avery yells, jumping up and down.

"Uncle Matty got you a present," Sofia says as Avery runs into the house as if she's here all the time.

"Well, well, well." Sofia folds her arms over her chest. "Damn, girl, you."

"Oh my God." I hear from behind her and see Matty putting his fist in front of his mouth, hiding the smile. "He's going to lose his mind. I hope the Ring cam catches it."

I don't have a chance to ask him what he means because Avery comes running back. "Momma, they bought me a tea set," she says, "to have tea." She grabs her bag. "It's a good thing I brought the tiara." She unzips the top of her bag and takes out the tiara gently and puts it on her head. "I knew it was going to be a special day." She turns to Sofia and asks her, "Can we do the tea party now?" Sofia just nods her head.

I look from them over to Stefano, who is just looking at me, his eyes moving up and down as he takes me in. If I thought my nerves were shot before, that look just pushes me out into orbit. It also makes other parts of me really happy that I shaved. "Daddy," Avery says, walking to him, "I'm having a tea party." She started calling him just Daddy two days ago. At the beginning she would call him Dad Stefano, but then one day, she was just like Daddy.

He takes his eyes off me and squats down in front of her.

"That's fun. Tomorrow, how about we have one at the house? I'll come and get you after breakfast."

"Okay," she agrees with him before she turns to Matty. "I can't have too hot water. I'm going to burn my skin off," she informs Matty, who just nods at her.

"Okay, get out of here," Sofia tells Stefano, who walks outside and I take him in. He walks down the steps wearing blue dress shorts and a light-blue button-down linen shirt, with the top two buttons open at the top.

"Hi," he says softly when he stands in front of me. All I can see is him and all I can smell is his scent, and it makes my mouth water at the same time certain parts of my anatomy want to feel his touch. "Where are your keys?" he asks me, his teeth clenched together. My hand comes up and shakes a bit when I open it. He grabs the keys from my hand and turns to toss them to Matty. "See you guys tomorrow." He then slips his hand into mine before turning and rushing us both back to his car.

"Call me if you need anything," I instruct over my shoulder at Sofia as my feet try to keep up with Stefano, but the door slams in my face. "That was rude." I look over at him but don't take my hand out of his.

"No," he says, stopping by the passenger door of his car, right in front of me, boxing me in. He puts his hands beside my head, stepping in closer to me. "What would be rude is me pushing you against this car and finding out what you are wearing under that dress." His voice is low as he presses into me a bit. "That would be rude."

"Yes." I try hard not to show him how much he affects me, but my voice comes out breathlessly. "That would be rude." My eyes stare into his, and I can see his head coming closer and closer to mine. "There are cameras," I finally say, "all around the house."

"Oh, I know," he assures me, "trust me, I know." He opens the door for me. "Besides, when we do this, it's not going to be a five-minute thing."

I look at him. "I certainly hope not," I mumble as I get in the car, jumping when he closes the door. "I should have taken my vibrator out," I tell myself while I watch him walk around the car. My nipples literally perk up, and I have to close my eyes and think of anything that will stop me from asking him to take me home and have his way with me.

"Are you okay?" I hear him ask me and my eyes fly open. I was so busy trying not to react to him that I didn't hear the car door slam.

"What?" I ask, blinking my eyes rapidly as my chest heaves, and my heart beats what feels like a million times an hour. I don't know anything right now. You could ask me what my name was and I don't think I could even answer that. My head is spinning, this week has been pushing and pulling me in every single direction. It's all too much, and what little thread I have been hanging on to is starting to fray.

"Are you okay?" he asks me again, one of his arms resting on the car door as his hand is on the steering wheel, while the other hand is on his leg, but I really wish it was on mine. I could picture him reaching over and putting it on my leg. His fingertips roaming up my bare leg until it's underneath it. "Addison." I hear my name, and I snap out of my daydream.

My face feels like it's been lit on fire. "Yeah," I answer, avoiding looking at him. My mouth is so dry I'm having a hard time swallowing. "Yeah, I'm fine." I turn to put my seat belt on before I hold on to the door handle so tight my knuckles are white. I look out of the window, seeing the trees pass by. We get to the corner of the street and he stops. "Nothing." The word comes out of my mouth and all I can do is go with it.

"What?" he asks me and I turn to look at him. Just like that night, all those years ago, we are back at the same spot more or less. He took the first step that night, asking me to come to his room. I didn't know then what I do now, but even then, I knew I wanted to spend the night with him. But now that I've already had him, all I want is to see if my memory is anything like the real thing.

"The question you asked me before," I explain, my heart beating so hard in my chest, I'm surprised he doesn't hear it himself. "You asked me what I was wearing underneath this dress." His eyes go the darkest green I have ever seen. "The answer is nothing."

"Addison," he growls, and I can see his Adam's apple go up and down as he swallows. "Be very clear right now." We look at each other, our eyes having a secret conversation. His eyes ask me if I want him to take me home. My eyes say there is nowhere else I want to go. He just nods his head and turns in the direction of his house.

His car picks up speed. "Okay, I might have lied a little bit," I backtrack as we get closer and closer to his house. I shake out my hands nervously. "I'm wearing a bodysuit, so it's like clipped." I point at my vagina. "But unclipped, there is nothing there."

"I'm going to need you to stop talking right now," he states, his jaw tight, and his teeth clenched together. "The last thing I need is to pull over and fuck you in this car."

My mouth opens in shock and then closes and then opens again, nothing coming out. He puts the car in park and I see we are in his driveway. "Now, this is your last chance," he says, looking at me. Fuck, the way his lips fall, the way his hair is pushed back, the way I want to taste him, it's the most overwhelming feeling I've ever had.

My hand comes up to touch the door handle, this time pulling it open. "Is the front door open?" I ask him and don't even wait for him to answer me. I just open the door and step out. My knees feel like they are knocking together. The butterflies in my stomach are at an all-time high, and the only thing I'm wishing for is not to throw up all over his porch.

I reach for the handle of the door right before I feel his hands on my hips, pulling my ass into him. He bends his head, and I can feel his breath on my neck. "Do you know how long I've wanted to do this?" he whispers close to my ear, and my body shivers.

"Do what?" I whisper, holding my breath as I wait for him to answer.

I close my eyes, waiting for the touch to come. I close my eyes, willing it to come, but instead, he says, "It's better if I show you." He puts his hand on mine, opening the door.

Twenty-Two

Stefano

I push open the front door. "After you," I say. I don't know why but it feels like an eternity before she takes that first step into the house.

She puts her hand on mine that holds her hip, intertwining our fingers. It feels like someone just sent electric shocks through me. My body is one big, tight nerve. It's been one big, tight nerve this whole fucking week. I'm so out of my comfort zone, it's not funny. At this point I've been winging it, hoping she wants what I want. She takes a step into the house, her hand never leaving mine. "Upstairs or downstairs?" She looks over her shoulder.

"I just want to put it on the record that I did have plans to wine and dine you tonight," I clarify, kicking the door shut with my foot.

She turns to face me, her hand slipping out of mine but she doesn't step away from me, instead she takes a step, closing the distance. "Are you saying that you wouldn't have tried to sleep with me tonight?" She looks up at me, the twinkle in her eye.

I shake my head. "Do you know the hell I've been through this week?" I ask her, my hand coming up to push her hair behind her shoulder. "Having you close but not close enough." I lean down and rub my nose along her neck. "Giving you the space you needed but wanting to be in your space." I kiss her right where I can feel her heart beating just as fast as mine. "I've been trying really fucking hard not to scare you away." I trail kisses back up to her jaw. "Every single night I wanted to come into your room and slide into bed with you." She shivers under my touch and I fucking love it. I love that I have this effect on her, it's the same effect she has on me. "I want you in my bed," I spell out to her, "tonight, tomorrow." I kiss her lips softly. "Every fucking night." Being next to her and not being able to act and do the things I've wanted to do has to be the hardest thing I've ever done in my life. I tried to be subtle about it, sit next to her, touch her when we are standing side by side. Watch the ridiculous shows she watches just so I can hold her hand. My favorite thing to do lately is just sit with her and look out at Avery. Except it would be with her in my lap or sitting in front of me while I kiss her neck.

"Well then, you should have just come to my room." She puts her hands on her hips. "Because I was waiting for you to make the first move." She leans her head back and nibbles my jaw, my cock straining so bad to get into her. "It's a good thing I didn't have my vibrator here, or else you would have heard the buzzing."

"Addison," I hiss out her name.

"Stefano," she moans out mine, and all I do is close my eyes and count to ten. I have to count to ten or else she would be over my shoulder as I carry her to my bedroom. I get to four before she says, "Touch me."

Yup, it is at that moment I snap. My eyes flicker open and all I can see is her. Instead of throwing her over my shoulder, I wrap one arm around her waist and pick her up. Her legs wrap around my waist, her arms around my neck, and then her mouth is on mine. Our tongues attack each other's as I move toward the stairs. Our heads move side to side as we try to deepen the kiss. Once we get into my room, I stop right in front of the couch that faces the bed. She lets go of the kiss and looks around. "Finally made it into the bedroom." She smirks at me as she slips her legs off my hips. She stands in front of me, tossing one shoe to the side followed with the other one. "It's a lot different than I thought it was going to be."

She looks around and I chuckle. "How so?" I try to focus on the conversation but all I can do is watch her. She has a hold on me I don't even think she knows about.

"I was expecting leopard." She laughs at her own joke. "Black satin sheets, for sure." Her hands go to the side of her skirt and the sound of the zipper fills the room, and every comeback I had is out the window. I don't even know my own name at this point, all I can do is watch her hand. "Maybe even leather walls." She keeps talking but my eyes never leave her hips as the skirt falls to her feet. "Also, I may look different," she says, standing in front of me wearing just her white body suit. It looks more like a swimsuit. "I have stretch marks."

"You are even more gorgeous than you were back then," I cut her off, "and you were the top of the pyramid back then. My mouth waters when I look at you." I can't stop my mouth.

"My hips are fuller." She moves her hand up her hip and I can't help but lick my lips. "My breasts are also a bit fuller but also not as perky." She looks down and her voice trails off.

"Shut up," I snap. "Don't say even one word negative about you or your body," I say, my teeth clenched together, and her eyes snap back to me. "Your body brings me to my knees. I want to spend all night worshipping you and your body." I don't add in that I'm going to spend the rest of my life worshipping her because I don't want to push her too fast, but there is no way I'm letting her go after finally finding her after all this time. "Show me."

"I'm already half naked," she says to me.

I immediately kick off my shoes to the side to join hers. My hands go to the third button of my shirt and then the fourth, before I just pull it off me. "I've already seen that." She folds her arms over her chest, cocking her hip. My hands go to the button on my shorts and then the zipper. I pull the shorts off, leaving me in just my boxers, my cock outlined, showing her how hard it is.

"Is this better?" I ask.

"Yes," she whispers out and then slides a hand between her legs and I hear the sound of snapping, and then in one fluid movement the white bodysuit is over her head. My hand goes to my mouth as I take her in.

"You're fucking exquisite!" I exclaim to her and she looks down shyly. I walk over to the bed, getting on it in the middle as her eyes watch me. "Are you coming?" I hold out my hand to her and she walks over to the bed, putting one knee on, then the other, and she crawls over to me. "You are beautiful," I tell her as she bends over and slides her tongue into my mouth. One of her hands slides under my head while my hand comes up and rubs the back of her leg, all the way to her ass. She lets go of the kiss before she throws her leg over me, putting her hands on my chest, sitting right on my covered cock. I groan as the heat from her pussy seeps through my boxers. "That's not playing fair," I groan between clenched teeth. My hands come up to cup her tits as she moves her hips back and forth on my cock, my fingers pinching both her nipples at the same time. She bites her lower lip as she moans, right before she falls forward and kisses me. Her hands come to hold my face as she slides her tongue into my mouth.

"I want to do something." Her words come out breathlessly as she moves down, kissing my chest, her hair tickling me as she trails her tongue down the middle of my chest. "For the life of me," she says, stopping right on top of the band of my boxers, "I can't remember sucking your cock." All I can do is watch her as she peels the boxers down over my cock as it springs loose. I lift my hips as she peels them off me, tossing them to the side. My head comes off the mattress as I watch her. "Yeah, I don't remember this at all," she says, gripping the base of my cock and then her tongue comes out. She licks from my balls all the way up my shaft, and I can't help the way my head falls back as her mouth covers my cock. "Definitely would have remembered having you in my mouth," she declares. I watch her as she swallows me from the tip to the middle of my cock, her fist working with her mouth. Each time she tries to take me deeper and deeper.

"Fuck," I hiss when she sucks and twirls her tongue around the head of my cock. Her fist going faster and faster, I can feel my balls getting tight. "I'm going to—" I don't even finish because she takes me into her mouth again, sucking me into the back of her throat.

"Good." She smirks, taking the head into her mouth, her fist never stopping. "Means I'm doing it right."

I can't even answer her because I'm coming in her mouth, and the only thing I can say is her name. "Addison." She swallows every single last drop, smiling when my cock falls out of her mouth.

"Yes," she says, getting up on her knees almost as if she's standing proud, and she should be.

"That was—" I start to say but my head is slower than my hands because I'm already flipping her onto her back. "My turn," I say as she sits in the middle of the bed, her arms back on the mattress, legs propped up and spread.

"Now, I definitely remember you doing this," she confirms, her voice quivering when I kiss her inner left thigh.

"Are you sure you really remember?" I ask her, right before I lick through her slit, all the way up to her clit. "I know I remember this for sure." I suck her clit into my mouth, and she tries to squeeze my head, making me laugh. "Do you remember this?" I ask her as I slide two fingers into her as I nip at her clit. This time her head goes back, her hips lift off the bed. "Someone wants more?" I tease her as I eat her pussy with everything I've got. I lick, suck, and bite all the while finger-fucking her. The sound of her moaning fills the room and I know she's about to come because I can feel my fingers being squeezed tighter and tighter. "Want to come on my finger"—I flick her clit—"or my tongue?"

"Both," she says, and I smirk at her.

"Rub your clit, then," I instruct her. She moves one of her hands to replace my tongue as I slide my tongue into her, with my fingers making her even wetter. "You taste like heaven," I say, and she thrusts her hips up, getting my fingers in all the way to my knuckles.

"Stefano," she breathes my name, her hand leaving her clit as she runs it through my hair. "Remember that time—" she says but stops when I rub her G-spot.

"What time, baby?" I tease her, my fingers slowing down.

"The time in the bathroom." I listen to her and I know exactly what she's talking about. It was a memory I used over and over during the years. "When I was coming and then you rammed your cock into me."

"Yes," I tell her, my fingers picking up speed.

"I want that, please," she begs me, and I swear I would give her whatever she wants. "Fuck me like that again."

"Okay," I agree, "but after, I get to fuck you how I want."

"Deal." She moves her hand to her clit, moving it side to side ferociously, my fingers picking up the speed. "I'm almost there."

"I know," I say, my tongue sliding in there with my finger and I feel the spasm around my finger and my tongue.

"Stefano," she cries as she spasms once, twice, and then I pull my fingers out of her and quickly ram my cock into her. I slide it into the tightness and I have to stop as soon as I'm balls deep. Both of our moans fill the room. "Fuck me," she groans, falling to her back, her legs wrapping around my waist. "I remember you fucking me harder."

I get up on my knees, her legs dropping to the sides. I pick one up and place it over my shoulder as I hammer away into her. My hips thrust into her as my thumb works her clit, her pussy squeezing me so hard as she comes or continues coming from before. I press her ankle that is next to my lips in a kiss as I slow down the pace of my fucking, but my thumb works her clit, faster and faster. Right when I know she's going to come again, my hands move to the sides of her as I thrust into her harder and harder. My balls slap her ass, her hands holding my forearms as I take her over the cliff again. She soaks me as she spasms over my cock again and again. I slow down my speed until she's done. "One more?" I ask her, or maybe I'm telling. This time I fall onto her a bit but then move her legs over my forearms, opening her up even wider.

"Yes," she pants out as I move my cock all the way out and

then slam back into her.

"So fucking tight," I say, looking into her eyes. "Watch my cock," I tell her, and her eyes go to between her legs. "Watch your pussy take my cock." I push all of me into her, then pull out again, so slow we both groan. "Your pussy was made for me," I say, slamming into her, "my cock was made for you."

Her eyes never leave my cock. One of her hands goes between us as she slides her fingers around my cock, her touch shooting through me. I take my cock out of her, pushing her leg back, and my mouth lands on her wet pussy. I kiss her pussy like it's the last thing I'm going to do on this earth. My tongue slides into her as I move my face side to side before licking her slit to her clit and biting down on it. She lifts her hips for a second and calls my name over and over again, "Stefano." I move back, sliding my cock into her. "Yes," she hisses with one leg over my shoulder again, the other one stretched out.

She's so fucking open to me, I slide into her slowly, but my hand comes up, and I rub her clit with two fingers, faster and faster. Her moans get louder and louder every single time I bury myself balls deep in her. In and out slowly, but my hand moves vigorously from side to side. "Oh my God," she says, her eyes closed as she takes in the feeling. I know she's close. I can feel it. I also know she hasn't given me a big one yet. I know I want it. I want her to cry out for me. I slip my cock out of her and slide two fingers into her, harder and harder. "Yes," she moans, and I know she's right here; she's on the edge. Right when she's finally going to come, I slam into her. She screams my name as the both of us come, and her juices soak my cock as I empty myself into her over and over again. I don't think I've ever come this hard in my life. I roll to the side when both of us go limp. Wrapping my arms around her, I take her with me. My cock still buried in her. "That was—" she says, moving the hair away from her face. "That was—"

"Better than anything I've ever dreamed of," I finish her thought as she buries her face into my neck.

"But can we do that again?" she asks, laughing.

I can't help but laugh because I've never been this fucking happy in my life. "Oh, we are going to do that a couple more times before the night is over."

She unburies herself from my neck. "Promise?"

I look down at her, kissing her lips. "I promise you everything."

Twenty-Three

Addison

"Are you sure you want to get dressed?" Stefano asks me as I step out of the shower, and he hands me a plush white towel. "I really like you naked." He leans in and kisses my wet neck.

"I'm not going to the kitchen and eating naked," I counter, wrapping the towel around myself. "What if someone rings the doorbell?"

"We don't answer." He smirks and winks at me, and I just laugh as I watch him walk away from me, naked. His backside as good as his front side. I grab another towel before I flip my hair over and wrap it, twisting it up to soak up the water. He comes back a couple of seconds later dressed in boxers with a black shirt in his hand. "Here you go." He hands me the shirt.

"Thank you," I say nervously, which is the silliest thing since I just spent the last two hours, maybe even three, learning every single inch of his body. I know there isn't one place on my body he hasn't kissed, licked, bit, or sucked. I let the white towel fall from my body and put the black T-shirt on.

It's huge on me and it's in the middle of my thighs. "Fuck." I look over at him and Stefano just comes to me. One of his hands holds my hip while the other comes up so his thumb can rub my cheek. "You're so fucking sexy in my clothes." His voice is low. "Every single time you take my breath away, but in my clothes." He leans in and softly kisses my lips. "It's even hotter than you naked."

I smile shyly. "Are you sure about that?" We both laugh together.

"Okay, let me get you downstairs so I can get you fed and then have my way with you on the counter while you wear my shirt." He slips his hand in mine as he pulls me to the kitchen.

"I'm pretty sure we can make it back to the bedroom," I joke and he stops mid step and turns to me.

"My cock is ready to go now." He points down at said cock. "I'm meeting him halfway."

"Fine," I concede, like I'm not the one who is going to benefit from him taking me on the counter.

We walk down to the kitchen. "What do you want to eat?" He looks over at me as he lets go of my hand and pulls open the fridge. "I've got a lot of stuff for breakfast," he mentions and I lean on the counter.

"Did you?" I fold my arms over my chest, trying not to laugh.

"Well, I was hopeful I could charm you into coming back home with me," he confesses, and I roll my eyes. "My mother said you liked me enough to sleep with me once, chances are you would sleep with me again."

"You told your mother we were going to sleep together?" I screech.

"I don't really tend to talk to my mother about things I do with my dick." He shakes his head laughing. "But my mother tends to talk to me about what she thinks I should do with my dick."

"Oh my God," I say, putting my hands on my face, feeling the heat rise. "How the hell am I supposed to face her the next time I see her?"

"She knows we've had sex before," he reminds me, grabbing the fruit out of the fridge. "We have a daughter."

"I know but"—I put my hands on my head—"you were literally with someone a month ago."

He stops moving. "With someone is a big word."

I glare at him. "Did you or did you not bring her to a family wedding?"

"Yes," he admits, and he's about to say something else when I hold my hand up to stop him from talking.

"There is nothing that you can even say after that, so my advice is to just stop talking." My glare does not leave my face.

"Duly noted," he says. "I'll also note that it took me less than two point three seconds to walk away from her." I roll my eyes. "You can roll your eyes all you want, but it's the truth. The minute I found you and Avery, it was over."

"Whatever," I mumble, not wanting to ever have this conversation because it's super awkward, and the last thing I want to sound like is that I'm needy. I walk over to the drawer to grab a knife to start cutting the fruit.

"You can 'whatever' all you want, baby," he says softly and I look over at him. He drops what is in his hands before coming over and standing behind me. His hands go to my hips, and he squeezes them. "It's you." He bends and whispers in my ear, "It's always going to be you." I turn my face, our eyes locking, my mouth going dry, my hands trembling just a bit as my heart races in my chest. I reach up with one hand to cup his cheek. "It will always be you." He leans in to kiss my lips softly. "Avery and you"—his eyes stare into mine—"will always be my top priority."

I swallow down the lump in my throat and all I can say is one word in a whisper, "Okay." He smiles at me and then walks back to the fridge.

"So what do you think about omelets?" he asks me and I just nod my head.

"What can I do to help?" I reply to him, and he hands me the container of mushrooms.

"How does ham, onion, and mushrooms sound?" He takes out the clear deli meat bag and grabs a white onion. He points at the container in my hand.

"Cheese," I tell him. "You have to have cheese."

"Yes." He puts the things on the counter next to me before walking back to the fridge, pulling open the stainless-steel door, and grabbing the bag of shredded white cheese. "Swiss is all I have."

"That works." I walk over to get two cutting boards. I open the plastic film, grabbing a couple of mushrooms out and start to quarter them.

"What is going through your head right now?" he asks me. He grabs a knife out of the drawer, then closes it with his hip, before coming back over next to me, cutting off the end of the onion.

I side-eye him and shrug my shoulders. "It's strange we share this connection." I grab another couple of mushrooms. "We share a daughter, and I don't even know your favorite food."

He chuckles next to me. "I don't know if I have a favorite food," he states, dicing the onion. "My yaya." I look over at him. "That is my father's mom. She makes the best pastitsio."

"What is that?" I ask him as I grab more mushrooms.

"It's this pasta bake. There are these long noodles that you put in a pan and then add meat sauce on top of the noodles." He smiles as he tells me. "And then it's topped with béchamel. It's so good."

"Sounds delicious." I smile at him.

"It's so good. I'll ask her to make it for us when we go see her," he says as if it's not a big deal. "What's your favorite food?"

"Probably chicken potpie, but with homemade crust that is flaky and buttery."

"Sofia's great-grandmother makes the best," he shares and I nod my head.

"There is nothing she can't cook and it's always the best thing I've ever eaten." I chuckle. "Her potato salad is hands down heaven."

"Her chicken fried steak with gravy," he counters, and I groan. "I've never seen my uncle Matthew shut up faster in my life."

We both laugh. "So," I start, "where do you work, exactly?" We've skated around the fact that he's here, but we've never discussed him staying here permanently. I was under the impression he would get to know Avery and then he would jet out of town, coming back a couple of times a year. I think I tried to tell myself that to prepare for when he did leave. I also tried to tell myself that I wouldn't care, but it's evident to me it's really going to suck when he does leave.

"I work all over, really," he says, sniffling as he finishes cutting the onion. "The head office is in Washington." My head spins as I think about how far away that is from us. "But I was in San Francisco right before the wedding."

I gasp and look over at him. "That's on my bucket list, I've been to LA before, San Diego but San Fran," I tell him, "I've never been, but there was this special on television once. My dream is to watch the sunrise over the Golden Gate Bridge." I shake my head. "Above the clouds." I smile at him. "It's magical from the pictures I've seen." It was going to be my graduation gift to myself but, well, having a baby canceled that.

"I didn't really sightsee. I was in the office for seventeen hours a day."

"Well, I highly recommend it if you go back," I tell him, even though I've never been.

"Noted," he says, putting the onion in a bowl before placing the knife and the cutting board in the sink. "Do your parents know about Avery?" I look at him as he walks over to get another cutting board and knife before standing next to me. "I know they kicked you out and all that." I see his hand grip the knife handle, his knuckles turning white. "But did they know you gave birth?"

"I don't know," I answer him honestly. "After they made me choose her or them, I left town." I avoid looking at him, embarrassed my family did that to me. The hurt simmers under the embarrassment, especially since his family has welcomed us with open arms, never once judging me. "My sister was on my side for a bit after I left, my brother, well, he's always been a dick, so he was on my parents' side. We would text and talk daily, but then she quickly changed her tune when my parents threatened to withhold her allowance from her." I shrug, trying to push away the sting of tears. "After that, I erased them all out of my life." I take a deep inhale. "I wasn't going to share the best thing I've ever done with them." I look at him. "They didn't deserve her." I smile thinking of the little human we created together.

"I'm sorry you did that alone," he says softly.

"It's okay." I turn and lean my hip onto the counter. "I will never, ever regret Avery." I stop talking for a second. "With that being said…" He looks over at me as he dices the ham.

"We didn't use protection this time. I want you to know I'm protected."

He nods his head. "Doesn't matter to me," he assures me, putting down his knife, turning to face me, his own hip on the counter. "But just so you know, I've never been without a condom."

"The condom didn't work the last time." I try to make a joke.

"Look at what we created without even trying." He smirks at me. "Can you imagine if we tried?" His eyes darken.

"Yeah, because that would be smart." I fold my arms over my chest. "Let's have another child together when you don't even know where you will be in a month."

His eyebrows pinch together. "Where do you think I'll be in a month?"

"Well," I say, wanting to kick myself for saying anything, "probably in Washington working."

"Why would you think that?" he asks me, and I throw up my hands.

"Because that is where your office is," I reply, trying not to sound like this bothers me. "How can you have an office in Washington and live here?"

"I don't have to go to work every day," he says calmly. "That's the perks of owning the business, plus I never work in the office, I'm always off-site."

"It doesn't matter." I turn away and walk to grab a frying pan.

"It does matter if this is what is going through your head." He watches me put the pan on the stove and walks over to grab the olive oil.

"Nothing is going through my head." I avoid even looking at him as I turn the knob for the stove. The clicking sound fills the silent room.

"Addison," he says my name, "we are going to have this

conversation."

"And what conversation is that?" I move the pan around, making sure the oil spreads evenly.

"You aren't going to look at me?" he calls me out.

"I'm cooking," I say, looking at him for a second and then looking away, afraid he's going to see even though I prepared myself for him leaving, it still bothers me.

"I'm not going anywhere," he says, and my head whips around to look at him. "I'm here with you. You are here with me. I finally have you in my life. I finally feel." He shakes his head. "I'm fucking happy. I might have to take business trips a couple of times a month, but this is my home." He looks into my eyes. "This is our home."

Twenty-Four

Stefano

I feel the bed move beside me before I open my eyes. "Where are you going?" I ask her as she walks over to the bathroom door. My eyes are glued to her perfect ass as her hair moves from side to side.

"I'm going to shower before we go and pick up Avery," she mumbles, looking over her shoulder. "Even though we showered before bed, I'm pretty sure I still smell like sex."

I laugh, turning on my side and propping my head up with my hand. "Well, we had sex a couple more times after the shower. That could be why."

She turns to face me, showing me her whole naked body, and my cock, already at half-mast, is now full-blown hard for her. "A couple?" she huffs. "We had sex three times alone during the middle of the night." She shakes her head. "You're worse than a teething child in the middle of the night wanting comfort."

I grip my cock in my hand and toss the covers off me. "I need some comfort now," I tell her, and she glares at me, which makes me laugh even more because she wants me just as much as I want her. She just doesn't like to admit it.

"You are going to need to self-soothe," she tells me, slamming the bathroom door. "And don't come in here."

"Fine," I pout, getting up and looking over at the clock on the bedside table, seeing it's a bit after eight in the morning. "I'm going to go make coffee."

"You do that!" she yells, right after I hear the sound of the shower turning on. I grab a pair of shorts and my phone before walking downstairs.

The kitchen is a little bit of a mess, making my cock even harder. After she finished cooking, or maybe in the middle, I remember getting behind her on my knees and tongue-fucking her until she snapped and rode me in the middle of the kitchen floor. "Best omelet I ever had in my life." I chuckle as I fill the dishwasher right after the coffee is started.

I pull up Sofia's number and press call. It rings once before she answers. "Well, well, well," she sings into the phone. "If it isn't the baby daddy," she greets, laughing.

"That would be me," I say. "How is she?"

"She's amazing," she gushes, and I can't help the smile that fills my face. "She's still in bed. She spoke with your mom last night and was informed that princesses get breakfast in bed, so…"

"Oh my God," I reply, shaking my head.

"She is taking full advantage of it." She laughs. "Why are you up?"

"Quick question," I say, looking over at the stairs to see if I'm still alone. "How hard would it be to take Addison away for a week?" I whisper.

"Away for a week?" Sofia asks me, confused.

"Yeah, I want to take her and Avery to San Francisco," I fill her in, and she gasps. From the minute she told me it was on her bucket list, I had already started to make plans in my head. But then I knew I had to make sure she could leave work.

"Does she know?" Sofia asks me.

"No, it's a surprise," I tell her, looking over my shoulder the whole time. I put the phone to my ear, so she doesn't hear anything.

"She's going to freak out," she states, the excitement already in her voice making me smile even more.

"Yeah, so how would that work?" I ask her as I finish filling the dishwasher.

"I can check the calendar."

"Okay, that is good." I'm really hoping I can do this for her. "Please let me know and keep it a secret if you can."

"Ugh," Sofia says, "just take her."

"What?" I ask, shocked.

"Just take her," she repeats. "I'll cover for her, and I know the girls would want her to go."

"Are you sure?" I don't even know why I bother asking her instead of just hanging up and start the planning.

"Yes," she assures me, and I can feel the smile on her face. "You better not fuck this up, Stefano, or else."

"Thank you," I say to her and quickly hang up. I run up the stairs, two at a time, walking into the bedroom and still hearing the shower going.

I pull up my father's name and press the green button. "Hey there," he answers after half a ring.

"I don't have a lot of time," I rush out, sitting on the bed, watching the bathroom door. "I'm surprising Addison and Avery and taking them to San Francisco," I tell him. "Do you think I can get a suite?"

"On it," he says. "I'll make the arrangements and send you the confirmation. Today, right?"

"Yeah," I say, getting up with the nerves filling my body. "I've never done this before. I am going to call for a plane." I look at the bathroom door when I hear the water shut off. "She is coming," I say in a whisper. "Shit."

"I'll take care of everything. All you need to do is get her to the airport," my father confirms with glee.

"What about clothes and stuff?" I ask him.

"Your mother will have a field day," he mumbles, "but it'll all be at the hotel."

"Okay, text me the details."

"Will do," he says and disconnects. At the same time, I hear the handle of the door unlock and the door open.

She walks out wrapped in a white towel, her long hair piled on her head. "That shower was amazing," she moans. "Why are you here?"

"It's my bedroom." I try to act cool, folding my hands over my chest. "Why?"

"What's wrong?" She just stares at me. "Did Sofia call?" Worry fills her face. "Is everything okay?"

"Everything is fine," I reassure her. "I just came to ask you if you wanted breakfast in bed." I come up with an excuse.

"Is that code for you want a blow job?" She folds her arms over her chest.

My eyebrows pinch together. "As much fun as that sounds—" I start, and the phone beeps in my hand, making me look down.

Dad: Plane will be ready in an hour. Suite booked at the Fairmont.

"I have a surprise for the two of you," I say. "So how about we table the blow job for tonight?" I wink at her. "Let's go get our girl so I can get this surprise underway."

"What kind of surprise?" she asks me and I shake my head.

"It's not a surprise if I tell you." I walk to her and bend down to kiss her lips. "I love that you smell like me." I suck her neck, and she pushes me away.

"You left a hickey on each of my inner thighs," she grouses, "and my ass."

"Did I?" I feign ignorance. "I would need to see the evidence before I confess."

"Oh, I'll show you," she says, and when the towel falls, I lick my lips. "You are too much." She grabs the towel from the floor, putting it in front of herself. "We have to go and get Avery, and I have to run home to get a change of clothes," she informs me, walking around the room, trying to gather her things.

"What? Why?" I say, watching her slip on the bodysuit.

"I'm not going to do the walk of shame in front of Sofia and Matty," she huffs, turning to grab her skirt, showing me that the bodysuit is a thong, and I moan out when she bends over.

"You don't think they will know we spent the night together?" I ask her as she shimmies her hips into the skirt.

"I have no idea, but I won't help them come to that conclusion. Now, are you going to shower and meet me downstairs?"

"I might need you to wash my back." I wink at her, striding to the bathroom.

"I think you can do that all on your own like a big boy." She laughs, walking out of the room.

"I'll take a rain check for tonight," I say to the empty room as I quickly shower. I put on a pair of jeans before grabbing a white T-shirt. I slip my sneakers on before grabbing my phone and heading downstairs to the kitchen. I see her wiping down the counter, and she looks up at me. "I made you a coffee to go."

She points over to the thermal cup at the corner of the counter. I walk over to her, turning her to face me before I lean down and kiss her lips. "Thank you," I say softly.

"You are very welcome," she replies, putting her hands on my hips. "I'm ready to go when you are."

"Lead the way," I say, knowing she is in for the surprise of her life in about forty minutes.

I drive her over to her house, and she quickly changes out of her outfit from last night before turning to me. "What should I wear?"

"Casual," I tell her, and she nods. Turning back to her closet, she comes back out a couple of minutes later wearing high-waisted, blue-and-white striped shorts, with the sash tied in a bow and a white short-sleeved T-shirt. She slips on her leather flip-flops before walking over to the bathroom, taking her hair out and combing it.

"Ready?" I ask her when she comes back out of the bathroom. She nods and slides her hand in mine as we return to the car to get Avery. She is sitting on the steps with Sofia and Matty.

We get out of the car and can hear Avery clapping her hands. "Momma!" she screams, running down the steps toward Addison, who holds her arms out and picks her up.

"Hi," she says, leaning forward and kissing her neck. "How are you?"

"I had breakfast in bed," she says, and Addison looks at Matty and Sofia.

"Your mother-in-law informed her this is what princesses do," Matty deadpans. "It was fun for everyone," he says sarcastically.

"Thank you so much," Addison says. "We really have to have a chat about this royalty thing."

"Stone called Ryleigh *princess* once," Matty remembers, laughing, "she stuck her heel in his toe."

I nod, laughing at the memory. "Thank God it was off-season." Then I turn to Avery. "Guess what?" I bend down and kiss her. "I have a surprise for you and Mom."

"A surprise?" she says with a squeal. "Bye, Aunt Sofia and Uncle Matty." She princess waves her hand at them.

"We've been dismissed," Matty says, looking at Sofia. "That hurts."

"I'll kiss it and make it better," Sofia soothes.

"Eww." I cover Avery's ears. "There is a child."

"Oh, please." Sofia gets up. "Have fun with the surprise." She winks at Addison, who looks at me.

"They know what the surprise is?" she asks me as I move her away from them and toward the car.

"You'll know soon enough," I tell her as she puts Avery in her car seat.

"For the record, I hate surprises," she declares, huffing and walking away from my kiss. "Like hate-hate." She opens the passenger door.

"Noted," I tell her right before she gets into the car and slams the door. I laugh and look up toward the sky. "Please let her not freak out."

I start the car and make my way over to the private airport in the industrial part of town. I pull into the parking lot before turning off the car. "Let's go," I urge, getting out of the car before she asks me questions. The chain-link fence shows a hangar with two planes outside. One plane has the stairs down with a rug.

"Where are we?" Addison asks as she looks around.

I get Avery out of her seat. "Look, an airplane." She points at the plane as I walk around the car and slide my hand into Addison's.

"What are we doing here?" Addison asks again, her teeth clenched this time as we walk toward the chain-link fence.

"It's a surprise," I tell her, holding her hand even tighter when I feel her slip away.

We walk over to the glass door, and I pull it open and step in. The long desk faces us, with the woman standing up and smiling. "Mr. and Mrs. Dimitris?" she questions, and I nod. "Right this way," she says, turning and walking out of the side door onto the tarmac.

Once we walk outside and head closer to the plane, I look at them. "Surprise," I say nervously.

"Is that a plane?" Addison asks me, her face filled with shock. "Is this a private plane?" She continues to look at me and then back to the plane. "Are we taking this plane?"

"We are," I confirm, and she gasps at the same time Avery jumps up and down.

"I never went on a plane," she says, clapping her hands together. "Momma, did I go on a plane?"

"No," Addison says, shaking her head, the shock all over her face. "I didn't pack a bag."

"Don't worry about it," I assure her, once we get to the stairs leading to the plane. "I got it." I put my hand on her lower back, almost pushing her toward the stairs.

"What do you mean, you got it?" She turns, asking me through clenched teeth. Avery is already on the fourth step.

"It means trust me." My hands come up to hold her face. "I promise I have you." My thumbs rub her cheeks.

"I literally have nothing but my purse," she says, looking at the plane, seeing Avery talking to the attendant, who is squatted down in front of her shaking her hand.

"Everything is being set up at the hotel," I tell her, and I can feel her start to shake in my hands. "Hey," I say as she blinks away tears, but one escapes, "why the tears?"

"I can't afford this," she whines as if I stabbed her, "this is too much."

"Baby," I say softly. "You raised our daughter for four years without a penny. Trust me, I owe you a lot more than a trip." I lean forward, the need to kiss her stronger than anything I've felt.

"But work," she finally huffs, putting a hand on her forehead.

"Taken care of." My hands fall from her face. "Let me give you this." I don't know if I'm asking her or begging her. "Please," I beg, "let me do this for the both of you."

Twenty-Five

Addison

"Momma," Avery yells from inside the plane, "they have a couch in here!"

I smile at her and then look back at Stefano. "This is not normal."

He chuckles and wraps his arm around my waist, pulling me closer to him. "Baby, nothing with us will ever be normal." He bends his head to kiss my lips. "As normal as things can be."

"I don't think you guys would know how to do normal if it came and bit you in the butt." I shake my head. His arm drops from around my waist as his hand finds mine before he puts his other hand on my lower back, guiding me to the stairs. I walk up the first step, and the only thing going through my head is how crazy this is.

"Welcome aboard," the attendant says, standing with her

hands in front of her. "We will be ready to go when you are."

All I can do is nod at her and move to the side so Stefano can step in. "I want to sit by the window," Avery says, walking over to the four seats on one side with a table in the middle. "Dad, can I sit in that one?" She points at the one chair facing out the window.

"You can sit anywhere you like," he replies, and I'm not even going to lie, I feel my chest rising and falling as I try not to freak the fuck out.

"Relax." Stefano leans down and whispers in my ear.

"Easier said than done," I mumble, making him chuckle as he kisses my lips softly before walking over and getting Avery buckled in her seat. He sits right next to her and then motions to me to come on over with his hand.

I inhale deeply and exhale before walking to the chair facing him and sitting down. The sound of the plane starting makes Avery squeal, the smile on her face is everything. She's always been a happy kid. Always been a kid who just accepts what I tell her with no pushback, like when I couldn't buy her the *Frozen* sneakers, and she stared at them for the longest time before just shrugging and walking out with me. It broke my heart so much I went back to get them the day after and ate ramen noodles for two weeks. I blink away the tears as I watch her and Stefano together.

He's got his head next to hers and his arm around her, as he explains everything that is happening. When the plane starts to move, she looks over at him with her eyes big and her mouth in a big O. She puts her two hands on the armrests when the plane picks up speed and the pressure makes her back stick to the chair.

"My ears feel funny," she says, putting her hands over her ears.

"When we get into the sky, it'll feel better," Stefano assures her and she just nods at him.

She looks out the window and gasps, "Momma, look, we are in the clouds."

I smile at her as I turn to look out the window. "Pretty cool, right?"

The ping for the seat belt goes off, and Stefano unfastens his seat belt and then unfastens hers. "Just for a minute so that you can look outside," he tells her as she gets on her knees, looking out the window.

"Where are we going?" I ask Stefano, who looks over at me with a smirk.

"It's a surprise," he repeats, earning him a glare which makes him laugh. "Last one, I promise."

"I don't know, but something about that statement makes me not believe you," I accuse him. The attendant comes over to hand us water before coming back with a huge fruit plate. "Who is going to explain to her that this isn't the way travel is done?" I point at Avery, who is looking out the window while she eats strawberries. "No one travels like this."

He rolls his lips when I ask, "How often have you been on a regular airplane?"

He rolls his eyes. "Plenty of times."

"Name five," I demand, holding up my hand and he ignores me and turns to talk to Avery.

"Do you want to go watch a movie on the couch?" He points over to the other side, where a couch seats five people. Avery nods her head and he gets up from his seat before reaching over and picking her up.

I watch the two of them sitting on the couch as they watch a movie Avery chose. He will do anything she says. I wonder when she'll use it to her advantage for real. I sit in the chair, looking around, wondering how I got here. I get up from my chair and walk over to the couch. I'm going to sit on the other side of Avery when he moves over so I can sit next to him.

Avery is now lying down on the other side with her feet in his lap. "Hi," he says, putting his arm around my shoulders. "How're you doing?"

"I'd be doing a whole lot better if I knew where we were going." I look over at him.

"You're beautiful when you get that look on your face," he tells me, kissing my lips softly.

"What look?" I ask him, settling next to him.

"The look where you are going to kill me but still like me," he teases, and this time I can't help but throw my head back and burst out laughing.

"You aren't going to tell me?" I prod him, and he shakes his head.

"You are always the one in charge. Let someone else take care of you for once." His voice is soft as he raises his hand to touch my face. "Be the queen for the week."

"A week?" I whisper-shout. "I can't be away for a week."

"I spoke with Sofia—" he starts, and my eyes get big.

"You did what?" I shake my head, ready to jump out of my seat.

"I called Sofia." I close my eyes tight while my stomach rises. "I asked her if I could take you away for the week."

I get up and walk over to my purse. Taking out my phone, I see missed messages from them.

Sofia: Addison is out this week.
Shelby: Is she sick?
Sofia: Nope, her baby daddy is surprising her with a trip.
Clarabella: Shut the front door!
Presley: She's going to have to get so down and dirty.

Sofia: I think they got down and dirty last night.

Shelby: On the nondate. Bahahaha

Clarabella: She rode that pony like a rodeo queen.

I shake my head.

Me: I am not out this week. I might be out for a couple of days.

Sofia: I approved it and we are changing the locks if you come back.

Me: I am not taking the week off.

Shelby: You haven't taken a vacation since you started.

I put my head back, closing my eyes. I haven't, that is true, but I tend to save my vacation days for the days when Avery gets sick.

Me: I took a week off last year.

Clarabella: Because Avery was sick and then you got whatever she had.

Me: Still took the week off.

Presley: I agree, you aren't allowed back at the office this week. Enjoy the D.

Presley: I mean vacation.

Shelby: Yes, send all the pictures.

Clarabella: Not all the pictures. I don't need to be waking up to a dick picture.

Presley: Yes, let's not forget when you sent us an ass picture.

Clarabella: It was a blurry shot and the kids took it.

Shelby: I swear I saw ball sack.

Clarabella: You did not.

Sofia: Do not send me that picture to confirm or deny.

Presley: Also, first thing we do when you get back is have a recap of that nondate.

Clarabella: Yes, we should discuss how that co-parent meeting went.

*Me: **Our co-parenting meeting went great, thanks. Sofia: She did have a huge smile on her face this morning. And if it's any indication, by her outfit, they didn't make it very far.***

"Everything okay?" Stefano asks me, and I look over at him.

"No," I growl between clenched teeth. "I was told not to come into work this week."

"Oh, good," he says. "See, now you can relax and unwind."

I put my phone down, my head spinning, when I hear, "I'm hungry."

Stefano puts his hand up to get the attendant's attention. She comes over and talks with Avery, who orders a turkey sandwich and fries.

We eat lunch, and by the time we look out the window, it looks like we are descending. We sit in the seat with Stefano next to Avery, his arm reached in front of her to stop her from flying out, apparently. The landing is perfect and Avery claps her hands as soon as the plane stops. "Are we here?" She looks out the window as I unfasten my seat belt.

I stretch my legs, watching Stefano grab Avery and put her down in front of him. "I'm going to go out first," he tells her, "and wait for you. But hold on."

"Okay," she says, listening to his every word. He walks down the steps, looking back every single step to make sure she is okay.

A black truck is parked on the side with the driver standing by it. I walk down the five steps to the tarmac where Stefano waits with Avery holding his hand. He slips his other hand in mine before walking over to the truck.

"Welcome," the driver greets, opening the back door of the truck, "to San Francisco."

The minute he says where we are, I stop in my tracks and gasp, "What?"

"Surprise," Stefano says over his shoulder as he places Avery in her car seat. I look around to make sure I heard what he said and to be sure I'm actually in San Francisco. The tears fill my eyes, making my vision blurry, and I blink them away but one escapes anyway.

"They have a TV in here!" Avery shouts, making me laugh while I wipe away the tear.

Stefano comes over to me, grabbing my face in his hands. "Hey," he says softly, his thumbs rubbing my cheeks.

"This is—" I start to say without letting the lump in my throat bother me, but the tears come anyway. "This is too much."

"No." He smiles as he kisses my tear from my cheek. "It's never going to be enough." I look up at this man, who was just a memory to me not long ago, but now the man is reality and he's everything you could wish and hope for. Maybe even more than I wished for. "Now, let's go. There is one more surprise."

"Please, I don't think I can take it," I say, putting a hand on my stomach. This is all more than I have ever dreamed of. I get in the truck and look out the window, taking everything in. We pull into the hotel, and I look up when I see the name. I close my eyes, not even trying to think about how much this is going to cost him. The door opens on both sides, the man holding out a hand for me to help me out. "Thank you," I say, stepping down and walking around the truck to see Stefano with Avery. His hand is always holding hers.

"Mr. and Mrs. Dimitris." The man comes up to us, and I don't correct him and neither does Stefano. "Welcome to the Fairmont. We are honored to have you."

"Excited to be here," Stefano says to him.

"If you will follow me, I'll take you to your floor," he says, and I look around seeing the hustle and bustle of people. We walk up the four steps toward the brown doors that are opened for us. My mouth hangs open as I walk into the lobby. The beige marble floors are shiny, with the ceilings high, and the molding looks like artwork painted in gold, and pillars are all over the room. It's the prettiest hotel I've ever been to. I don't even hear what the man is telling Stefano as we walk to the side, going straight to the elevator.

"Don't we need to check in?" I ask him, and he just shakes his head.

"Already done," he replies, getting into the elevator after the man. I watch him press the eighth floor out of nine. "Also, my parents are in town." My mouth hangs open. "Or will be. They should be arriving shortly. They will give us tonight." I tilt my head to the side. "They probably won't because they want to see Avery."

I don't say anything because the elevator doors open and facing the car are two brass doors. "Welcome to the penthouse suite."

Twenty-Six

Stefano

I watch her face when we walk into the suite. Her eyes roam the living room with the baby grand piano and I have to roll my lips to stop from laughing. "You okay?" I ask her when I walk to her.

"We are going to have a conversation," she hisses under her breath, "a serious, serious conversation."

"I look forward to it." I nod as I slide my hand in hers.

The concierge is still giving us a tour, but Avery is the only one talking to him. "I'm not kidding," she says in a whisper, but her tone is stern. I lean in to kiss her, seeing that Avery has her back to me. "Did he say this has three bedrooms?"

"Not sure," I say, looking at the man whose name I didn't even catch because I was too worried about Addison freaking out.

"How many bedrooms?" Addison asks the man, who smiles

at her, and I want to throat punch him. Even though he's close to his sixties, it's stupid since I'm holding her hand, and it's clear we're together.

"There are three," he says. "If you go through that door right there." He points at the glass door. "It's the outdoor patio." He puts his hands in front of him. "It has access to the library and the formal dining room."

"Library?" Addison asks, shocked, and he nods proudly.

"I think we are good. I don't want to keep you," I tell him. "We will have a look around."

"I will have everything set up for the tea in a couple of hours." He looks at us. "The clothes are already away and hanging."

"Thank you," I say and watch him leave the room before turning toward the door. The minute the door is closed, Addison folds her arms over her chest and glares at me.

"Avery," I call her name and she sticks her head in the room. "Grand-mère sent you a couple of things." My eyes look at Avery, who jumps up. "I think it's in one of the closets." She turns to run out of the room.

"You left your mother in charge of buying us clothes?" she grumbles between clenched teeth.

"I did," I say softly, "but in my defense, I don't think I gave it enough thought."

"Really?" she retorts, making me chuckle, but the chuckle leaves when I see how pissed she is.

"Listen, you were in the shower," I start to tell her, "and then I wanted to surprise you, so I called Sofia. Then I didn't know how much time I had, so I called my father." I hold up my hands. "Obviously, I didn't know he would go to the extreme."

"Extreme?" she screeches. "A three-bedroom penthouse suite with a library." I roll my lips to stop laughing. "With a baby grand piano." She points over to the piano. "I've stayed in my share of suites before"—she looks around—"but even this is a little bit out of my comfort zone."

"Momma, Momma!" Avery yells from somewhere in this place, her voice echoing. "Look at this," she says, coming into the room dragging something blue and sparkly behind her. "Look, it's Cinderella's gown."

"Oh my," she says as she picks up the dress that is bigger than her. "Oh my," she repeats as she grabs the dress from Avery. "This is…" She holds out the dress that literally looks like a replica of what Cinderella wore.

"Can I put it on?" Avery asks, jumping in the same spot, her hand flopping up and down. "I want to wear it today."

"This is," Addison says as she looks at the dress. "This has to have cost—" She doesn't get anything out because there is a knock on the door.

"You should answer that, it might be Princess Kate to have tea with us," Addison deadpans and all I can do is kiss her lips. "We are having a conversation." I kiss her again. "This is over the line."

It's at that moment we both look down and see Avery looking at us. "Um," I start to say, "I like your mom." I close my eyes, thinking how dumb I sound right now.

"Aunt Sofia and Uncle Matty kiss all the time," she says. "Do you like her like that?"

"I do," I confirm, looking at Addison, who is staring at me and not saying a word.

"We are having many conversations tonight," she grumbles between clenched teeth.

"Noted," I tell her as the person knocks again. "But in my defense, have you met my mother?"

"Stefano," she seethes as I walk away from her, going to the front door, pulling it open, and seeing my father and mother standing there.

My mother just smiles big at me. "Bonjour." Hello, she says, coming in and hugging me.

"I tried to stop her," my father says, "but well."

"Grand-mère!" Avery shouts with glee, running over to us. My mother quickly lets me go to scoot down, opening her arms for Avery. She runs in them, and my mother just kisses her head.

"Ma puce." Beauty, she says. "I missed you." She covers her in kisses. "Tu as grandi." You grew, she says to Avery, who just looks at me.

"You got bigger," I translate for her.

"Where is Addison?" my father asks me as we walk into the living room. Addison is still looking at the dress.

"Momma, look," Avery says to her and she looks up at my parents. "Momma and Daddy kiss," she tells them, and when I look over at Addison, it looks like she wants the room to swallow her.

"Is that so?" my father says, trying to hide his smile. My mother's eyebrows just shoot up.

"Yeah, on the lips like Uncle Matty and Aunt Sofia," Avery elaborates, and Addison just closes her eyes.

"This is fun," I say sarcastically.

"Why is this room so small?" my mother complains, walking into the room. "Markos, did you not book them a suite?"

"It's the biggest one they had, Vivienne," my father relays, walking over to Addison. "Hello, dear," he says. "Sorry for intruding on the family vacation, but—"

"Oh, please," Addison replies, "the more the merrier." I can tell she's one second from freaking out and trying to hide it. "Thank you for booking everything," she says while my mother goes to her and gives her a big hug, "and this." She holds up the dress. "We need to perhaps talk about dresses."

"Oh no," my mother says, putting her hand to her mouth, "did it not fit?" She looks outraged. "I gave them the measurements we took the last time. I had the whole line made."

"I'm sorry," Addison says, "the whole line?"

"Well, the last time Avery said she loved all the princesses, so I called my seamstress, and she made me them all." She looks at my father. "We have to redo them."

"No," Addison says quickly, "I meant they are—" She tries to think of the words and then looks at me.

"Mom, we have to tone it down a touch." I walk over to stand next to Addison. "We love it, but she can't wear this."

"Of course, she can wear this," my mother states. "She is wearing it today." She looks over at Avery. "Did you find the shoes?"

"It comes with shoes?" Addison mutters from beside me, but all I hear is my mother and Avery.

"We should go check your room." My mother holds out her hand for Avery, who grabs it and they walk out of the room. My mother looks over her shoulder as if she just won the lottery.

"Dad," I say and he shakes his head.

"Listen, I know." He holds up his hands. "I had the same conversation with her, but this is her first grandchild."

"There is the guilt I was waiting for." I put my arm around Addison's shoulder.

"So I'm assuming," my father says, putting his hands in his pockets, hiding the smile he wants to make, "you haven't seen what she bought you?"

"What she bought me?" Addison asks, pointing at herself.

"I might have asked her to buy you a couple of things for the vacation," I confess, and I can see her head is ready to explode. "Dad." I turn to him. "Thanks for this."

"Oh, son." He walks over to the couch. "Trust me, this makes me happier than you will ever know." He sits. "Also, you owe me. I stopped your uncle Matthew from coming."

"Stefano," Addison says from beside me, "I'm going to need you to take me to the room where the clothes are."

"I don't think we need to do that," I deflect, shaking my head. "You look fine the way you are."

The knock on the door comes again. "Who is that?" Addison looks at me, and it's my chance to run away.

"I'll get it," I say, walking over to the door and pulling it open, finding five people standing there. "Hello."

"We are here to set up for the high tea," the woman in the front says as I move out of the way for them to come in. "Where would you like us to set up?"

"Wherever you think," I say and Addison comes out of the living room. "They will set up for tea."

"You should go change!" my father yells from the living room. "I'll wait here."

We walk down the hallway past the billiard room and hear my mother and Avery talking in the second bedroom. "I love tea parties," Avery says from the bedroom. "Do you think I need a crown?"

"Of course, my love." I hear my mother, and Addison looks at me.

"Fine," she grumbles, "I'll give her the tea party, but we have to have limits." She holds up the dress. I just nod. "Silence isn't golden," she mumbles as she walks into the master bedroom. "There are no closets?" She looks around the bedroom and I point at the wall on the side. "Here we go," she says and I sit on the king-size bed, waiting for her to freak out. I know this is too much for her, but knowing how much my family loves her is everything. Knowing for five years she didn't have any support and now she has us is, well, there are no words for that.

"Stefano." She comes out of the walk-in closet. "There is a floor-length cape dress." She walks back into the closet. "There are also more clothes in here than I own at home."

I get up, walking over to the closet, and see both sides stuffed as if we live here. "If it makes you feel better, she bought clothes for me also."

"That does not make me feel better at all." She shakes her head, and fifteen minutes later she walks out of the closet wearing a long floral skirt with a sleeveless white shirt. "These shoes—" She lifts her dress. "These are the ones from *Sex in the City*. They are the Carrie shoes." She points at the blue shoe. "They also cost eight hundred and ninety dollars," she huffs. "Trust me, I know because they are my dream shoes."

"You look beautiful," I compliment her, "so, so beautiful." I get up and she looks at me as I wear my beige linen suit. "Shall we go?"

"Sure," she says as I slide my hand into hers. "I'm doing this for Avery," she mumbles to me as we walk out, "and for your mom."

"Thank you," I say as we walk toward the living room. There is a woman in the corner playing the harp.

"Our daughter is going to have to marry the King of England at this point." She side-eyes me as we see the outside patio has been transformed with a round table in the middle. The table has trays of food all over it and of course teapots everywhere.

My parents are taking pictures of Avery, who is dressed like Cinderella, with a crown on her head. "Show the shoes, my love," my mother urges her and she smiles as she picks up her dress and shows us glass shoes. "You are a true princess." My father looks at my mother with all the love in the world. I know she pushes it, but this is how she shows her love. What I didn't tell Addison is the number of times my mother has cried because she missed so much. The number of times she calls me to make sure I'm making them feel loved. This is her way of making up for lost time. "I love you so much."

We walk out onto the patio but Addison doesn't follow me, so I stop. "I can't go out there," she says to me as she wrings her hands in front of her.

"What, why not?" I ask her, wondering if she is sick.

"I can't mess up the bottom of the shoes or else we can't return them," she says softly.

"Addison." I grab her face in my hands. "Those shoes are never being returned, my love." I see how her eyes get big when I call her my love. "Now, let's have tea with our daughter."

Twenty-Seven

Addison

*H*e stands in front of me, this man who has literally thrown my world upside down, asking me to have tea with our daughter. Our daughter. The tears so evident in his eyes that he wants to give this moment to our daughter. If I wasn't sure I loved him before, I love him now. This whole day has been out of a dream. It's been out of a fairy tale, to say the very least. Being swept away in a private plane to my bucket-list destination. Then to have this suite that is four times the size of my apartment, to having a whole closet full of clothes that I would only dream of buying. To walking out to a harp playing for a tea party for a four-year-old. It's literally the definition of a fairy tale. These things don't happen, at least I didn't think they did.

"Okay," I give in and take a step forward, even though inwardly I cringe thinking about the fact I can't ever return these shoes.

The pair of shoes that were going to be my gift to myself after I booked fifty clients, are now on my feet. "Oh, there they are," Markos says, looking at us and smiling. He also has changed into a suit, his hands in his pockets.

"Momma," Avery says, coming over to me wearing her Cinderella gown, looking like a princess, the sound of her dress swishing along the way. Her hair is softly curled with a new tiara on her head, this one with baby-blue rhinestones to match the dress, obviously. "Look at my glass shoes."

"They aren't real glass," Markos assures me. I chuckle and shake my head as she lifts her big poofy dress to show me the clear plastic shoes. "Vivienne knows someone who—" I laugh because whereas this would have shocked me, I don't know why I've come to expect it.

"Look at them," Vivienne says, the smile on her face from ear to ear. She also has changed into a beautiful baby-blue lace dress that fits her amazingly. "We should get a family picture."

"Yes," Stefano agrees, slipping his hand in mine, "let's get a family picture."

I walk with him to the corner of the patio and stand next to him. He places his arm around me, pulling me to his side, with Avery in front of us. Vivienne takes the picture and then I call over one of the people who are setting up this tea party. "Would you mind taking a picture of us?" I then look over at Vivienne. "Come on, Grand-mère," I say in the best French I can muster. She comes over and stands next to me as Markos goes on the side of Stefano. The five of us smile for the picture. "Now, just the three of you," I tell Vivienne and Markos as they stand with Avery. Instead of standing behind her, Vivienne gets down to Avery's level and Markos follows as they hug her in the middle. The picture is so beautiful, I know I'm going to get it framed for her room.

"Now, shall we have tea?" Vivienne asks, clapping her hands as Avery walks over to the table.

"Vivienne," I call her name softly and she looks over at me. The smile on her face fades as she comes over to me.

"Is everything okay?" she asks me, the worry etched over her face.

Her hands reach for mine. "I just want to thank you," I say nervously, "for everything you've done for us."

"Oh, Addison." She smiles. "I'm just thankful you aren't keeping Avery from me." She blinks away the tears and all I can do is squeeze her hand.

"I will never keep her away from you," I say honestly. "My girl deserves all the love in the world." I look over at Avery, who is sitting in a chair with Markos and Stefano on each side of her as she explains to them how to drink tea. They both hang on to every word she says as if she's describing how the sun and moon work.

"We would do anything for the two of you," Vivienne assures me softly and I look back at her. "Nothing can take the place of your mom," she says gently, "but I'll be here for you in whatever you need even if it's to talk about Stefano. Or complain about him. I love my son but no one is perfect." She tries to make a joke of it, but all I can do is try not to become a blubbering mess in front of her.

I swallow the lump in my throat, breathing out slowly before I answer her, "You've known about her for two weeks and you've done more than my mother has ever done for us. And she's known about her for her whole life."

"Are you guys going to join us?" Markos asks from his seat, holding a teacup with his pinky up. "She's already eating all the cakes." I look over at Avery, who has chocolate on her cheek and also whipped cream on her nose. Stefano grabs a napkin and cleans her face and she just smiles at him, the two of them scrunching up their noses at each other.

I stand here while Vivienne walks over to the table and Markos gets up to pull out her chair. She kisses his lips softly before sitting down and grabbing one of the linen napkins to put across her lap. Stefano gets up from his chair and comes over to me, bending his head. "Are you staying here so you don't scuff the shoes?" he whispers in my ear and I can't help but chuckle. "Do you want me to carry you there?"

"I'm good," I reply, looking down and taking a step and then another one. He pulls out the chair for me, just like his father did to his mother. "Thank you," I say and he bends his head and kisses my lips.

My eyes go big in shock, as he moves over to his own chair. "So we can assume you two are together?" His mother doesn't skip a beat.

"We are," Stefano says at the same time as I say, "We haven't discussed it."

His parents just look at us. "I remember that," Markos says and Vivienne just rolls her eyes. "I sent her a fish."

"Oh, mon dieu." Oh my goodness. "He sent me a living fish." She throws her hands up. "Who does that?"

"Well, good news for me." Markos smiles at her. "I wore her down."

I can't help but laugh at him as he tells us the story of her freaking out and returning said fish. My stomach hurts from laughing so hard. Stefano sits rolling his eyes while he leans over and puts his arm over my leg.

I don't even know how long we sit at the table, but the sun slowly goes down. Avery, of course, is the center of attention as she gets back up and walks with her dress. It's not long before she comes over and climbs into my lap. "How about we get you a bath?" I ask her, and she just nods.

"It's the time difference," Vivienne observes. "It's nine o'clock for her."

The five of us walk inside. "Give me a kiss." Vivienne squats down in front of her. "How about tomorrow we take you to see some puppies?"

"Um," I say nervously, "absolutely not." My tone is sharp. "No pets allowed in our place."

"We are going to visit one of my places," Markos explains, "there is a puppy class early in the morning."

"Can I go see the puppies?" Avery looks at me and I just nod my head.

"We'll call you tomorrow when she wakes up," Stefano says to his parents, who just nod at us. They walk out of the room with their arms locked around each other.

"They could stay here," I say when Stefano closes the door and then glares at me. "What? It's a three-bedroom suite. I can share with Avery."

"You can share yourself in my bed is what you can do," he grumbles and then walks back toward where the two bedrooms are. "I'll get the bath going," he tells me and side by side we get Avery ready for bed. By the time her head hits the pillow, her eyes are already closed, no matter how she fights it. I look down at her in the middle of a king-size bed, looking like a real princess in a big bed.

Stefano slips his hand in mine, pulling me out of the room and then heading to the master bedroom. "Are you tired?" he asks me as he leans down to kiss my neck, making me smile. I don't have a chance to answer him before his mouth covers mine. Needless to say, I do slide into bed, with him of course, since he wrapped me in his arms and refused to let me go. I was going to wait for him to fall asleep and then slip out, but sleep took me first.

I feel a soft kiss from beside me as the bed goes down. My eyes struggle to open. "Baby," Stefano says softly, as he pushes the hair away from my face. My eyes flicker open and I see Stefano and it looks like he's already dressed.

"What time is it?" I ask, stretching my arms from out of the covers.

"It's almost five," he answers me. "My parents just came and got Avery."

"What?" I ask, so confused. "Why?"

"One, she's been up since three thirty," he tells me, and I just look at him. How did I not hear any of this? "Three hour time change is a killer. She is going with my parents to have pancakes."

"It's five a.m.," I repeat, getting up on one elbow.

"Can you get dressed?" he asks me. "The car is going to be downstairs in about ten minutes." He leans forward. "It's a surprise." I glare at him. "Okay, fine, we are going to watch the sunrise at a special spot." My eyes go big, and my heart speeds up. "So can you be ready?"

"Yes," I mumble, pushing him away from me. "Move." I push him again, walking to the bathroom and washing my face and brushing my teeth. Going to the walk-in closet, I wonder if I should just wear the outfit I came here in. Instead, I grab a pair of jeans off the hanger and look for the price tag, but of course it's not on them. I slide my legs in the jeans and then just grab a white short-sleeved crop top that sits right about the waist, showing a little bit of skin. I bend to snatch up my shoes before walking back out to see Stefano sitting on the bed, waiting for me. When he hears me, he looks up, and my feet move to stand in front of him. "I'm ready," I tell him and he lifts his hands to grip my hips, pulling me to him.

I put my hands on his shoulders, looking down at him, my hair falling to the front. He tilts his head back. "You are so beautiful." His voice is a whisper, and if I wasn't looking at him, I don't know if I would have heard it. "You take my breath away." I lean down and softly kiss his lips. I have no choice but to do this to keep my lips busy, because if they aren't, I would say things I shouldn't. I would tell him, watching him be a father to our daughter has been the most beautiful thing I've seen. I would tell him the minute he kissed me again all these years later, it was just like it was back on the first day. I would tell him I am hopelessly in love with him, just the thought of me admitting that to him scares me more than I can ever imagine. "Let's go," he urges softly, getting up and slipping his hand into mine. We take the elevator down to the lobby where it is eerily quiet, the person behind the desk looking up and smiling at us.

The driver sees us and opens the back door of the black car. "Good morning," I tell him as I get into the car. The city is still pitched in darkness. Stefano gets into the car beside me, both of us quiet as we make our way over to the bridge.

"Here we are," the driver announces, stopping the car and getting out to open my door. I step out and I feel like I'm one among the clouds. The top of the bridge sticks out from the clouds, the two red lights at the top of the bridge blinking.

I literally catch my breath for how beautiful it is. The driver is telling Stefano where to go, but all I can do is look out into the city in the distance, the lights trying to cut through the thick fog. Stefano leads me over to the lookout point, which is a big rock. A couple of other people also have the same plan we do. Stefano sits down on the rock and pulls me down to sit in the middle of his legs. "This is—" I press my back to his chest as he wraps his arms around me, his head next to mine, looking out. "This has to be one of the best moments of my life," I declare softly, turning my face to look at him. "Thank you." I kiss his cheek and then look out into the distance and watch the black sky turn a soft golden color. The sun peeks out slowly at first and then moves higher and higher in the sky. And the higher it gets, the more the fog fades away on the horizon, and the lights in the distance slowly dim. I don't know how long we sit here, the both of us not saying a word and just taking it in. Both of us are in our own thoughts. I wish I knew what he was thinking. I wish I knew what was going to happen now. I wish all these things while I secretly tell him and the universe, I hope he stays with us.

Twenty-Eight

Stefano

"Yes," I hiss, moving my hands from her hips to her tits as she grinds down on my cock, my back to the headboard.

"Stefano," she moans out my name, making my cock twitch inside her. She arches her back as I roll her nipples between my fingers, right before pinching them. "Yes." She picks up speed, moving up and then slamming back down on me. Her head goes back, making her hair rub against my thighs. "I'm almost there."

"I can feel you, baby." I watch her eyes close as her movements get faster. I lean down, taking her nipple in my mouth, sucking it, and then biting it. Her pussy squeezes me so tight, we both hiss. "Let go," I tell her before assaulting her other nipple. It's all she needs before she lets go. Her pussy convulses around my cock, and when I know she's done, my hands grip her hips and I turn her on her back, my cock still buried in her. "My turn," I growl as I pound into her over and over again. My forehead is on hers as I slide my tongue into her mouth. "It's so good," I say as I pull out of her all the way to the tip, and then slam back into her. "It's always so fucking good." She wraps her legs around my hips and then her arms around my neck as she lifts her hips up to match my thrusts. She moans out again, my mouth swallowing her moan and two seconds later she is swallowing mine. I plant myself into her as I bury my face in her neck, her legs slowly slipping away from my hips, giving me the chance to turn to my side, again taking her with me.

She buries her face in my neck, at the same time the alarm on the side table goes off. "Good morning," she mumbles as I turn to grab the phone and turn it off.

"Good morning to you," I say, "although, any time I wake up with your mouth on my cock is a very good morning."

She retorts, "You were poking me in the back with that thing. I thought it was code." I can't help but laugh as she pushes me away. My cock sliding out of her, I go to reach for her but she's faster than me this morning. "I'm going to clean up and you are going downstairs to make us coffee. It's back to work, mister, for the both of us."

"Ugh," I moan, tossing the covers off me and grabbing a pair of shorts from the floor next to the bed where I took them off last night before sliding into bed.

"I see where our daughter gets the early morning shine from," Addison says over her shoulder, making me smirk as I walk out of the bedroom.

Instead of going downstairs, my first stop is Avery's bedroom. Peeking my head in, I see she is in the middle of the bed on her stomach, but she's sideways. Seeing that she is okay, I finally make my way down the stairs toward the kitchen. I grab two cups for coffee before turning and taking the milk out of the fridge. Once the coffees are done, I take both cups upstairs to the bedroom. The sound of the shower is still going by the time I walk back into the room. I take a sip of my coffee before placing both cups down on the coffee table. I think about maybe joining her in the shower, but right when I'm debating, I hear the sound of feet hitting the floor. I sit on the bed and watch the doorway, seeing her shadow on the floor before she walks into the room. Her tiny hands rub the sleep away from her eyes. "Morning," I say to her and she grunts, making me chuckle a bit.

"Where is Momma?" she asks as she comes to the side of the bed where I'm sitting.

"She's in the shower." I kiss her neck. "Did you sleep good?" I ask her and she nods her head. It's been two days that we've been back from San Francisco. The week flew by in the blink of an eye. As soon as we got off the plane, we headed to Addison's house to make sure everything was okay. We stayed for a couple of hours until we headed out to my house, where we've been for the last two days. "Do you want to go and get some breakfast started?" I pick her up and put her on my lap, wrapping my arms around her and pulling her close to me. She lays her head on me as she nods. My chest fills so much it is sometimes hard to breathe, but at the same time I feel a dread. Today for the first time since I found her, I'm going to work. I mean, I was working before but today I'm flying out and going into the office to have a couple of meetings.

"Do I have daycare today?" She looks up at me, and I nod. She climbs off my lap, and I stand.

"Go get dressed," I tell her, "then meet me downstairs." She turns and walks toward her bedroom. The shower turns off as I grab her cup of coffee, walking to the bathroom. When I open the door, I find her wrapping a towel around herself. "Avery is up." I hand her the coffee cup. "I'm going to go make her breakfast."

"Don't you have to pack?" she asks me, and my stomach tightens.

"I'll drop Avery off and then come home to pack," I say to her. "Are you hungry?"

"Not really, I sort of ate already today."

I shake my head. "That you did." I kiss her neck and then kiss her lips before returning downstairs to start breakfast.

Avery eats some pancakes and fruit before we all usher each other out the door. I put Avery in my car before walking over to Addison's. "I'll call you later." I wrap my arms around her. "And I'll FaceTime you for dinner."

"Okay," she says softly, "fly safe." She kisses my lips. "See you on Saturday."

I nod at her, giving her one more kiss before I open her door and she gets in. I hold my hand up as she pulls out of the driveway before I get into my car. I take my time driving Avery to daycare, and when I park she hops out. I walk way slower than I should, stopping at her classroom door, I squat in front of her. "I'll call you tonight," I tell her, "and then this weekend we could maybe go to the zoo."

"Okay, Dad," she says, not even giving a shit that my heart is breaking right now. She has no idea the hold she has on me.

"Give me a hug and kiss," I tell her and she walks into my outstretched arms and kisses my cheek. "I love you," I say to her and she just runs into her class, turning and waving at me before joining her friends who are shouting her name.

Packing is a piece of cake. I've done this before so many times, I can do it with my eyes closed. Even when I get on the plane, I think to myself that this is the longest I've been in one place. The flight flies by, and two hours after I left my house, I'm walking into our office. "Holy shit," my partner, Levi, says when I walk in, "he's still alive." He's dressed in what for sure was a suit but he took off his jacket. We've been friends since our first day in college when we took computer coding together. The two of us were at the top of the class and then we just started hanging out together. We opened the company together and fast-forward about twelve years and here we are.

I laugh. "I worked every day," I tell him as I walk over to my office, open the door, and feel the stuffiness come out. I dump my bag on the love seat in the corner before walking over to my desk. The mail has been piled up. "What time is the meeting?"

"We can start whenever you are ready," Levi says to me.

"I'm good to go," I state, grabbing my laptop from my bag and heading to the conference room.

"The war room," Levi says, coming in with his own laptop in one hand and a bottle of water in the other. "I don't know about you," he says, sitting down, "but I love, love, love these times." He leans back in his chair, waiting for the rest of the staff to come and join us. "How have things been?"

"Good." I try not to smile big, but I can't help it. "Amazing, really."

"You look good." He rocks in his chair back and forth. "Saw a couple of pictures of your daughter and your…" He trails off, making me laugh. "What are you calling her?"

I chuckle and look down at my hands and then declare, "Mine." He just laughs. "You should try it."

He looks at me, his eyebrows pinching together. "Are you crazy?"

"What?" I lean back, mimicking him. "The proverbial bachelor can settle."

He chuckles. "Not my thing."

"Until you find the right person," I tell him, and he huffs and rolls his eyes at me.

"I'll take your word for it." He leans forward, unbuttoning his cuffs and rolling up his sleeves. "The only woman I've had in my life for longer than one night is Eva, and that's only because she's always been my wingman. She knows all my secrets and is always there when I need her."

"You mean she wouldn't touch you with a ten-foot pole," I remind him of what she told me the last time she came in, and I joked about them dating.

"That also." He points at me. "She can smell my bullshit a mile away." He stops talking when more people come in and say hello to me.

The seats are all taken as we go through our list of clients. "Okay, people," I say, clapping my hands, "let's get this done." I know we have to go through our client list and see if they have any needs. Then we have to go through our waiting list to see which clients we are going to be taking on in the next couple of months. I lean back in my chair as Levi starts in on the first name on the list.

I don't even feel the time go by. "We should order in food if we are going to keep going," Levi suggests, and I look down at the corner of the computer screen and see that it's a little past eight thirty at night, and I start to panic.

"I have to head home," I hear someone say as I look beside my computer for my phone and I find it empty. I jump out of my chair, ignoring everyone voting on staying or going. "I'm with whatever," I say, rushing to my office and finding my phone on my desk. I turn it over to see Addison tried to call me once, but then I have ten missed FaceTimes from Avery.

I sit in the chair and call Addison first. She answers after two rings, and I can tell she was sleeping. "Hey, did I wake you?"

"Yeah," she mumbles, "I must have fallen asleep with Avery," she whispers.

"She's sleeping?" I say, putting my head back and my eyes

closing.

"Yeah, she had a busy day. Apparently, she was teaching the class how to wave like a princess. It's hard being Avery." She chuckles, and picturing her is just making it worse, even with my eyes closed. "How is your day?"

"Good, we just stopped to get something to eat or finish, I'm not sure. I saw the time and ran to call you," I tell her, looking up when I hear people start walking in the hallway. "I think we are going to be ending it. I'll call you when I get to the hotel."

She yawns at the same time that she says, "Okay." I disconnect the phone and put it back on my desk.

Levi sticks his head into my office. "We will reconvene tomorrow at ten," he says. "Get some sleep. You look like shit."

"Thanks," I mumble, getting up and making my way over to the hotel two doors from the office. I check in and make my way up to the bedroom. The sound of the door clicks closed once I walk in.

I toss my bag by the bed and call Addison right away; she answers after one ring. "Hi," she grumbles, and I press the FaceTime button. The sound of ringing fills the phone. "Are you FaceTiming me?"

"Yes," I confirm, putting the phone in front of me as the white circle goes around until she fills the screen. "Hi, beautiful," I say softly.

"You look tired," she notes. "Why don't you get a shower and go to bed?"

"I will in a bit. I miss you," I admit to her and her mouth goes from a smirk to a full-blown smile.

"Do you?" she asks me, turning on her side, and I wish I was sliding into bed with her.

"I do." I smirk at her. "How is Avery?"

"She's good," she says, and I can feel her holding back

something.

"She tried to FaceTime me," I tell her and she smiles sadly.

"Yeah. We called you from my phone together and then she went to her bedroom." She trails off. "I found her under the covers trying to call you."

I close my eyes and it feels like someone kicked me in the balls, and then came back to kick me in the mouth after I fell to my knees to cup my balls. "What did you tell her?"

"You were at work, and you would call her when you weren't busy. It's totally normal for a parent to go away for work. Your dad used to do it."

"I know, but I didn't. He didn't come into my life after deserting me for four years," I groan.

"You didn't desert her, and I see what Sofia was talking about being dramatic with the family." She softly giggles. "Go take a shower, and you can call her tomorrow. Then she can guilt-trip you and you can come home and bring all the stuffies you find in the airport."

"Should I order them now?" I ask, and her eyes go big.

"That was sarcasm," she retorts. "You aren't going to buy her anything because then she is going to think that she is going to get something every time you go away."

"But she will," I assure her and she rolls her eyes.

"Goodbye," she says, "call me tomorrow."

"Night, baby." I look at her and she disconnects. I order some food before taking a shower and eat in my bed before going to sleep. "This is my life," I say, hunkering under the covers.

I don't even know when I fall asleep, but the phone ringing fills the room.

I sit up in bed, looking around before I realize where I am. I get the phone and see that it's Avery calling me. I press the connect button and see her sitting in the car. "Dad," she says, her voice high. "See, Momma, I told you he would answer."

"Hey," I say, lying back down in the bed, "how are you, my beautiful girl?"

"Good, I'm at daycare," she reports, and the back door opens and she jumps out.

"Already? Okay, have a great day," I tell her and she hands the phone to Addison.

"Why didn't you call me?" I ask her.

"Because I knew you would be sleeping, and if you are anything like me, you tossed and turned all night long, so I was being nice."

"You missed me." I smile into the phone.

"I have to go," she deflects. "Say bye."

"Bye, Dad, call me tonight," Avery says, and then the phone hangs up. I lie back down in the bed, turning to the side and seeing it's just after eight. I get up and get dressed to go to work, grabbing a cup of coffee right before walking back into the office. The joy I used to get walking into the office feels like it's gone.

I nod at the receptionist, who greets me when I walk in. Most people aren't even in yet, so I go through the mail I have on my desk. By the time Levi gets in, we get back into the war room, and just like the night before, it's after nine when I finally look up. After lunch, I didn't even see the time move. I felt like I looked down at it after one in the afternoon, and then we started talking about our next client. It would be a big one that would keep me working for days on end. I am not going to lie. I was itching to get started, especially since I was the one who wanted this company.

Everyone gets up, this time slower than yesterday. I look down and see I don't have any missed calls, but I have a video. I grab my stuff and head to my office, sitting down and opening Addison's text. I press play on the video, and Avery's face fills the phone.

"Hi, Dad. It's me, Avery. I'm going to bed, and Momma won't let me call you because you're busy." Her voice trails off sadly. "Call me tomorrow. I love you." She gives the camera her princess wave before it turns off. My hands grip the phone as my eyes close.

"We fly out tomorrow morning at six thirty," Levi says, sticking his head into my office. "Meeting starts at eight sharp."

"Sounds good," I say, getting up and putting the phone in my back pocket, "then we've got to talk," I tell him, and he just looks at me, nodding. "Let's nail this client, and then we talk, yeah?"

Twenty-Nine

Addison

"Is Dad coming back tonight?" Avery asks me when she gets on the chair in the kitchen. It's been four days since he's been gone. Four long fucking days. Four days I've felt like I'm in a daze. Four days I've felt like the hours are years. I went four years without him, and now I can't even go four days without him. It's insane and also something I will never, ever admit freely.

"Not tonight, sweetheart," I reply and she groans. I look at her and I want to say, "Girl, same," but instead, I shake my head.

"How about we have a pedicure night?" I try to change her mind. It hasn't been easy with her these past few days, and I wonder if she thinks he won't come back for her. I was even going to cave and ask him if we could go and stay at his house tonight, just so she knows he's coming back. I have no idea if this is a good idea or not. I have no idea because I've never had to do this before. It was always her and me without anyone between us, but now it is all about her dad. Where is he? What is he doing? Do I think he misses her? It was fucking brutal, and as the day wore off, so did communication with Stefano, which I refuse to think about. He went from calling me at night to just sending a quick text. Which I only answered in the morning. I would send out a text, hoping he was up, but the text only got answered after I was at work. Yesterday, all I got was a "good night" text after midnight. I refuse to think about it, but I know deep down that change is coming. I also know, no matter the change, I will say I am okay. I survived worse than being left by Stefano Dimitris. I will pretend I am okay and I will do it with a smile on my face. I will do it for my daughter.

"Can I paint my nails red like Grand-mère?" she asks me and I close my eyes.

"Only your toes, not your hands." I compromise and I think she knows it, so she smiles as she eats her pancakes. I have time to wash her hands quickly when she is done before ushering her to the car. I have never been late in my life, and I am not about to start now. I continue with our routine.

Dropping her off, I kiss her and head to the office. I don't even try to call Stefano this morning because it was past eleven when he returned to his hotel room. Or at least that is the time he sent me the text. I didn't answer him back. I saw it come in and swiped it away while I spent hours on Instagram looking up wedding ideas.

I'm the first one in the office, so I open the shades and then make myself a coffee before walking over to my desk. The front door opens, and I look up to see Sofia and Shelby walk in, talking to each other. They look over at me as I smile at them, making them both stop. "What is wrong with you?"

"What?" I get up, shocked. "Why would you ask that?" I

gasp.

"I don't know, you look like your dog ate your homework," Sofia replies.

"And then your fiancé sent you a love letter meant for someone else," Shelby cuts in, making me gasp again because that happened to her. I don't have time to answer her before the door opens, and Clarabella and Presley walk in, almost bumping into the two women.

"What is this?" Clarabella asks them, then looks at me.

"Did someone die?" She puts her hands to her chest.

"Do you think if someone died, they would be just standing around?" Presley laughs at her and then looks at me. "Oh my God, are you pregnant?"

"What?" I squeak. "No." I shake my head. "We've had this discussion every single day since San Francisco. I'm on birth control."

"I'm here to tell you that nothing is one hundred percent safe unless you suffer abstinence." Presley raises her eyebrows as she talks. "Which, from the stories we got, you are not."

"Good God," I mumble, "what makes you think anything is wrong?"

"You don't have the ray of sunshine you usually do," Shelby answers.

"You smile and stuff, but the past two days you've been," Sofia says, "sad."

"I have not," I defend, shocked, "I'm fine."

"No, you are not," Clarabella says. "It's okay to miss your man."

"I don't miss my man," I lie. "He's not even my man." Sofia just snorts at that one.

"When Ace went away after he and Shelby got together," Presley says, looking at her sister who just glares at her. "She came to work with a Cheeto in her hair."

"I did not," Shelby retorts. "Was I out of it? Yes." She folds her hands over her chest. "Did I miss him? Yes. Was I a mess?"

"Also yes," Clarabella answers for her, earning her a death glare. "You showed up for an appointment with two different shoes!" she reminds her, and I quickly look down to see I have the same shoes on.

"It looked like the same shoe." Shelby stomps toward her office. "One was black."

"And one was navy blue." Presley rolls her lips. "We told the couple she was color-blind."

Shelby gasps. "Is that why the groom kept telling me what the colors were of the flowers in front of me?" she asks. "He would even say, 'that is a nice blue shirt you have on,'" she mimics the man, and for the first time in four days, I laugh.

"After hearing this"—I motion with my hand in a circle—"I think I'll be okay."

"Color-blind?" Shelby ignores what I just said. "Incredible."

"What were we supposed to say?" Clarabella asks us. "You were a mess."

"I was not!" Shelby shouts to them.

"You showed up with your hair unbrushed and thought you had the amazing beach waves. The back of your head was a rat's nest," Presley shares.

"I'm not talking to you two," Shelby pouts, turning around and looking at me. "I wasn't that bad."

"I believe you," I pacify her, nodding my head, and she flips me off, and again, I can't help but laugh.

I'm about to answer her when the phone rings. I answer it, and the three of them go to their offices. No one comes back out to talk to me and I have a bride and groom who come in the afternoon to discuss their upcoming wedding. The three of us sit down and go over every single detail. I fly out of the office a little past four o'clock, and I'm only a couple of minutes late picking up Avery.

She talks the whole way home, reminding me about her memories from San Francisco. It feels like I have a whole weight of the world on my shoulders. I grab her hand and start walking to the front door when I hear Avery shriek beside me. "Dad!" she yells, letting my hand go and running to Stefano, who squats down enough to catch her.

"There she is," he says, grabbing her under her armpits and pulling her toward him. "I missed you," he tells her, then looks up at me.

I smile at him, trying to fight the lump in my throat. My feet make it to them. "Hi," I greet him awkwardly, holding my hand up.

"Hi," he replies softly, twisting his body to lean down and kiss my cheek.

"Are you surprised?" he asks me, then looks at Avery. "I missed you so much I came right back."

I put my hand to my stomach, and I swear to God, I think I'm going to be sick all over the grass. "Why don't we get into my car and go have dinner at the house?" he suggests to Avery, who is very okay with this plan.

"You can just take Avery, and the two of you can have some alone time," I cut in, not sure I'm able to have this conversation right now.

He looks at me for a second and then back at Avery. "Or we can stay here."

I guess he really wants to get his ducks in a row before he leaves, I think to myself. "Okay, I'll follow you in my car, then," I say to him, and he just looks at me, not sure what to say.

"Dad." Avery uses her hands to turn his face. "Remember the

puppy that licked my face?"

"Yes." Stefano nods his head as we turn, and he walks to his car, looking over at me. "You'll follow me?"

"Yup." I nod at him, turning to walk to my car. Sitting back in my car, I follow him to his house. I don't think I've ever been this nervous, not even when I had to tell my parents I was pregnant. I park beside him, and Avery gets out of the car and goes into the house, as if she lives here, which—I mean—she will some days.

He opens the front door and she kicks off her shoes. "I'm going to play in my room," she states. I want to tell her to stay there because I'm a chickenshit and I know deep down inside, I don't want to have this conversation. But instead, I kick off my shoes and follow him into the house.

"Do you want pizza for dinner?" he asks me over his shoulder, and I nod my head.

"Sounds good," I say, walking into the house and going to sit on the couch. I sit at the edge of the cushion while Stefano places the order on his phone.

He comes into the living room, stopping midway to the couch. "Is there something going on?" he asks me, unsure.

I look at him and do a fake smile. I know it's a fake smile, he knows it's a fake smile. "Listen, I think we need to talk."

"We do," he agrees, coming over and sitting down next to me. The nerves in my stomach crawl their way to my throat.

My neck suddenly becomes like a heater. "I get it," I say the words. "I understand."

He does not make a move to hold my hand, instead he leans back onto the couch. "You understand." I nod. "What is it you understand?"

"Well, I think it's pretty obvious." I avoid looking at him and instead I turn my head and scratch my neck, pretending it's itchy.

"Well, it's not obvious to me, so why don't you tell me what you understand."

"This isn't for you," I finally say it. "You have to go work and even though you tried to—I don't know—be happy here. You aren't." I look at him and he stares at me with his mouth hanging open. "I understand, trust me, I know."

"You understand." He says his words in a whisper.

"I know that we are going to have to come up with a parenting plan." I put my hands together to stop them from shaking. "She starts school soon, so you are going to have to come up and see her when you can, of course. And then, of course, whenever you come home here, she can come and stay with you." I literally think I'm going to vomit. I jump up, shocking Stefano as I rush away from him, running to the bathroom. I shut the door behind me and close my eyes, counting to ten. I breathe in through my nose and out through my mouth. "It's going to be fine," I say, walking over to the sink and turning on the cold water. "It's going to be fine." I wet my hand and then tap my cheeks. "It's going to be fine. You'll be fine." I close my eyes, take a deep breath in, and open the door, screaming when I see him standing there. "Holy shit, you scared the bejeezus out of me."

"Good," he declares, his tone tight, "hopefully now the real Addison is with me, and not whoever left that room." He points at the living room, making me pissed.

"I was trying to help you," I growl between clenched teeth.

"Trying to help me?" he asks me and I never will get over how hot he is. Like today when I saw him, I couldn't help but stare at him. His hair is longer than I'm used to and his beard looks like he hasn't trimmed it since he left. He also looks a touch tired, but I thought it was because he was feeling guilty about what was going to happen. "How were you trying to help me?"

"Oh my God." My hands fly up. "I don't know why I have to spell it out for you. I know." I fold my arms over my chest.

"You know?" he replies, and I don't know why but I think he's smirking at me. "You know I've had the worst four days of my life?" he asks. I don't say anything, only because he doesn't wait for me to answer him. "That for the past twenty-four hours I was huddled into a room, trying to make the logistics work so I don't have to go into the field anymore." My mouth opens. "I mean, I will still have to go into the field, but it'll be two days... tops. I'll get what I need and then come home. I spent over six hours on the phone with Casey Barnes discussing it," he informs me. "Five hours and fifty-five minutes of him threatening me also, by the way." He holds up his hand to make sure I don't speak. "Rush home to my girls because I'm miserable without them." If I wasn't so pissed, I might sigh, but I am, so I don't. "Guilt eating at me for missing bedtimes. I've missed too much already. I'm not missing more. Put my foot down, spoke with who I needed to speak to. I'll do my part for the business because I'm good at it and because I like it, but I'll do it from nine-to-five in the comfort of my house."

"Stefano," I whisper.

"Rush home with a plan to wine and dine you and ask you guys to move in with me." His voice gets louder. "Only to be given the cold shoulder and then you sit there and tell me you know." His eyes almost glare at me. "Not even a kiss. Four days I've been gone, and you aren't even happy to see me."

I know he's throwing a lot of stuff at me. I know I need to focus on what he is saying, but the only thing I can zoom in on is: "You want us to move in with you?"

"Um, yeah," he says like I should have known this. "Didn't you know?"

I roll my eyes at his last remark. "Addison, I'm in love with you," he declares, his voice soft and quiet, which makes my heart literally skip a beat. "Like, so in love with you." I blink away the tears. "And it has nothing to do with Avery. It has to do with when you hold my hand, I feel a sense of peace. It has to do with when you kiss me, my heart speeds up. It has to do with when you smile at me, I feel like I could take on the world with just you by my side."

"You." I put my hand to my mouth to stop the sob from coming out, but it's too late. "You aren't leaving?" He is in front of me in one step, his hands on my face, tilting it back to look at him.

"I'm not leaving," he reassures me, "not now, not ever." He finally lowers his head to kiss my lips. I put my hands on top of his.

"I didn't know that," I admit and then laugh out through the tears.

"No shit," he says, shaking his head. "I don't even know what you thought you knew."

"You are not picking a fight with me right now. Not after I spent four days practically sleepless because I was missing you," I grumble between clenched teeth, "and then you come home and kiss my cheek."

"You were being weird," he replies between clenched teeth.

"You were being weirder," I counter. I know it's not a good comeback, but it's all I have right now.

"When is your lease up?" he asks me. "Doesn't matter, it'll just sit vacant."

"It's over next month."

"So do you think you can move in with me tomorrow?" He smirks at me. "I mean, I would ask for you to do it today, but it's late. I have to feed my daughter, and then I have four days of sex to catch up on."

"Four days?" I can't help the smile that fills my face. "That's a lot of sex."

"I have faith in us," he declares, kissing my lips. "Now, let's go tell our daughter that you're moving in."

Epilogue One

Stefano

One year later

"How are you so calm, cool, and collected?" I look over at Casey as he just stands there looking down at his phone.

"Well, for one." He tries not to smirk. "I have no skin in this game. I'm here because they heard of me and took the meeting. And number two, I've been where you have been." I look at him, my eyebrows pinched together. "First thing I did when I had money was buy the farm my ex owned. No one knew it was me. I broke it to her in the middle of the barn, where I found her fucking someone else. It was a good day."

"So the moral of the story is?" I look out the window.

"Moral of the story is I won, one, by buying her farm and, two, by finding the love of my life, which wasn't her." He puffs out his chest. "Now, relax."

I'm about to say something to him when the door to the conference room opens, and a woman comes in. "Showtime," Casey says and I nod my head.

She's dressed head to toe in a designer outfit. "Hello, gentlemen." She smiles at Casey and then her eyes fall to me as she smirks.

"Kristina." I nod at her as she pulls out her chair, putting her phone on the table.

Her brother is the next one in, who looks annoyed that he was called into this meeting. Which doesn't surprise me since he actually has no idea what the fuck he's even doing. "I have a meeting in thirty minutes," he huffs, pulling out a chair, and I know he does. He's actually having an affair with his fiancée's best friend's boyfriend.

I don't bother even acknowledging him, because in walks the man of the hour. I have never in my life been more nervous, but I've never in my life hated someone more than I hate this man who is walking into the room next. "Gentlemen," he greets, smiling to me. All I can do is nod instead of wanting to throat punch him.

"Mr. Laurier." I nod at him. "How has your day been?"

"It's been good," he replies, pulling out the chair at the head of the table where the president usually sits. I look over at Casey, who pulls out the chair in front of him that is in the middle.

"Shall we get started?" I look over at them.

"Should we not wait for the rest of the shareholders?" Kristina smiles at me as she taps her finger on the table.

Gerald takes a deep exhale and looks bored AF and just wants this over with. They are the only three who we haven't shared the news with. News I'm ready to share with them. News I hope shatters their whole fucking world. "I think we can start without them," I state, looking over at Casey, who leans back in his chair. Cool, calm, and collected.

"Yes, let's," Casey says, smirking. "Knock them dead."

"Well, I don't want to drag this on, so let's get to the point. Since your company is public, and Casey has been looking into purchasing stocks to become a majority shareholder in Laurier Lumber for a while now." I look over at Casey, who just rocks back and forth. "I've met with several of the shareholders." I put my hands on the table. "And your numbers are, well, how do I put it?" I look over at Casey. "Fictitious." I look at the reaction of all three of them, the only one who isn't surprised by this is the man at the head of the table. "You see, I'm really good at my job."

"He's lying," Casey cuts in. "He's the best at his job, even I'm somewhat impressed."

"Thank you," I tell him. "Now, as future shareholders of Laurier Lumber, I think it's our right to see how much Mr. Laurier has, how do I put it?"

"I think it's called embezzling." Casey leans in like he's going to tell me a secret, but the whole table can hear him. Kristina, who smiled at me before, now just looks at me with big eyes.

Gerald suddenly sits up in his chair, now paying very close attention.

"Excuse me?" Mr. Laurier says, sitting up in his chair.

"You're excused," I say to him as I open the folder I placed on the table when we walked in. I hand them each a sheet of paper with columns and numbers. I slide it to them, Mr. Laurier snapping it up in his hands. "As you can see, the three of you have been, well—" I look for words to say. "Having a field day with funds that were not yours." I look over at Casey, whose face grimaces. "So, for the past couple of weeks, we've had the pleasure to show this to some of the shareholders."

"Past couple of weeks?" Mr. Laurier says. "Are you saying you went behind my back?"

"I am, in fact," I say, nodding, "saying that we went behind your back."

"I'm not taking the praise for this," Casey declares. "This was all Stefano. I'm just here because I knew someone." He looks at me. "Go on."

"This is bullshit." Mr. Laurier slaps the table with his hand. "I want you out of this office now."

I just stare at him while Casey laughs. "I don't think so." I laugh also. "You see, I sort of—" I move my head from side to side. "Kind of"—I snap my fingers—"am the majority shareholder."

"That's," Mr. Laurier shouts, "that's impossible!"

"But is it?" Casey asks him, then turns to me. "Go for it."

"Mr. Laurier," I say his name, "from my findings, you have been dipping your hand where it shouldn't go." I smirk. "But you aren't the only one." I look over at the other two. "You see your son, Gerald, has a hotel room that is booked four times a week with the company card." I look at him, and his face goes white as I turn to him. "And I don't think you are bringing clients there." I don't wait for him to say anything. "And, well, Kristina over here, she has a little bit of an issue that she needs help with."

"Shut the fuck up," she says, slapping her hand on the table.

"And, well, you." I point at Mr. Laurier. "There are the family vacations. The hotel suites. The private jets are all paid for by the company."

"I have an allowance." He shoots to his feet as his chair flies back. "My father started this company."

"He sure did," I confirm. "And we aren't even going to go into all that. Because if we went through all of it, your father would have been behind bars for the way he obtained some of his materials. But, in the end, I'm sure you will be handing it down to your kids." I look at the two next to him.

"It's a family tradition," he states.

"You have just the two children, then?" I ask him, and he is about to answer me when the door opens and in comes the other person I hate.

"What is going on?" she asks, looking around at her husband and kids. "Why the hell did you summon me here?" I shake my head and look down. How the fuck did Addison come from these people? My hands bunch into fists on the table.

"Mrs. Laurier," I say, my voice tight, "I was explaining to your husband and your two children that I now am the primary shareholder in the company." Everything I've done in the last year has paid off for this moment right here. Standing before her family, taking what they love the most away from them.

"This is fucking bullshit." Gerald jumps out of his seat, just like his father.

"No," I say quietly and stand. "What is bullshit is the four of you." I look over at Casey, and he just smirks. "I don't believe we've been formally introduced." I look over at the woman. "My name is Stefano Dimitris." They all look at me like it means nothing, and I guess to them, it doesn't. "You would know who I am if you were in your daughter's life."

They look over at Kristina, who holds up her hands. "I have no idea who he is."

"Not that daughter," I explain. "I'm talking about Addison." The minute I say her name, the blood drains from their faces. "I'm guessing from the reaction on your faces that you know who I'm talking about. You see, you turned your back on her over six years ago."

"Yeah, so what?" Gerald says. "She was stupid enough to get knocked up."

"Breathe," Casey says from beside me.

"I'd watch what you say." I look into his eyes. "You're talking about my fiancée and my daughter. So if you don't want to eat from a straw for the rest of your life, I would watch the next words that come out of your mouth."

"Are you threatening me?" He puffs out his chest.

"Nope, threat means I won't do it." I smirk. "This is me telling you that I'll make you eat from a straw for the rest of your life."

"What the fuck is going on?" Mr. Laurier says.

"What is going on, old man, is"—I look at him—"this is your last day working for this company." I look at Casey, who nods at me and gets up. "As much fun as this was." I take the other paper in the folder and hand it to them. "You will see, Casey bought two shares of the company." I smile big at them. "While I bought the other sixty shares. Which means…" I hold up a hand. "Which means I move to have you removed from the company," I declare. "All in favor, say aye."

"Aye," Casey says, then looks over at the four of them. "I guess you guys are opposed."

"Doesn't fucking matter." I clap my hands. "My shares are going to my future wife and my daughter. It's in her hands. But for now, for me, I want you out of your office tonight." Then I look over at her mother. "You turned your back on your daughter and tossed her out like garbage. She struggled to pay her medical bills while you spent forty-seven thousand dollars in the Bahamas in a weekend."

"She made her bed," her father retorts, "she had to lie in it."

"You don't know what you're talking about," the woman says. "You can't speak to me like that."

"Trust me, lady, the last thing I want to do is speak to you." I shake my head. "I thank fuck she didn't turn out like you." Then I look at her sister. "You should go to rehab." Then I look over at her brother. "You should also tell your fiancée she's not your type."

"Fuck this, I quit!" Gerald yells. "I won't stand here."

"You haven't worked a day in your life." I laugh. "You don't even know how to do your job. We've already hired your secretary to take your place since she has been doing your job since you started.

"You have until the end of the day to pack up your shit." I look at Casey. "You were right, this was fun, but I'm done." He nods at me, and I start to make my way out. "You fucked up, old man. Trying to do things like you were still in the fifties, thinking no one would know the difference," I inform him. "You fucked up even bigger when you turned your back on your daughter. You will never see the woman she has become, and you will never see the goodness that is our daughter." Then I look at her mother. "You were supposed to fight for her. You were supposed to be her strength and guide her, and instead, you chose to stand behind your husband."

"Don't speak to me that way," her mother seethes. "You don't know us."

"Thank fuck," I reply, "wouldn't even want to walk on the same street as you."

With that, I take one look at them and then walk out with Casey at my back. "How you feeling?" he asks me and I just look down. "I'm going to say that I'm happy as a pig in shit right now." I look over at him. "Do you know how pissed Matthew is going to be that we did this without him?"

I chuckle and shake my head. "Who do you think gave me the money to do this?" I look over at him. "He knew exactly what I was doing."

We walk out of the door and there standing by the truck is Uncle Matthew, Uncle Max, and my father side by side, all of them arms crossed over their chests. "Fucking hell," Casey greets, "you're a sight for sore eyes."

"Missed you, too, Casey. Or should I say, partner?" Matthew says.

"Why are you everywhere?" Casey asks him, chuckling.

"He's like those fruit flies," Max goads, "you think you killed him and then you look around and he's still there."

"It's my charm." He shrugs, then looks at me. "We good?"

I look back over at the company. "We're good."

"It was touch and go in there," Casey shares. "Thought for sure he would do something that I would have to end up cleaning but"—Casey slaps my shoulder—"he did good."

"Time to go home," I decide, taking a deep inhale, "and tell Addison."

Casey leaves us at the plane and we get in, and in twenty-five minutes I'm in the car on my way home while everyone else goes back to New York.

I pull into the driveway, looking up at the house I bought hoping I would be able to convince her to move in with me. The house I wanted to make a home in. A house that is now our home. She moved in the weekend after I asked her to. Our clothes now hang in the same closet. Picture frames are all over the house of our amazing life together. I can't help but smile while I look over and see Addison is already home. I grab the envelope on the passenger seat, putting it in my inside pocket. When I open the driver's door to step out, at the same time a yellow school bus pulls up in front of the house.

I walk toward the bus just in time to see Avery jump off the last step, her princess backpack bigger than her, but she insists on wearing it. She also insists on taking the bus. I'm not going to lie, I hate every single second of it, but Addison said we had to let her try it. I'm hoping that eventually she'll get tired of it so

I can drive her to school and pick her up.

"Daddy!" she shouts, running to me and jumping in my arms, knowing I'm going to catch her.

"How was your day?" I ask her, kissing her neck, and she giggles. Turning, I see Addison coming out of the front door.

"Good, I had art and I drew a picture for Grand-mère," she replies as I walk up the steps with her in my arms.

"Hey, you two," Addison greets us at the top of the stairs, looking down at us. I stop at the step under her, and she smiles at Avery before she leans in and kisses my lips.

"You're home early," she says to me, her smile makes my knees week.

"It went faster than I thought." I put Avery down.

"Go wash your hands and put your lunchbox on the counter," Addison tells her as she walks inside, then turns back to me. "You look like you have something you need to tell me."

I nod my head, turning and sitting on the stoop. "I do," I tell her, and she sits down right next to me. She puts her hand in mine. "I love you," I remind her and she just laughs.

"I think I knew that already." She leans in to kiss my lips. I just stare at her. "What happened?" Her hand comes up to hold my cheek.

"I did something today," I admit, taking the envelope out of my inside pocket and hand it to her. "That's for you."

"What is this?" she asks, turning the white envelope over and pulling out the white paper. She unfolds it and then looks at it, gasping when she sees the top.

"A year ago, when I found you again, and found out what your family did, I started a plan." She looks down at the paper, her hand shaking. "I didn't know if I could actually do it, but I wanted to bury them. I wanted them to hurt just like you hurt. If not more." She looks at me, the tears rolling down her face. "It took some time, but today I was able to bring you that."

"I don't understand," she says to me, and my hand comes up to wipe her tears away.

"Well, as of this afternoon, you are the majority shareholder for Laurier Lumber," I tell her the gist of it, "and your father is out. So is your sister and your brother."

"But how?" she questions in a whisper. "Why?"

"Because you deserve what is yours," I inform her. "Also, I wanted to make them pay."

"But…" She shakes her head. "…don't you see?" I just stare at her. "I won. Look at me. I have a beautiful daughter, who is healthy and filled with so much love. I have a man, who I like on some days and adore on most days. I have his family, who have accepted me with open arms, treating me like I'm one of their own. Never not once did your family ever make me feel that I'm not part of the family. I have the best job a girl can ask for." She puts the paper down in her lap. "Stefano, I won." She puts her hands on my face. "We won."

"We did win," I agree, reaching into my pocket, taking out the ring box. "Today they asked me who I was." I move out of her touch, her hands falling to her lap, getting on one knee. "I told them you were my fiancée." I open the ring box. "Addison, you have given me a life I didn't know I wished for. You have shown me what unconditional love is. You have made me a better man. You have my heart before, today, and always. I want to have more children with you. I want to have my ring on your finger, knowing that you will be forever stuck to me." She laughs at that. "I mean, technically, you are forever stuck to me, but this is so everyone knows."

"I'm yours," she confirms, "with or without the ring."

"Is that a yes?" I ask her, taking the ring out of the box and putting it on her finger.

She looks down and gasps. "This is—"

"It's on your finger, and I'm not taking it back," I tell her, and the door opens. Avery comes out, watching us.

"Why is Momma crying?" she asks, looking at me and then her mom.

"I asked Momma to marry me," I explain to her as she walks over to Addison, putting her arm around her shoulders. "I gave her a ring."

She gasps, too. "Do I get a princess dress?" she asks, making Addison roll her eyes. She has so many fucking princess gowns in our house. In my parents' house. Every single place she goes there is one waiting for her.

"You both get a princess dress," I tell them both. "Now, can I kiss your mom?"

"Ugh, again?" she groans. "I'm hungry." She turns and walks back inside the house.

"Glad she took the news well," I joke, leaning in and kissing Addison's lips. "I promise I'll never make you regret this."

Epilogue Two

Addison

Two months later

"This wedding is going to be the death of me," I mumble from my desk, looking down at the papers I just printed out. "Who the hell plans their wedding via email?" All I can do is shake my head.

"You would be surprised," Sofia says from the doorway to my office, rubbing her pregnant stomach. She's almost seven months pregnant, and for once in my family, it's going to be a surprise what she is having. I think it's a boy, but I could be wrong. A lot has happened in a year. I'm now officially one of the wedding event planners, my reception job given to Cathy, our intern turned office manager/reception/social media guru.

"I haven't even met this couple," I tell her. "Who would

entrust someone to plan their wedding without even meeting them?" I throw up both hands. "Like for real, we've booked everything just off the pictures."

"How many people at the wedding?" she asks me, sitting down in the chair in front of me.

"About a hundred people," I say. "Which isn't that many, I know, but still who picks their flowers from pictures?"

"Maybe she just doesn't care," Sofia puts forth, "maybe she just wants to marry the guy."

"I guess that must be it." I look down at the list of things that they've picked from pictures. "Well, regardless, I'll be meeting these two this weekend since it's their wedding."

Sofia throws her head back and laughs. "Well, *if* they will show up."

"One can hope." I cross both my fingers together on each hand. "All I know is Stefano is a tad tired about hearing about this wedding." I laugh. "He might have had a hand in picking some of the options because who tells their wedding planner, 'I don't have a vision'? My five-year-old has a vision of what her wedding is going to be like." Sofia can't help but laugh. "Needless to say, we are in for it. I may need to get a second job."

"Well, the good news is, this time next week, it'll all be over," Sofia reminds me, getting out of her chair.

"Good news is that in two days this will all be over. Stefano's parents are going to be in town to help me celebrate."

"I'll polish off my tiara," Sofia teases, turning and waddling out the door.

"Yeah," I mumble, looking down and making sure that everything is ready for the wedding in two days.

I SLAM MY car door two days later, looking around to see the hustle and bustle of people setting things up. I look at my watch and see the bride is going to be here in twenty minutes. I walk into the venue space and find the tables have already been set up. I nod at the waitstaff as I walk over to one of them to check and make sure it's set up in the way I had it in the picture. We opted for long tables instead of circular ones because she wanted it to be more intimate. It was my suggestion when she didn't want to do a seating chart.

The wooden tables have an off-white, almost beige, long runner down the center of the table. White roses and orchids are intertwined with green garland that runs from one end to the other. We went with beige plates and crystal glasses with gold rims to match the gold chairs. I'm not going to lie, if I was getting married, this would be what I would have chosen. My phone beeps and I look down and see a text from Sofia.

Sofia: Bride is early and she's in the bridal suite.

Shit, I look at my watch, she's thirteen minutes early. I walk through the back of the venue, headed out to the bridal suite. I take a deep breath in and open the door, the smile on my face is now frozen when I take in who is in the room.

"What is going on?" I ask, looking around at Stefano, who stands there with Avery. Behind him is Vivienne and his aunt Karrie on one side, and on the other side stands Sofia, Clarabella, Presley, and Shelby. I look around the bridal suite and white vases of roses fill the room. A rack of dresses is on one side and then wedding dresses on the other side of the room.

"Well," Stefano starts, "I know that you've been going nuts these past couple of months to plan this wedding."

"Yes, and my bride is going to be here"—I look at Sofia—"any minute."

"She's already here," Sofia states with tears in her eyes, and I finally take in everything in the room.

My hand goes to my mouth, before I look back at Stefano, who is now on bended knee. "Addison," he says my name.

"I already said yes." I can't help the tear that rolls down my face.

"I know, but this time, I want to know if you want to marry me today," he explains, and I gasp. Even though it's right in front of me, hearing it is another thing.

"Momma," Avery says, jumping up and down, "I get to wear a princess dress."

"Not yet," Stefano says. "She needs to say yes."

"Momma, you want me to wear a princess dress, yes or no?" She puts her hands on her hips, making everyone laugh.

"So there is no bride?" I look at Sofia, who just shrugs.

"There is a bride," Presley confirms.

"Yes, she's very low-key," Clarabella cuts in.

"So low-key, we didn't even see her," Shelby says, smiling. "Now, you." She points at Stefano. "Up and out."

"She didn't say yes," Stefano retorts, and I shake my head.

"We live together," I remind him. "Two months ago, I said yes." I hold up my hand.

"Where is my dress?" Avery decides that she's done with this conversation.

"Yes, let's get her dressed," Vivienne agrees, clapping her hands.

Stefano gets up and kisses me. "I guess we're getting married." He winks at me, and I just smile and swallow down the lump in my throat. "I'll see you at the altar." His thumb comes up to wipe away the tears. "I'll be waiting for you."

"I think I'm going to be sick." I run past him and straight to the bathroom, making it just in time for my whole breakfast to come up. Flushing the toilet and then closing my eyes as I push away the nausea that I feel. I grab a piece of toilet paper and wipe my mouth, breathing in through my nose and out through my mouth.

"This is not good," Presley whispers outside the door.

"It's a sign," Shelby says in a whisper, but it's louder than a whisper.

"It's no sign. She's fine. It's just cold feet," Clarabella hisses, and when I look over at the door, I see the shadow of feet.

"Is there a window in there?" Sofia asks. "What I'm saying is she might escape."

"No one is escaping," Stefano snaps. The knock comes on the door, and he doesn't wait for me to say anything. He just comes in.

"Oh, God," I say when I look at him, "Are you okay?"

I nod my head and feel like my stomach is going to lurch out. "Can you get me a water?" I ask him, and he grabs a bottle of water from the basket on the counter. He opens the white cap and hands me the little bottle of water. "Thank you," I say softly, grabbing it from him and then rinsing my mouth out while he turns on the water at the sink and starts to wet a white hand towel.

I can't help the flutter that happens in my stomach, as he squats down in front of me handing me the towel. "We don't have to get married," he soothes, his voice soft. "I did it this way so it's stress-free for you." He looks down. "But we don't have to do it."

"No," I say quickly, "I want to get married." I sit up straight and put my hand on his cheek, my finger playing in his scruff like it always does. I wait for his eyes to look up at me, and I can't help the soft smile that fills my face. "I think I fell in love with you the first time I met you." He smirks. "I mean, obviously, I found you attractive if I slept with you."

"Good thing," he replies.

I look down, suddenly nervous and then look up again. "I'm pregnant."

The minute I say the words, I think I hold my breath. "What?"

"I know, I know," I say, nervous that he's going to be pissed. "I think it's when Sofia got strep throat and then I got it. The meds must have messed with my birth control."

"That was over three months ago," he reminds me.

"I know, but with Avery being in school and then me being sick and then you giving me my family's company. Then my family going all fucking nutso and calling me." I'm just rambling at this point. The minute that he got home and handed me the papers with me being the majority shareholder, my phone started ringing. My father, my mother, my brother, my sister, everyone suddenly remembered I was alive. I was shocked, but then I did what I should have done all those years ago. I blocked their numbers, and they didn't exist.

I refused to speak of them in our home. I refused to give them space in my thoughts. I refused all that, but I failed miserably and the only one who saw this was Stefano. The more I pushed it away from my mind, the more I thought about it. Then my sister got me at work. She called me at my job, and that is where I drew the line. I would not let her into my work, so I took her call. It was very cold. The whole time I realized it was all about her and what she was going through now that she didn't have a job. Not once did she ask about Avery. I waited for her to stop talking before I told her I was sorry for her, then I hung up. She never called back. "Then this bride wanting me to plan her wedding in two months." I glare at him. "I was a little busy to realize that something was off. Then, well, my nipples started to hurt and the only other time that happened was, you know, the last time."

"Did you go to the doctor?" he asks me and I just shake my

head. "Somebody get Chase!" he shouts for his cousin over his shoulder, at the closed door, and I see the shadow of feet move away.

"What are you doing?" I ask him shocked, but I don't have time for him to answer because in this family it's like everyone is on speed dial.

There is a knock on the door and then Chase sticks his head in. "You rang?"

"How did you get here so fast?" I ask him.

"The minute you said you were going to be sick, I got four texts and one phone call." He smiles, shaking his head. "How is the patient?" He looks at me.

"I'm fine," I assure them.

"She's not fine," Stefano says. "She had strep three months ago." His eyebrows shoot together. "And now she took a test." He puts both hands on his head, making me roll my eyes and throw my hands up in the air.

"Does your throat still hurt?" Chase asks me.

"I'm pregnant," I inform him. "I don't even know why you were called."

"She was on birth control," Stefano says, and I seriously want the floor to open me up and spit me out, "and now she's pregnant. Is that okay?"

"One, congratulations." He slaps Stefano on the shoulder like he's the one who is carrying a child.

"He just put it in there," I finally snap out, "I'm the one doing all the work."

"Of course," Chase placates, trying to hide his smirk. "Congratulations to you. It's going to be fine, just stop taking the pill until you see your doctor."

"I did," I tell him.

"What else do you feel?" he asks me. "Any bleeding?"

"No," I reply. "I'm tired and hungry and cranky. Getting crankier as the day goes on." I look at Stefano, who hasn't stopped smiling since I told him I was pregnant.

"I think it'll be fine," Chase says, smiling at me, "but if you need me during the day, I'll be around." I nod at him. "So are you getting married or not?"

"What?" Stefano and I say at the same time, shocked.

"The cousins have a side bet going on," he shares, trying not to laugh. "I bet five hundred dollars that you would be." He puts his hand on his chest. "But Michael and Dylan said she would escape."

Stefano throws his head back and full-on laughs at the top of his lungs. "Like I would let her get away."

"That's what I said." Chase laughs with him.

I get up off the floor. "Get out," I tell him. "Let me get away," I repeat his words as I shake my head.

Stefano stands up. "Do you not love me?" He puts his hands on his hips and I glare at him because he knows how I feel. "Exactly, so I would not let you get away."

There is another knock on the door, and this time, Sofia sticks her head in. "Listen, I'm trying to hold off the pack, and I'm using my pregnant body as a shield but there are a lot of them and no one is good at listening in your family." She glares at both the men. "Are we getting married?"

"We are getting married," Stefano declares, then looks at me. "Right?"

"We shall see," I say, walking past them. "You'll know if I walk down the aisle." I walk out the door but not before I hear, "She's totally walking down the aisle," Stefano states.

"Totally," Chase answers him.

I walk into the room and see Vivienne there with Markos trying to calm her down as she wrings her hands. "Good, just the two people I need to see." Vivienne's face goes white, and Markos just stares at me.

"Are you okay?" Markos asks, the worry all over his face. "Whatever you want to do, we will support you."

"Yes," Vivienne says, "you don't need to be married. It's the twenty-first century."

"I'm going to marry your son," I assure her. "If you asked me this ten minutes ago"—I look over my shoulder at him as he comes out with Chase—"the answer would have been a maybe, but I may just have to get this over with."

"Aw," Chase says, "isn't that love?" The look I give him makes him stop snickering.

"I would like to speak to Markos, please," I tell the room. "Alone."

Everyone looks at everyone else, not sure what to do. "Okay, you heard the bride," Shelby announces.

"Well, she's the bride at this moment," Clarabella jokes, "but time will tell."

"If it makes anyone feel better," Presley says, "none of our weddings went off without a hitch, and Shelby and Clarabella both were engaged before to other people."

"How does that make anyone feel better?" Sofia asks.

"This? Coming from you," Presley huffs. "Wasn't your man engaged when you planned his first wedding?"

"Out," I command in my most stern motherly voice. Everyone's eyes go big as they slowly trickle out.

"If you want me to help you escape, I can," Markos says.

I laugh at his declaration. "Thank you for that," I say nervously, "but I don't need you to help me escape."

"Oh, thank God." He puts his hand on his head. "Because I would have to tell him where you are, so..." I laugh a full-on laugh.

"Good to know you would give me a head start." He smiles at me. "I know this may be weird, and, well, you haven't known me a long time, but I was wondering if maybe you would like to walk me down the aisle."

"What?" he gasps in a whisper.

"You've been like a father to me since you met me." I wring my hands together. "And if I'm telling the truth, you are a million times the man he is." I hold up my hands. "No pressure. If you want to say no, I get it."

"Sweetheart," he declares, "I would be honored."

I laugh and cry at the same time. "Thank you."

"Now, I'm not one to pressure you, but I feel like if you don't get dressed and walk down the aisle in the next ten minutes—" He looks over his shoulder at the door that we both know people are waiting at. "He's going to lose his shit and... Kaboom." His hands go to his head and make exploding signs.

"I know," I tell him, leaning in and whispering, "I'm doing it on purpose."

He laughs, and the door opens, and there stands my groom with a worried expression on his face. "What is going on?"

Markos walks over to him. "Let's step outside." He pushes Stefano. "I'll send in the girls." He looks over his shoulder.

I nod my head, and in twenty-seven minutes, my makeup is done. My hair hangs loose and is pinned up at the side, and I'm being zipped into my lace wedding dress.

Three minutes later, I'm slipping my hand through Markos's arm, getting ready to walk down the aisle. The minute the doors open, all I can see is Stefano as he stands there waiting for me wearing beige linen pants, a white buttoned shirt, and a matching beige vest. With tears in his eyes, he accepts my hand from his father, and five minutes later, I'm Mrs. Stefano Dimitris.

The end....

Dearest Love,

Well, look at this, another one bites the dust.

It fills the soul when two people find love, doesn't it?

Spring is in the air, which means wedding season is quickly approaching us.

Brides and grooms are preparing to take the leap and walk down the aisle.

Or.

A woman asking her best friend for a huge favor.

Just for a year.

A fake wedding.

Except.

What happens when they have to live with each other?

What happens when they have to share a bed?

What happens when everything starts to get blurry?

Will the vows they said to each other be real?

Will they honor those promises?

Time will tell!

XOXO

NM

MINE TO HONOR

EVA

Things were finally looking up for me.

I was my own boss. I owned my own house—and I recently was contacted by an older sister I didn't know I had.

Everything was perfect... until tragedy struck.

All the things that had come into my life were suddenly gone—except for one thing: my niece.

LEVI

I was a confirmed bachelor.

I was married to my work and committed to nothing more.

No woman was going to change that.

Eva is my best friend and needed a life-changing favor:

Marry her so she could gain custody of her niece.

A marriage of convenience that would only last a year, tops.

But there were stipulations we hadn't planned on.

Things got blurry—lines got crossed.

I will honor my commitment—I just hope I can walk away.